# The
# Rosary
# Garden

*A Famished Heart*
*The Rosary Garden*
*The Burning Boy* (2022)

# The
# Rosary
# Garden

## NICOLA
## WHITE

VIPER

First published in this edition in Great Britain in 2021 by
VIPER, part of Serpent's Tail,
an imprint of Profile Books Ltd
29 Cloth Fair
London
EC1A 7JQ
*www.serpentstail.com*

An earlier version of this work was published as
*In the Rosary Garden* by Cargo Publishing in 2013

The lines from 'Canal Bank Walk' by Patrick Kavanagh (p.247) are reprinted
from *Collected Poems*, edited by Antoinette Quinn (Allen Lane, 2004),
by kind permission of the Trustees of the Estate of the late Katherine
B. Kavanagh, through the Jonathan Williams Literary Agency.

1 3 5 7 9 10 8 6 4 2

Printed and bound in Great Britain by
CPI Group (UK) Ltd, Croydon, CR0 4YY

A CIP catalogue record for this book is available from the British Library.

ISBN 978 1 78816 411 5
eISBN 978 1 78283 644 5

To my parents, Seán and Mary,
who fed me books

# 1

*Dublin, 1984*

It was good to be early. A step ahead. He cruised the car to a gentle stop on the canal side of the street and killed the lights. There was a little humpback bridge at the end of the road with a lantern on the top of it. Pretty as a postcard. Through the arch of the bridge he could just make out a wall of water falling over a lock gate, a shadowy unspooling that sounded like someone exhaling for ever. It was good to watch, took the edge off his nerves.

On the dot of eight, a light came on behind the splayed bones of a fanlight. The door below opened and she appeared – silhouetted, alone. It looked like she had nothing but a small case with her and disappointment flooded him, but then he noticed the crossing of one arm over her chest, the way she leaned back as she came down the stone steps.

She stepped into the fall of a street lamp and he could see the bulge of her coat more clearly. It was good that she was trying to be discreet, even if the result was ludicrously noticeable. Luckily there was nobody else on the road to see. He scanned the front of the terrace again for movement at windows. Nothing. The trees along the canal were

1

in full leaf, blocking the buildings on the other side from sight.

He rolled down the window.

'Here!'

Her head swivelled in his direction.

*Steady!*

He called her name gently. Better to stay in the car, make her come to him.

She crossed the street and he reached over to open the passenger door for her. She put the case in the footwell and lowered herself slowly in beside him. He didn't want to look at her, so he fiddled with the keys.

'How're ya?' Her face was coming towards him. He ducked down and started the engine. 'We'll drive round a bit, eh?'

He checked his mirrors, pulled out slowly. He wasn't sure where he was going, but it seemed a good idea to get moving.

'No one saw me leaving,' she said.

He looked in the rear-view mirror.

'No one saw me. I did well, didn't I?'

She was such a poultice.

'Sure you did,' he said.

Her hand was still clamped to the front of her coat where the lump was, and she started to stroke the material above it. He should have told her to put it in the back.

They were headed into the city centre now. He didn't want to go too far, didn't want to get lost. Get her to hand it over, drop her at the train station. That's all.

'Tell me again about the family?' she asked.

'They're rich, cultured people. Aristocracy, I suppose you'd call them. Big house, ponies. She'll have the life of a princess over there.'

'They won't send her to boarding school?'

'No, they were very against that,' he said and made himself touch her, put his hand flat on her thigh and give a little squeeze. She'd put on the beef.

'What matters is that we get a fresh start,' he said. 'Nobody pulling us this way and that.'

She covered his hand with her own.

They were driving round Stephen's Green. Round and round. She didn't seem to notice that they were going nowhere. A set of lights changed to red and he took the chance to retrieve his hand.

'I have a little bed for her in the back.'

She twisted to look. It was only a laundry basket, but he thought it looked the business, padded out with sheets and things.

'I'll pull in up here and you can put her in, eh?'

He could feel her reluctance fluttering beside him.

'We won't let them bully us,' he said, 'will we?'

'No,' she said, 'we won't.'

The word *we* was all that was needed. He applied it sparingly, knowing she'd do what he wanted, for the hope it contained. She was too easily swayed. Soft in the head, really. She would have made a terrible mother.

# 2

Fitz and Ali were late. They got to the door of the nuns' parlour in time to hear the dry beat of a pair of clapping hands rise through a babble of voices.

Ali cracked the door open. Reverend Mother Mary Paul looked in their direction, one sceptical eyebrow raised even as she continued to clap for silence. The feeling of dread was only a reflex – Ali had to remind herself that the nun had no hold over them now.

A dozen of their former classmates gathered around in an untidy horseshoe with a few nuns and older lay teachers. Some big sheets of paper were pinned to the wall. GOOD LUCK TO OUR BRAINBOXES was painted across them, each awkward letter wrought in a different style and colour. An art project for reluctant first-years, probably. Ali tried to tuck herself out of sight behind a pair of teachers, slumping to lose height.

Fitz had insisted that they dress up for the occasion – their first time at St Brigid's without uniforms. She'd persuaded Ali to backcomb her hair and put on a baggy pinafore dress. With kohl round her eyes, she had looked bohemian in her bedroom mirror. Now she felt like a big demented farmgirl.

Mary Paul cleared her throat.

'Now that we're all *here*,' she directed a quick nod at Fitz, 'I wanted to express how very, very proud I am of the girls from our class of 1984 who are aiming to move on to university and third-level colleges. We hope there will be twelve of you who will be successful in this, if your results are good enough, and I have to say this would be a very proud result for St Brigid's, and a testament to the fine quality of teachers that we have here.'

Wrinkled faces creased deeper into smiles and a lukewarm spatter of applause emerged from the girls. Ali looked around and was relieved to see a couple of the others had also dressed for effect, one in a leather biker's jacket, another in a rainbow jumper down to her knees.

'I couldn't be prouder of your achievements, which is why you'll heed me when I say that wherever your God-given brains take you – to the highest levels of commerce or the halls of academe, or even the furthest reaches of the known world – promise me that you will not deprive yourselves of the real joys of womanhood. The fruits of the material world are very seductive, but they can't replace the simple satisfactions of home and family. Ireland needs intelligent mothers and wives just as much as she needs bankers and doctors. Think about that, and remember you can come back to see us at any time.' She raised her hands in exhortation: 'Our doors are always open!'

Again the girls clapped dutifully, eyes drifting to the buffet table.

'What the hell is the "known world" anyway?' Ali said sideways to Fitz. 'Does she think there's still a big undiscovered bit somewhere?'

'Don't be worrying your womanly brain with that.'

'How long do we have to stay?'

'Give it ten minutes, max. I can't look at that food with this hangover.' Fitz made a gagging face. Ali was ravenous.

With a bit of shuffling, Ali manoeuvred herself into prime position at the table and put three triangular ham sandwiches onto her paper plate. She was edging her way towards the cocktail sausages when a tremulous black shape docked beside her.

'Alison Hogan. Don't you look great?'

Tiny Sister O'Dwyer, not the worst of them. Long past teaching, but still in nominal charge of the gardening club, which Ali had joined in her first year and signed up for ever since, not entirely for horticultural reasons.

The nun's raw-looking fingers were already locked on Ali's sleeve, and she decided to give herself up to the old soul. It was easier than fighting her off, and more bearable company than she might otherwise get landed with. She peeled another paper plate from a stack, urged the nun to accept a finger of quiche and steered her to a pair of the straight-backed chairs that ringed the room.

Ali wolfed down her food while the nun talked about her gratitude for all that Ali had done for the Rosary Garden, stirring the air with her untouched plate.

'There's not many girls would put in the effort, but you and your friend Carmen – what is it you call her: Fuzz?'

'Fitz, Sister.'

'Well, you were both great. Always there at lunchtime. To be honest, it's become a trouble rather than a pleasure to me lately. You need to be able to get down on your knees in a garden, even more than in the chapel. The weeds would break your heart.'

'Sure, you'll get some new girls, Sister. Some young ones, with plenty of bend in them.'

'I suppose. It won't be me that trains them up, though. Sister Bernadette's taking over.'

Sister O'Dwyer nodded towards a tall nun who was talking intensely with Fitz. Sister Bernadette was known among the girls as Red Bernie, but Ali had never been sure whether it was because of the ginger hair that peeked out of the band of her short veil or her attachment to social justice. She was always recruiting girls to visit hospices or crochet blankets for Africa.

Mother Mary Paul clapped again, sharp as a rifle shot, and announced that there would prayers of thanksgiving in the chapel. Ali saw Sister Bernadette turn away from Fitz to put her plate down, and Fitz took the chance to signal to Ali. She held two fingers up to her lips, blew through them and pulled an invisible cigarette from her mouth.

'Is she blowing a kiss at you?' asked Sister O'Dwyer, alert to any hints of an unsuitable attachment.

'No, it's something else.'

Fitz was pointing towards the window now and Ali nodded her head.

'What's she doing?' said the nun.

'Let me help you up, Sister.'

It took a minute to ease Sister O'Dwyer into the small herd shuffling towards the chapel. Ali stepped back into the emptying parlour, where a couple of younger nuns in big blue aprons were clearing the tables. Fitz had disappeared.

She retrieved her overnight bag from under a chair and hurried back out into the corridor. One side was lined with glass cases full of dull geological specimens and stuffed animals whose fur had been bleached blonde by decades of sunlight slanting through the windows opposite. All these familiar things. She passed the arched alcove that housed a mural of the Assumption, Mary taking off into the wild blue, supported by a cushion of disembodied angel heads. Down the big staircase next, her lone footsteps echoing up through the cold hallways, the empty classrooms, the ranks of desks.

*I never have to come back again.* She was almost running now, past the cloakrooms to the double doors that led to the grounds. One push and she was out, the sun streaming down.

She thought Fitz would be right there, but she wasn't. She must have gone on to their usual smoking spot. Ali walked on into the grounds. The nets sagged on the tennis courts, weeds sprouting at the bottom of the chain-link fence. Summer-holiday shutdown. Passing the junior-school windows, she could see tiny chairs stacked up on tables.

She turned down the broad path that led to the Rosary Walk and climbed the four steps up to its gravel surface. Stone slabs, like miniature tombstones, flanked either side at regular intervals, ten on the left, ten on the right. Each slab bore a tile showing a scene from the life of the Virgin. The idea was to say your rosary while you walked, and if you got the pace right, you'd reach a slab at the end of each Hail Mary, completing a ten-prayer decade by the time you'd walked the length. It depended how fast you prayed, of course. Or walked. Before you turned round for the return decade, you could contemplate a life-size statue of the Pietà at the path's end, a whitewash-blurred tableau of the dead Christ balanced on his mother's knees. Mary looked down so calmly at the distorted corpse, oblivious to the strain on her thighs.

Halfway along the walk, a path led off to a small gate in a thick hedge. Ali lifted the latch and entered the shade of the Rosary Garden. She remembered Sister O'Dwyer telling them that the trees around it had been planted to shelter the little garden from the winds that blew down across the fields from the Dublin Mountains. That must have been a long time ago, for nowadays the garden was shaded to the point of gloom and the fields had become housing estates. With the trees in full leaf, it had an almost underwater feel, faint dapples of light moving across ivy-filled beds. A tiny building stood in one corner, all dimpled windows and painted-on beams. It looked like something from a Grimm fairy tale, but it was just the garden shed.

Ali scanned the garden. Perhaps Fitz had got caught up with the chapel crowd after all. A twig snapped somewhere nearby, and a blackbird flew from a hedge.

She moved deeper into the garden. Another sound reached her ears, a kind of high whimpering. It was coming from the direction of the shed, and now she noticed that the door was half open.

'Hello?'

'Aa – li?' The voice that came from inside the shed was Fitz's but sounded weirdly stretched. Ali's skin prickled.

She pushed the door open. Fitz was standing in the middle of the shed, her face as pale as milk and her fingers at her mouth. A smear of lipstick trailed across one cheek. She appeared to be standing in a nest of gardening tools – hoes, rakes and loppers meshed around her ankles. Her eyes were fixed on the floor: on a wire basket filled with smaller tools. Ali picked up a fallen rake that blocked her way, propped it against the wall. As she turned back she noticed a large mushroom or egg nestled among the tools in the basket. She wanted to go to Fitz, to free her from the tangle of handles – but she couldn't make sense of this thing. She stepped closer, wondering at the fuzzy halo around the edge of the egg.

Downy hair on a head.

Ali's vision blurred and wavered. She moved a little to the side and the object resolved itself – couldn't be undone now – as the top of a baby's head. She took another step towards Fitz and the body of the baby appeared, shoulders wrapped in white and the rest hidden by a brown paper bag. The rusting blades of pruning saws and secateurs bristled behind its head, but the baby was unmarked, and perfectly still.

'I was looking for matches,' said Fitz.

The baby's eyes were closed, but its open mouth was dry and flaking around the lips, and a horrible darkness brimmed inside. She waited for it to move.

'I was just looking for matches.'

Ali pulled her eyes towards her friend.

'For a fag,' said Fitz.

'C'mon!' Ali grabbed her arm and propelled Fitz out of the tumble of shed and into the garden.

Then they were running back to the school in a kind of dreamtime, slow and heavy, and her throat ached. Sister Bernadette appeared suddenly on the path in front of them, from nowhere, and Fitz ran ahead to her, streaming words.

The nun took control – Fitz was to go on to the school and get help, Ali was to come back with her, show her the place.

They ran shoulder-to-shoulder along the Rosary Walk and plunged into the garden. When they reached the door of the shed, Ali stood aside to let Sister Bernadette go in on her own. There was a long silence, a gap in time, before the nun reappeared, her face distraught, the features pulling themselves apart. She thrust an old china cup at Ali's stomach.

'Get me some water,' she said.

'What?'

'Go on.'

It wasn't until Ali was at the tap that she realised what her errand was. If the nun wanted to baptise the baby, perhaps it was alive. She hurried back, holding the sloshing cup at arm's length.

Sister Bernadette was waiting outside the shed, the child cradled in her arms. As she shifted her hold to reach for the cup, Ali was sure the baby's head moved.

'Is it going to be all right?'

But the nun just glared at her, then bent her head close in to the baby's, mumbling unsteady lines of prayer under her breath. She poured the water in a thin line over the child's face. It didn't flinch. Sudden tears fell from Bernadette's eyes onto the baby's still cheek, salt water following fresh. Ali noticed the baby was now wrapped in her own paisley-print scarf, and that her overnight bag was open on the ground.

Bernadette lifted a corner of the scarf to wipe the baby's face.

'That's mine,' Ali said.

Sister Bernadette turned hot eyes on her.

'You're a trivial, stupid girl, do you know that?'

She tugged the material in agitation, and the body of the child rolled in response, the cloth falling away to reveal a great purple bloom covering its back and neck.

An acid gush filled Ali's throat even as Bernadette moved to cover the little body again, now so obviously lifeless and broken. A crackle of static travelled through the air, a radio rasp. Ali turned to look at the gate, where the silver buttons on several Garda uniforms flashed in the bright sunlight beyond the garden.

# 3

A line of nuns occupied the six plastic chairs in the reception area of Rathmines Garda station. Vincent Swan could feel their eyes on his back as he walked up to the front desk and introduced himself.

'Detective Inspector Swan … from HQ.' Some old instinct kept his voice low.

The Garda at the desk nodded and disappeared. Swan tried a casual glance behind, but the nuns were still staring, except for an ancient one on the end, who had bent to her beads.

He had dropped Elizabeth at the station that morning, and the late start led to him working through lunch. When the call came, he was the only one in the office.

Swan would have preferred to go straight to the school, have a look at the scene and check that the tech guys were doing their thing, but the Rathmines chief, Munnelly, was anxious to get his station clear of nuns before the papers got a sniff of it. Swan could have pointed out it was Munnelly's fault for bringing them to the station in the first place, but there was no use getting retrospective. You just had to work from where you stood.

The desk Garda came back and pointed Swan to a side corridor where Superintendent Munnelly was waiting.

There was often a bit of jockeying when the murder squad was called in to assist the local Gardaí, but Munnelly didn't look put out. A little distracted and nervous, if anything. He led Swan to a back office for a briefing with the Gardaí who'd been first on the scene and a couple of women officers who'd been taking statements.

They ran through the facts of the incident quickly: where the child had been found and the apparent cause of death. The two schoolgirls who found the baby, and a nun they brought to the scene, were now at the station and had given initial statements. Yes, they'd been held separately; and yes, their stories tallied – mostly. But the nuns in reception were refusing to leave until their sister nun was free to go.

'How do you mean: their stories tally *mostly?*'

'There was some disturbance of the scene, sir.' This was from the youngest-looking Guard, a lanky fellow with crinkly hair.

'You were there?'

'Yes, sir. The nun moved the infant for the purposes of baptism, sir.'

'Why? The child was dead, I thought.'

The Garda shrugged. 'In case it hadn't been before?'

'So she moved it—'

'And poured water on it.'

'And rearranged the shed,' Munnelly added with a sigh. 'We answer to different authorities, eh?'

Swan held his tongue. He said he would start with the first girl who found the child.

'Carmen Fitzgerald.'

'Yes.'

The interview with the Fitzgerald girl didn't take long. She was a nervous little thing and too upset to be fully coherent. She kept going on about matches and cigarettes. He'd expected her to be wearing some kind of uniform, but she was in jeans and a blouse, with smeared scarlet lipstick on her mouth, and mascara under her eyes. Not like the schoolgirls of his day.

'What year are you in?'

'I'm not in any year. We left in June.'

'I don't understand. Why were you in school?'

'They had us back for a reception. The ones who were going to college. Can I go home soon?'

Home would be a nice house in Rathgar, or some other leafy address. No wonder she was upset. She was the kind of girl that bad things shouldn't happen to. After the good school, she would probably take an arts degree at college, maybe spend a year in Florence or Paris and return to tennis clubs, marriage, children with cod-Irish names.

'Off you go. We might have to talk again.' Swan turned to the Guard by the door. 'Can we give Miss Fitzgerald a lift to … where is it, pet?'

'Eh … Donnybrook.'

*Close enough.*

As the girl left, Munnelly came in. 'Do you think you could see the nun now?'

Swan pretended to consult his notes before agreeing.

He hadn't been close up with a nun since he was ten and at national school. They hadn't been especially cruel to him, though they were quick enough to snap a ruler across small knuckles. Back then he had a dread of them just because they were so alien-looking – towering pillars of blackness. When they patrolled the aisles of desks, the folds of their habits would brush against your bare arm or leg, soft and cold.

This nun was younger than he expected, pale and tall, with a touch of Deborah Kerr about her. He read her statement aloud and she listened solemnly, absolutely still.

'I have a few questions,' Swan said, putting the page down on the table.

'And I have one for you.'

'You go first,' said Swan.

'The baby. Where is she now?'

'I haven't been to the school yet, but I expect the body is still there while our officers piece things together. Then it'll be brought to our mortuary.'

Sister Bernadette raised her hands to the table, watching her fingers slowly interlace as if they had a life of their own.

'And then?' She addressed her hands.

'Hopefully, we find her people and there can be a burial.'

'If there is anything our order can do …'

'Sister, my doctrine is a little rusty – what was the point in baptising a dead child? Surely its soul had already departed.'

The look she gave him had only a hint of pity in it.

'There is always a point in doing what you can.'

'You said in your statement that the child was naked when you took it from the bag?'

'I found something to cover her with, something to hand. I didn't want people – the girl was with me – to see it.'

He was tempted to press her harder about handling the child, but he didn't have enough of the whole picture yet. See the place it was found, locate the mother: those were the pressing things.

Sister Bernadette was adamant she knew of no girl or member of staff being pregnant.

'It can be hard to tell.'

'I'm not a naïve woman,' said the nun. 'I see plenty of the world.'

Swan was tempted to let the other girl go home too, so he could get to the convent, but Munnelly said her recall was particularly good. Swan looked through the pages of her statement and conceded. He asked one of the female Guard to come with him to the interview room.

Alison Hogan was drawing some kind of diagram when they entered. The sweet diligence of her face was at jarring odds with her bird's-nest hairdo. She was dressed like some kind of vampire shepherdess.

She blushed as he introduced himself to her, put a hand over her drawing.

'I was doing a sketch of the shed for the officers,' she explained. 'I'm good at maps.'

Eager to please, despite the hairy get-up. Another nice middle-class girl. Good at things.

'May I?'

It was a bird's-eye view of the shed, with neat lettering pointing out features: 'door', 'bench', window'. There was a little oval shape in the centre: 'basket'. In the middle of the oval was an X. No word for it.

'Sister Bernie – she shouldn't have moved it, should she?'

'How's that?'

'You're supposed to leave things as you found them. That's what they do on television.'

'Indeed they do.' Swan smiled and laid her statement on the table, turned a couple of pages. 'You say the baby was wrapped in a white cloth. Sister Bernadette and your friend say it was in a paper bag.'

'It *was* in a brown paper bag, but there was something white wrapped around the baby – inside the bag.'

'What kind of cloth was it?'

'Just cloth-cloth,' said Ali. 'You know. Like a sheet or something.'

'How much time passed between you and your friend leaving the shed and you coming back with Sister Bernadette?'

'Not sure. Two minutes. Three?'

'Could there have been someone else in the garden – someone you didn't see?'

The girl's eyes widened.

'I don't know ... maybe ...'

'I don't want to put anything in your head. No one you saw?'

'No.'

Swan continued to scan the statement. There was a thin plastic cup of water by the girl.

'Do you mind?'

She shook her head and he took a sip from it. It was stale, with an aftertaste like pencil lead.

'When do I get my bag back?'

'The bag you say the nun took the scarf from?'

'Yeah, it's got a lot of stuff I need.'

'Not for a while. Sorry.'

The girl pursed her lips.

'Do you get on well with the nuns?'

She shrugged. She was going quiet on them.

Swan turned to the woman police officer, a sensible-looking sort, with thick black hair pulled back in a knot.

'She's been a great help, hasn't she?'

'Good enough to join the force, I'd say.'

'I'm sure Ms Hogan has even loftier plans than that. College, isn't it?'

'Well …'

'What are you going to study?' asked the officer.

'Law.'

Swan and the policewoman shared a smile.

'No offence,' explained Swan, 'but some solicitors are a great trouble to us.'

The girl looked upset.

'I'm sorry, you've had a dreadful morning. Why don't we let you get back to your mum and dad?' He went to give her hand a pat, but she flinched away from him.

'I don't have a dad. He died.'

'I'm sorry to hear that.'

'He was a solicitor.'

'Ah.'

'I'll just go and see if there's someone waiting for you,' said the Guard.

Swan walked the girl towards the reception area. She was taller than he had realised, eyes on a level with his own.

'We may need to talk to you again, Alison, and in the meantime I'd be obliged if you kept the details to yourself, eh?'

The girl asked if there was a toilet she could use. Swan flagged down one of the station Guards for directions and said he'd meet her at reception. The flock of nuns had departed. Only two people sat on the line of orange chairs: an ample woman in an unusual tweed garment and a floppy-haired young man hunched in concentration over a tightly folded newspaper.

'Anyone here to meet Alison?' Swan offered.

'I'm her mother,' the woman said, pressing an anxious hand to her chest. 'Deirdre Hogan. Are you in charge?'

Swan claimed he was.

She rose and came towards him, her layered wrap swirling about her. The garment was held together by a Celtic brooch the size of a saucer. Mother and daughter obviously shared a taste for exotic costume.

'Is it true about Ali finding a baby?' she asked in a low voice.

'Well, she was one of the people there. We just needed a word with her.'

'Is she all right?'

'She's been very calm, actually – very grown-up. You should be proud.'

This didn't soothe the woman. She looked round quickly at the young man, before taking a step closer to Swan.

'It's not fair …' she said.

'What's not?'

'Once would be bad enough. But twice – it's beyond sense. You see, it's happened before.'

# 4

Ali woke sweating from a dream. She'd been on her knees in the Rosary Garden, trowelling through sooty clay while Sister O'Dwyer stood over her, crying, begging her to come to the chapel, that prayers would start soon. Ali tried to explain that she had to find something first. She looked down at her trowel and there was half a worm on it – a white worm as big as a finger – writhing, blindly searching for its lost half.

The morning light leaked through her thin curtains. She was telling herself it was just a dream when she remembered what wasn't a dream, and images from the day before flooded her mind.

Ma and Davy had treated her so gently when they collected her from the police station, and later Davy went out and got a bucket of fried chicken and a bottle of white wine for dinner, as if her brush with death called for something – not a celebration, certainly, but an occasion outside everyday rhythms.

After they ate, her mother went to visit a friend in hospital, and Ali went to her uncle's room to sit side-by-side across his bed and watch a spy film on RTÉ2. They didn't talk much. Davy said he felt a bit stunned by what had happened, so he couldn't imagine how it was for her. They'd shared a half-bottle of Southern Comfort until her eyelids drooped and she lost track of who was who in the film. She didn't even remember getting to bed.

She hauled herself up on her feet and washed the remains of her make-up off at the sink in the corner of her bedroom. There was a shower next to the sink, like a plastic phone box parked against the wall, a remnant of the house's former life as a warren of bedsits. Ali used it as a wardrobe, hanging her clothes from the top edge, inside and out. She picked yesterday's dress off the floor and hung it over the layers already there. Then she changed her mind and bundled it into one of the boxes of junk under her bed. She didn't feel like seeing it again. When tears started, she sat on the floor and waited for them to pass, like weather.

Davy was down in the kitchen reading a newspaper, his fringe almost touching the page. When he noticed her, he made a half-hearted attempt at hiding it.

'Just looking at the jobs,' he said.

Davy had come to stay with them three weeks earlier. He was trying to find a job in Dublin, saying there were none to be had down in Clare. Each morning he would phone a few companies from the Yellow Pages and ask if they'd anything going.

'Saves the feet,' he'd say.

'But not my bloody phone bill,' Ma complained. 'You need to get out there.'

Ali liked having him around. He was the baby of his family, nearer her age than her mother's, and had a quick energy to him that altered the dull atmosphere of their house. He pottered around at all hours fixing things, hacking back the garden, surprising them. But he hadn't landed so much as an interview for a job.

Davy shook out the newspaper and began to fold it up. 'I didn't want you upset. I just thought I'd look – there's hardly anything.'

Ali tugged at the paper and he allowed it to escape. She found a small headline and a paragraph underneath. *Dead Baby Found in Convent.* It was a strange relief to see the words there, out in the world. The matter-of-factness of it.

'I thought it might be worse,' she said.

Her mother appeared in the doorway. 'That's only the start, apparently.'

She was wearing a loose dragon-print kimono over her nightdress and her dark-dyed hair sat in a careless knot on top of her head, like a cast member of a slovenly *Mikado*.

'Seán O'Loan told me the Guards were trying to keep the lid on it, but he expects the press will soon be crawling all over it.'

'When did you talk to *him*?' said Ali. 'I thought you were visiting Angela Farrington and her new hip.'

'Well, when I came out of the hospital I had a while to wait for the bus, so I dropped into Lamb's and he happened to be there.' Ma had assumed her posher voice. She was a lousy liar.

'You told him all about it, didn't you?'

Ma took down the gas lighter and stood silent by the cooker, waiting for its tick-tick sparking to ignite the gas. The blue flames flattened as she put the kettle down and turned back to her daughter.

'Well, I don't know *all about it*, do I? You've told us very little. What harm if our friend gets to know something ahead of the pack?'

'The policeman said I wasn't to say anything, and you go straight to a journalist. You could get me into trouble.'

'*You* didn't say anything. I did. It's my affair and I'll take the responsibility.'

'Oh, it's your *affair*, all right.'

'You're a cheeky little pup—'

'Ah, stop it now!' said Davy.

Ali felt a stab of shame, just a little one. She wasn't comfortable with the men her mother hung around with. No doubt the media crowd in Lamb's were entertaining, but Ali couldn't get past the fact that all those men had homes and families to return to, and dinner waiting in the oven. Her mother was never invited to share that dinner or sit at their tables.

The doorbell rang. They all looked up the hall to where the big panelled door was framed by threads of daylight.

'Well, it won't be for me,' said Davy.

Deirdre Hogan moved, closing the kitchen door as she went. Davy and Ali listened to the muffled exchange on the threshold. The other voice was a man's, and there seemed to be some kind of negotiation going on.

After a minute, her mother reappeared.

'Love?' she started, and Ali bristled. 'Seán sent a photographer.'

'What!'

'He says they're doing an article, but they've no photos to go with it. All he wants is a quick snap.'

'No way.'

'I'll just have to give him your school photo then.'

'Very funny.'

'It's the only decent one I have.'

Her sixth-year photograph sat framed on her mother's dressing table, under a fine film of talc. In it Ali wore her uniform, a hairband and a submissive chin-tucked smile. She hated the girl in that photo.

'Hal-oo-oo?' The photographer was walking down the hall.

'You're *unbelievable*.'

Her mother opened the kitchen door. The man had a big canvas bag over one shoulder and a tripod in one hand. He looked around impatiently.

'Is there a cosy corner somewhere we could do this, ma'am?' He smiled at Ali and held out his hand. 'Eamonn Owens at your service.'

Ali stood up. 'I need to go and change.'

'Change? Change?' said the photographer, 'sure aren't you perfect as you are? A lovely young one. I've snapped all the great and the small – you're safe with me.'

'How about the garden?' said her mother.

Eamonn looked doubtful, then his expression changed.

'A garden was where this thing – this *awful* thing – happened, wasn't it? Yeah, the garden would do.'

He shot off through the back door and down the steps. Ali got up and checked her reflection in the kitchen mirror. She was wearing an old black jumper and her hair was pulled back in a ponytail. No make-up, no frills, just get it over with.

It was lucky that Davy had so recently managed to create something like a patch of lawn by getting down on his knees with a pair of old shears, but a thicket of creepers and shrubs still held sway over most of the garden. On fine nights, she and Davy would sit out on a rug, with candles in jam jars, drinking strange cocktails created from the furthest reaches of her mother's drinks cupboard. Those nights felt like ages ago. Ali clutched the metal rail as she went down the steps, thinking of escape, but not acting on it.

The photographer asked her to stand under the old apple tree and to look back at the house over his shoulder. It was uncomfortable to be examined so intently. The lens was huge, and the clicks kept taking her by surprise. The side of her mouth started to flutter in a nervous spasm.

'Don't smile,' he warned, 'think of … well … something sad.'

Ali let her eyes drift out of focus and allowed the pictures to rise in her mind – the garden, the shed – and with them the feeling that the last twenty-four hours, including this ludicrous photograph, were an elaborate hallucination over which she had no control.

Something was shifting in her mind, trying to surface, to make itself known.

It flickered into life.

The camera clicked on, but Ali was somewhere else, twelve years in the past.


*Because it was so heavy, she held the box across her arms. She hadn't noticed when she lifted it, but now it felt clammy against her skin, the cardboard sticky. Ali went down the farmhouse stairs one by one.*

*The door to the living room was shut and she had no hand free to open it. She was wearing her party shoes for Christmas Day, the black patent ones, and she lifted her right foot and pressed a shiny toe to the door. It swung open without a sound. The family were all there. Her cousins on the floor playing with their toys, teenage Davy crouched over something too. Ma looking sad and strange in her tight dress and make-up, Uncle Joe bare-headed for once, his hair plastered down, wearing his mass-suit.*

*They didn't see her, not at first. Ma looked up, and the others followed her gaze.*

*'What have you got there?' Ma asked.*

*'I found it,' Ali said. 'I found the doll.'*

'Turn your head. Chin up, but look at the ground. Almost there.'

All of them looking at her. The photographer, now, looking at her. The shame.

'Is that enough?' she said. 'Can that be enough?'

He took the camera from his face, and she headed straight for the house, leaving him to follow in her wake.

Her mother showed Eamonn out. Low voices mumbling by the door, a few exaggerated sighs. Ali waited in her bedroom until the coast was clear, then went down to the phone.

Their telephone was a black wall-mounted payphone in an alcove under the stairs. They left the money drawer open so that the same well-worn ten-pence piece could be circulated round and round.

Ali hooked the coin out of its cranny and put it in the slot. She pressed button A when Fitz answered.

'My mum's trying to keep me away from the phone,' Fitz said, 'you're lucky you got me.'

'How're you holding up?'

'I don't know. Fuck, Ali, I keep seeing the little face.'

'Yeah …'

'Could hardly sleep a wink.'

'Me and Davy got a bit pissed – that helped.'

'Your uncle's cool. I like him.'

'Did you say anything to the police about where we were on Sunday night?'

'No, they didn't ask. Did you?'

'I only thought of it afterwards. It gives me the creeps …'

'Hey – you won't believe this – a reporter from the *Independent* phoned this morning and I had to pretend I wasn't here. I said I was my sister.'

'You didn't talk to them?'

'No way. My dad says they're vultures. Did they try you?'

'No calls … but there was a photographer here, and my ma let him in.'

She told Fitz about her mother talking to Seán O'Loan. 'I feel like a right fool.'

She waited a beat for Fitz to contradict her, but Fitz just changed the subject to how horrible the police station had been.

A few seconds of silence opened into a chasm. Ali suggested that she could come over, but Fitz said it wouldn't be a good idea – they were about to have lunch.

'What are you having?' asked Ali, desperate to get back to normal.

She heard Fitz let out an impatient puff of air.

'Salad or something. It's not interesting.'

Ali let her go. The instant she put the receiver back on the cradle it rang, vibrating through her hand.

'Hello?'

'Hello. Am I speaking to Alison Hogan?' The elongated vowels had a velvety cadence that was somehow familiar.

'Yes, that's me.'

'Great. My name's Mary O'Shea ...'

The rest of her sentence was lost, drowned out by the panicked flurry in Ali's head. *Mary O'Shea*. Of course she knew the voice, but the voice should be coming out of a radio, not out of their cracked old phone. Ali tried to catch hold of the flow of words as they poured into her ear, suddenly seizing on the name 'Seán O'Loan'.

'... so Seán said it would be all right for me to give you a little bell and see how things stood.'

'I see ...'

'He said you were a very smart girl. Going to do law, he said.'

'I hope so – if I get the results.'

'And he said your mother was a wonderful women; a strong independent spirit was what he said.'

That didn't sound much like her mother, but the outside world judged things differently. Ali looked up to see the independent spirit pass by, still in her kimono, carrying a tray full of mugs and glasses to the kitchen.

'That's nice ...' Ali waited for her mother to get out of earshot.

'Look, here's me going on,' said Mary. 'It's hard to have a proper chat on the phone. I know you must feel absolutely shattered, but I was wondering whether you and I couldn't get together for a little talk. I'd really appreciate it.'

'I don't know ...'

'How about coffee at the Shelbourne? Just the two of us.'

# 5

Swan placed the pristine copies of the *Press* and *Herald* on the table in front of him. There was nothing on either front page, so he'd sit for a minute, enjoy his coffee and the dark peace of the Gravediggers on a summer's day. The barman leaned his crossed arms on the counter, surveying his own paper spread flat on the wooden surface. A burst of bronchial laughter carried over the top of the wooden screen that separated the small back bar from the front of the pub. He had passed two aul' wans on his way in, drinking glasses of stout side-by-side, merry as girls. Here in the back there was just the whisper of pages turning, the slow tick of the clock and the gurgle of cisterns beyond the brown lacquered toilet doors. All it needed was the thump of a collie's tail on the floor and you could believe you were in some country town.

He should have gone straight back to HQ from the convent, but took a little detour instead. He needed to see what the papers were saying – he needed to think.

Kavanagh, the chief superintendent, had phoned him at home that morning, just after seven, to say he wanted a quick finish to this case, it had too many 'knobs on'. Crudely put as always, but he understood what Kavanagh meant – this one had knobs, bells and miraculous medals all over it.

A dead baby in a convent – that was slaughter and religion, for starters, with a background of sexual activity. The fact that it was one of the most affluent schools in the city brought in money and class. Coming hot on the heels of the 'pro-life' referendum, when the country had screamed itself into a bitter divide over whether it loved its foetuses more than their mothers, this delicate atrocity was sure to keep the fires aglow. No wonder Kavanagh was jumping around like a bluebottle on a window.

Swan turned back to what he'd been putting off: checking through the evening papers to see what they'd got hold of. The press announcement wasn't scheduled until later, but you never knew. One of those girls could be the daughter of some blow-dried RTÉ journalist.

He opened the *Evening Press* and was assaulted by toothy grins on the social-diary pages. The high life in Ireland the previous day had consisted of a reception at a stud farm in Naas and the opening of a gallery in the Powerscourt Centre. All the photographs featured good-looking women with big hair and big earrings. It was a world that Swan rarely came into contact with, but it was the world that girls like Alison Hogan grew up to inherit.

That thing the mother said about the girl having found another baby at a relative's farm clung to him. Buleen, she said the place was. Ali Hogan was just six at the time. He hadn't got much more of the story from her before the girl appeared and Mummy clammed up. It was grisly luck all right.

If he could find someone to look into it, though, he could have some answers ready, in case the press or Kavanagh got hold of it. He tried to think who he knew in Clare or thereabouts, reaching for his coffee and enjoying a thoughtful sip. It was cooling now, but the brandy gave a nice gingery kick. If one of the lads happened into the pub, he would look as innocent as a lamb.

As a teenager, Swan had inherited a suitcase of old paperbacks when his Uncle Tony died. They were the first books, apart from school books, that he could call his own. He propped them up on the mantelpiece in his bedroom, with two bricks for bookends, and felt himself a man of the world. Half of them were green-spined Penguins by a man called Simenon, and he had spent weeks of one summer lying on his bed reading through them, lost in the pale stone and twisted staircases of Paris, mouthing words like *préfecture* and *gendarme* and imagining what an Algerian might look like. Maigret, the morose detective, would pop into bars throughout his working day for a quick drink, but never got drunk. The French didn't go for swilling bucketloads of Guinness and licking the foam from their faces. No, they supped one small crystalline drink, and on they went with their day.

That was the main lesson he'd taken from Maigret. The fact that he signed up with the Gardaí at the end of that summer was coincidence, really. College hadn't been an option. His father wanted him to come and sell furniture with him in the shop in Phibsborough, but the Saturday afternoons Swan had spent there throughout his teens – squeezed between bedroom suites and veneered telephone tables – felt like being trapped in a vault. His father standing, looking out the window, so forbearing, whistling through his teeth and dreaming of the pub later, the camaraderie of men and the bottomless pint.

The papers had the story on their second and third pages, a four-inch column in one and a double column with big headline in the *Herald*. All they said was that the body of a newborn infant had been found in the grounds of St Brigid's, Milltown. Mother sought. Nothing about the injuries. Good. Nothing too specific about the whereabouts. Good. The *Herald* filled in some background on St Brigid's, which included the information that the convent housed forty nuns. Just as a matter of record – hint, hint. He could see that the nun-angle might grow in the coming days.

Was it feasible that a nun might have given birth? It didn't seem likely; it seemed like the stuff of jokes about sexy nuns and randy priests that the tough boys down the lanes would tell. *Candles out before bedtime, Sisters.* And it wasn't a possibility that he – a man with two decades of police work under his belt – had had the balls to confront the Reverend Mother with.

Mother Mary Paul had greeted him that morning with level eyes, professional to professional, had walked him around the grounds and answered all his practical questions. As she spoke, she kept withdrawing a crumpled hankie from a sleeve, touching it briefly to her impressive nose before tucking it back into the pendulous folds of her sleeve. It seemed a preventative measure rather than a real mopping operation. Or maybe it was her way of expressing a kind of regret.

The school grounds were impressive, but depressing

– the gloom under the big trees, the holy statues watching over emptiness. They stood together for a while on the raised path they called the Rosary Walk and took in the view. It was a fine bit of land they had still, but, beyond an ugly brick wall, new houses pressed in around them, the march of the suburbs.

That was the moment he should have turned to her and asked plainly about the ladies of her community, but his brain would not form the correct words. Instead, he'd made another appointment to see her in the morning, in her office. He rationalised this as building a steady relationship, but knew he was just putting it off, hoping for a lucky break elsewhere.

Beyond those convent walls, dozens of detectives and Gardaí were going door-to-door along the quiet streets, searching for a woman known to be pregnant but with no baby to show for it, tapping into gossip, nosing out illicit liaisons, sudden weight gain or families where there might be 'a bit of a problem'. By the time he got back to the office, something might have been shook from the tree.

The barman stretched his arms above his head and roared out a long yawn. He pointed at Swan's coffee cup and raised an eyebrow.

'Maybe half a cup,' said Swan. The barman lifted the coffee flask from its dock and reached up for the brandy bottle with the other.

'Just the hot stuff, Joe.' He wasn't going to break the Maigret rule, especially during a wave of self-doubt.

There was something so bleak about the nature of this crime, the pathetic waste of it. What was there to say about a baby? There was no story to a person whose life could be counted in hours. It wasn't like the student nurse coming home alone after a dance, or the father of six stabbed in a pub fight. Until they found the baby's people, she floated alone, just an idea of a life.

No one had come forward to claim her yet. But things were ticking along, and now he had a new piece of the jigsaw. He looked down at the sealed bag beside him on the bench. What was inside might be a key.

Swan had parted with Mother Mary Paul outside the Rosary Garden. A lone Garda sat inside the gate on a rusty chair, looking eager for a chat, but Swan nodded briskly and passed into the gloom. A filament of cobweb stretched and broke across his face.

He paused and passed a palm over his cheeks, took in the scene – a few mossy benches, a rockery that looked more like a plum pudding than the side of an Alp, beds filled with indistinguishable green plants crawling over each other. *Ground cover* – the phrase came to him from one of his wife's gardening programmes.

The shed in the corner fitted in with the atmosphere of shabby romance, with its little cottagey windows and tiled roof, but green algae crawled up its painted walls and the bottom of the wood-slat door had gone soft and gappy. There was always a thin line between romance and rot.

Had the shed been a stopping-off point for whoever had the baby? Maybe they went in there to get a spade, but were disturbed by the girls. It would have been hard to get out of the shed without being noticed.

Two Technical Bureau personnel were still at work

inside, but said Swan was welcome to have a quick look. The interior was unexpectedly dry, the floor covered with dregs of desiccated peat moss. Chalk marks and smears of fingerprint dust showed on the floor and walls.

'You taken much out?' asked Swan.

'Not really,' answered one of the men, pulling down his mask. 'A few items that might have been weapons – but look at it.' The shed was filled to the gunnels with all kinds of metal tools, not to mention hundreds of old pots, boxes, bits of string and netting and a stack of dusty deck-chairs. They were going through it all, bit by bit, and so it happened that Swan was standing there when the other masked man lifted a deckchair from the stack and opened it to reveal a bundled knot of white concealed in its striped fold. The luck of it warmed him.

A mother-of-pearl button gleamed on an edge of it, and they could see some brownish staining in the depths of its folds. It could be the white cloth that Ali Hogan said the baby was wrapped in. The technicians slipped it gently in a bag, and agreed Swan could take it straight back to the labs. Well, it would get there soon enough.

The front section of the pub was growing noisy, the door opening and closing, letting in sweeps of sunshine. Three men in black suits came through and stood together at the bar. Glasnevin graveyard was next door, so funerals were a common part of the custom. He wondered whether the regular intrusion of mourning was one of the reasons he liked it here.

Enough wondering. Swan leaned back to root for coins in his trouser pocket. He picked up the evidence bag, walked over to the phone cupboard at the back and rang the office number. Declan Barrett, the newest recruit to the murder squad, answered.

'I'm on my way in.' Swan pulled the folding door tighter to damp the background noise. 'Did pathology call yet?'

The baby's body had been moved to the morgue late the previous evening. A tiny thing stranded on an adult-sized slab. No larger than a loaf of bread under the cloth. Full autopsy would take about a week to come in, if he was lucky, but he'd put in an urgent request for a rough estimate of the child's age and time of death.

'Just a tick, boss,' said Barrett, a slight stress of his voice managing to make the word 'boss' sound like a bit of a joke between them. The lad was giddy with his new posting. He'd better settle down soon. 'Here it is: estimated time of death between twenty and sixteen hours before forensics got to the scene at three p.m. yesterday. Newborn infant, female, approximately two to three days old, cord cut approximately five inches from the body and healing, body washed of vernix, some fibres present. Now I've looked up the medical dictionary, and apparently the vernix is waxy stuff that coats it when it's born—'

'Barrett, I know what vernix is.'

'So I figure the baby was washed and cared for.'

'Do you now? Have they checked the wounds?'

'No – the pathologist can't get to it yet. Backlog. I'll call again: harry them a bit.'

'Is Considine about?'

'Gina?'

'She's not Gina to you, Barrett.'

A pause. Swan could hear a muffled remark and someone laughing.

'She's on a call with Hannigan. Anything I can help with?'

'No.'

Swan hung up on a wave of irritation. Barrett's keenness needled him out of all proportion. And so did the fact that Sergeant Gina Considine was every detective's preferred support these days, and not just his. She was smart and hard-working. The other detectives gradually overcame their chauvinistic prejudice once they realised how good she could make them look.

This was a case Swan wanted her opinion on. He shuffled the coins in his hand and thought for a moment. Seeing the child last night, and the fullness of its features, made him suspect this wasn't a case of neonatal panic. There had been an incident last year, a baby left in a carrier bag under a bench by the Royal Canal. He had seen into the bag himself and could never forget the look of the poor scrap – smeared with a mixture of what looked like wax and old blood, its froggy little body squashed into shrouds of newspaper and plastic bag. Suffocated at birth, they said. Hard to tell if the lungs had ever drawn air, the eyes ever registered light.

A bubble of hopelessness rose in him and all at once he was aware of the heat and claustrophobia of the booth. He lifted the receiver once more, put in a coin and dialled his home number. Across the square from the Gravediggers, in a terraced red-brick house, a phone rang and rang. He imagined the sound echoing round the hallway, ricocheting off the dark furniture salvaged from his father's shop. He imagined Elizabeth walking downstairs towards the sound, or turning her head among the flowerbeds at the back, rising slowly to her feet. He let it ring until there was no hope of an answer. She hadn't come back yet.

# 6

Ali looked up at a torch-bearing maiden poised on the balustrade of the Shelbourne Hotel, the thin copper drapery emphasising rather than veiling the statue's voluptuous figure. She remembered staring at these figures when she was small, her attention caught by their prominent breasts; her father laughing when he saw what she was looking at, and she'd got embarrassed, but he'd swung her hand back and forth, making her body twist, forcing her to smile.

If only she could remember more of him. At least she could still feel that sensation of her own small hand in his large one, the comfort of that.

When he was alive, the two of them would go into town on a Sunday morning. After mass in Clarendon Street they'd buy Sunday papers from a man with blackened fingers and walk hand-in-hand to a nice hotel like the Hibernian or sometimes the Shelbourne, and Daddy would read his papers while she drank lemonade through a straw and ate her way through a little dish of salty, bitter-skinned peanuts. Often an acquaintance of her father would stop by to talk and she would try to look as well behaved as she could.

She hadn't been in the Shelbourne since – the days of expensive little treats long gone. The entrance hall was the same: high Georgian mirrors and walls the colour of mint ice-cream. And right in the middle of the hall stood Mary O'Shea, surrounded by a gaggle of hotel staff, eager with laughter.

'Oh, Mary, you're killing us,' said one, clutching his stomach.

'That's the best yet,' said another, holding on to the edge of the reception desk for support.

Even the chandeliers seemed to favour Mary, the light haloing her bobbed golden hair and winking from her polished nails as she waved her hands around.

Ali stood outside the group for a moment, wondering how to make herself known. She thought about walking back out of the place, but just as she started to turn she heard 'Alison?'

Mary O'Shea walked out of the circle of men to stand in front of her. Ali caught the look of deprivation in their eyes, before she herself was caught in the lovely beam of Mary's attention.

'Most people call me Ali.'

'So I will too, Ali, I will too.' Mary slipped her hand through the crook of Ali's arm and set off through a sofa-filled lounge. 'It's a bit public here, isn't it? Let's try the bar. Michael?'

Mary didn't even break stride or turn round. One of the reception staff, still pink with merriment, simply drew close behind them, a dog to heel.

'The bar's open, isn't it?'

'We can open it.'

'Good man.'

They settled onto a leather bench in a corner of the panelled room. An island bar took up most of the floor, a wooden command centre armed with upturned bottles. The air smelt faintly of ashes and stale beer.

'This is fine,' Mary declared.

'Grand,' agreed Ali.

A big, embarrassed-looking lad in a dicky bow appeared behind the bar counter and started to switch on lights.

'Can I get you ladies anything?'

'I was just going to have a coffee,' said Mary, 'but it's so hot, I don't know. What do you think, Ali: gin and tonic?'

Ali agreed, even though she hardly ever drank gin, associating it with the juniper tang of her mother's lips when she kissed her on her return from a party or the pub.

Mary fished about in her handbag. She brought out a tiny tape recorder and a gold compact, which she flicked open with one hand and circled in front of her perfectly made-up face. She tipped her chin up and rolled her glossy lips back to reveal an even row of small teeth.

'You look great,' Ali said, and Mary threw a smile at her.

'Bless you, but you should see it first thing.' She snapped the compact shut and threw it back in her bag, then turned her full attention on Ali.

'What happened at St Brigid's is important,' she said. 'Very big. There's going to be a lot of attention paid to this case. Even the British papers will be writing about it—'

The boy appeared with their drinks and put a small dish of peanuts in front of Ali. Tiny ones with their skins on, lathered in salt. Ali smiled. Mary caught her expression, misunderstood it.

'No flies on you,' said Mary. '*What does she want from me?* you're asking yourself. Well, I have a question for you.'

Ali met Mary's eyes, facing up to her challenge. This was worse than the police. But exciting too. If someone saw them together – imagine. She took a sip of her drink. It tasted clean and sour.

'How often do you hear the voice of a girl your age on radio or television?'

Ali shrugged.

'There's a lot talked about young people – your lack of respect, your promiscuous behaviour – but who gets to hear your voice? This case will be chewed over by doctors and bishops and government ministers, all men of course, but you were on the spot. The mother could be another schoolgirl. I want to hear what *you* have to say.'

'I don't know that I've anything to say. I just happened to be there.'

'Maybe you think you've nothing to say because all your life people have told you to listen, not speak.'

'Maybe …' Something stirred inside Ali, some obscure part of her spontaneously inflating. She had a vision of people applauding, rising from their seats. She took a big gulp of gin.

Mary's hand reached for her little recorder, fingered a button on it.

'Do you mind?'

Mary O'Shea was as famous as you could be in Ireland. She had a show on the radio, a Sunday newspaper column and *The Late Late Show* wouldn't go near the subject of women's rights without Mary in the studio. Even Ali's mother, who approved of very few people, loved Mary. She'd shout, *Go get 'em, girl!* at the radio when Mary lured some old reactionary out onto the gangplank of his own absurdity.

'The thing is,' Ali began, 'the policeman – the detective – said I wasn't to talk to anyone.'

Mary's brows lifted a centimetre, she widened her smile. The Dictaphone went back in the bag.

'Not a problem. The recorder's just handy – I'm desperate at shorthand. I wouldn't print anything against your will, or anything that would harm the case. I am *scrupulous* about that kind of thing. Did I tell you I went to Brigid's myself?'

'The nuns mention it all the time.'

'Probably as some kind of dire warning about condom-waving feminists.'

Ali laughed. 'Just a bit.'

'I hear Mary Paul's in charge now. She was the bane of my youth. She taught me history in second and third year … most of the oppressed or massacred "didn't help themselves", I seem to recall.'

'She doesn't teach now. Too busy imposing the rules.'

'Was she there yesterday?'

'Not in the garden, well … yes, in the garden later. They were all there at the reception, the nuns.'

Ali started to explain why they were at the school, and Mary asked if she could take notes at least. Ali suddenly couldn't think of a reason why not. When she got to the part where she entered the shed and saw the baby, Mary asked, 'When you saw it, what did you feel?'

49

The gold Biro hovered an inch above the page. The brown eyes skewered her.

Ali paused. 'I thought it couldn't be real.' Her face felt hot. 'Fitz was in a state. I wanted to get us away from the shed.'

'And now?'

'Now?'

'How has it left you?'

She could see an image of herself as the photographer had posed her that morning: wistful, misted in sadness. But that wouldn't do for Mary. Mary would want her to be tougher.

'I feel angry.'

Mary stopped writing.

'How d'you mean?'

Ali shrugged, she hardly knew what she meant. 'The way things are … this country.'

'Ah.' Mary sat back against the upholstery and smoothed the material of her skirt over her thighs. 'Did you get Sister O'Dwyer for sex education?' she asked.

'No!'

'That's what we got. She handed out booklets and made us read them in silence; it was all diagrams of Fallopian tubes and cell division. She'd sit up at the high desk in front of us – possibly the most innocent nun in Ireland – and she'd say, *Ask me anything*. One brave girl asked how the seed got from the man into the woman, and Sister O'Dwyer pretended she hadn't heard. Told us to turn to the next page.'

Ali laughed.

'And that was very advanced for the sixties,' said Mary. 'What did you get?'

'We got a man. Not just a man of course, a *doctor*. We were twelve or thirteen. He talked to us for a whole day. Most of it was about the Billing's method and secretions, and how to fend off your husband's advances. Because men can't help themselves, he said.'

'It's no joke, getting pregnant.'

'No. But they always go on about how men want sex, like it's their particular thing, not the women – we only go through with it to be kind. Can't women want it too?'

Mary smiled a slow smile and smoothed her hair. 'It takes a while to get past the programming.'

Ali took another sip from her glass, thought how nice it would be to be as comfortable in the world as Mary O'Shea.

'You know the referendum?'

Mary sighed as she nodded.

'No one made the men account for their sperm, did they?'

'A fair point.'

'Each little tadpole a potential human soul. No, it was always about those murderous women, those precious eggs.'

'*The most dangerous place in the world is in a woman's womb,*' intoned Mary, a notorious quote from an arch-bishop. 'Why do you think the baby died?'

Ali looked away.

'I don't know,' she said.

They fell silent for a moment, Mary looking down at her notebook, Ali stirring the ice-melt in her glass with a plastic swizzle stick.

'I had a great friend at school,' said Mary eventually. 'Barbara, her name was. We went to the Gaeltacht together one summer, had a rare time – the boys, the ceilidhs, bonfires on the beach. We ran wild. But when we got back to school, Barbara said her mother had decided she should go to boarding school in the country and that she was leaving St Brigid's at Christmas. She went really quiet. I stupidly thought it was because she was so sad to leave me. I wrote to her at the new school, but she didn't answer. It wasn't till years later that I found out the truth of it.'

Ali nodded to show that she understood.

Mary picked up her drink and cupped it in her hands, leaning towards Ali.

'Did that happen to any girls that you know?'

Five minutes before, Ali would have said 'no', but as Mary talked, the face of a girl called Eileen Vaughan had risen in her mind. Eileen had been Fitz's best friend. It was only Eileen's sudden departure from school at Easter that left Fitz free to be friends with Ali. There were rumours through the school that Eileen Vaughan had been dabbling in drugs. Fitz wouldn't discuss it. Ali realised now there was a more obvious explanation.

'I think maybe it did. The same as with your friend. A girl left suddenly early this year, no mention of it afterwards, like she'd never been there.'

'When was this?'

'March, I think.'

'Hmm.' Mary counted on her fingers. 'Can you give me her name?'

Ali looked into Mary O'Shea's clear eyes. 'Sorry.'

Mary frowned, disappointed with her. 'Look, Ali. This thing will probably never go to court. They'll find the poor girl who gave birth and send her to psychiatric for a while. It's a tragedy, and a national disgrace, but it's hardly a state secret.'

Ali shrugged. She was thinking of Fitz being angry, not the police.

'Who's the officer in charge? The one who made you promise not to talk to people like me?' Mary made it sound like a game, a matter of poses being struck.

'He's called Detective Swan, I met him in Rathmines Garda station, but he said he worked at the Phoenix Park.'

'Is he a small, dark man – neat, reasonably attractive?'

'Well … I don't know about attractive.' Maybe he was, to someone of Mary's age. Her own mother thought the oddest men were lovely.

'I know him! He's in the murder squad. I talked to him once at The Gate, at a Wilde play. Not many detectives you can say that of. Maybe dragged along by the wife. A foot taller than him, she was.'

'It's not that I don't want to talk to you, Mary, but he'll know it was me.'

'Sure weren't there others who saw the same thing? All the nuns hanging about?'

'Well, no, not inside the shed …' She was going explain how only three of them had seen the child lying in the basket, when she stopped herself. The gin was making her stupid.

'What do you mean, the shed?'

'In the Rosary Garden. It was in the shed. I don't … I told you, I can't talk this way.' Her face felt terribly hot.

Mary held her hands up in mock surrender.

'We're on the same side, Ali. Want another drink?' She pointed at Ali's empty glass. Her own was hardly touched.

'I'm fine, thanks.'

Mary dashed off a few more squiggles on her pad.

'Look, I have to meet someone here in five minutes. I could talk all day, but we'll need to finish up. I'll write something for the paper tomorrow. It's nothing to worry about, but I will mention you and talk about the type of place St Brigid's is. I'd love us to keep in touch – as this thing unfolds. You've got integrity, and you express your-self well.'

'You won't make it sound like I've been pushing myself forward?'

'Ali. Don't worry. We've nothing to fear from the truth. As somebody must have said sometime.'

Mary opened her bag again and took out a business card. She wrote two numbers on the back and handed it to Ali.

'The top one is my answering service. They can page me wherever. That other one is my home number, so I'd appreciate it if you kept it to yourself.'

Ali smiled at the rectangle of card and slipped it into the back pocket of her jeans. Fitz would be amazed. She was about to get up when Mary stalled her with an out-stretched hand.

'Can I ask you one more thing?'

'Okay.'

'Do you think the baby died of natural causes? Sorry. It's a horrible question. Do you?'

'No.'

'No, you don't think so; or no, it didn't?'

'I think it didn't.'

They looked at each other for a minute.

'Oh, well, I'm sure they'll make a statement later today … so I'll wait to find out, with the rest of the gang.' Mary was putting away the notebook and pen, gathering herself.

'The back of the neck,' Ali said in a small voice. She lifted a hand to her own nape. 'It was all bruised. And down her back.'

She could still feel the squeeze of Mary's hand on her arm as she stood in the Ladies. She shouldn't have told. But Mary had stirred her up with kind words and the notion that she had something say for herself.

The ladies' toilets were walled and floored in sand-coloured marble. There was a stack of tiny towels by the oval basins. Her face in the mirror was flushed, her eyes strange to her. She filled a basin and washed her face and hands in cool water. She took one of the towels and buried her face in it, the loops of thread caressing her skin.

*The first one was lying under a towel. A grubby yellow towel.*

*Ali had been looking for her present, the doll called Baby Joy. That's what she asked Santy for, because her friend Maura Griffin in Dublin said Baby Joy was just like a real* baby, not a stiff girl with nylon hair and clicky eyes. She liked the idea that it would be close to real, like someone new to care for. But there was only one present under the tree for her that morning, a plastic cookery set threaded to a big sheet of cardboard. Her cousins seemed to have loads of stuff. She couldn't make a fuss, not there in her uncle's house, everyone in their good clothes.

Before Christmas, she wondered whether she would get more presents that year because of her daddy dying. It just came into her mind, but she feared that Santy knew. You shouldn't think that kind of thing.

She sidled up to her mother's chair.

'Does Santy come again if he's forgotten to bring something?'

Ma laughed, but it wasn't a kind laugh. It was sharp and drew the attention of the other grown-ups to her.

'What are they like, these days! No, he doesn't.' Ma had a tiny glass in one hand. A tissue poked out of the fist of the other. Ali moved away, slipped into the hall and made her way up to the back bedroom.

She hadn't been snooping, not really, though that's what Aunt Una said afterwards, angry with her. It was just that her cousin Roisín had told her about the big wardrobe upstairs. That she had seen presents hidden there. That Santy didn't exist.

The wardrobe was huge, separating two single beds. It had a mirror on its front and she watched herself approach, her moon-face looming above the velvet party frock that was painfully tight around her ribs that year, and so short that she could see her bare knees.

*She opened the door and her reflection slipped sideways and away in a shard of light. A smell of mould rose to greet her. She parted the heavy clothes that hung there, looked down among the wire hangers and shoes scattered across the bottom. There was no present. When she stepped back from the wardrobe, she saw there was a shelf above the clothes rail and could make out some folded blankets there, but no glint or flash of wrapping paper. Still, she felt a high shelf was the very place you would hide something if you wanted to keep it away from children, and it was also the kind of place where a present might get shoved to the back, might get accidentally forgotten in the rush.*

*She was looking all round the room for something to stand on, when she found the box.*

*It was under the left-hand bed, right up against the wall. It was larger than a shoebox. It was the size of a doll box. A box that someone had forgotten to wrap and had forgotten was under the bed. Ali lay flat on the lino and slid under, through a thick layer of dust, to pull the box out to the light. There was a curly pattern on the top and she could read well enough to make out the words 'Baby Joy'.*

*Her heart beat fast as she lifted the cardboard lid and saw a crumpled yellow towel covering the doll, its sleeping face just visible through a gap in the folds. She had been right all along, and that sense of rightness was stronger than any scratchings of doubt about the griminess of its wrapping or the odd appearance of the doll.*

*Baby Joy was supposed to look a little ugly, Maura Griffin said so.*

*Ali moved the towel. The doll's chest and shoulders were*

*naked, and the colour of the body was strangely mottled,*
*like the skin of her legs when they had been too close to the*
*fire; and although the doll was sleeping, it had a kind of*
*annoyed expression too, as if the dream it was dreaming*
*was something that called for huge concentration. Ali put*
*a hand to the shallow valley on the front of its chest. Cold*
*softness. Not plastic, more like rubber.*

*She would bring it down and show her mammy.*

Ali scrubbed at her face with the towel until it stung, and
flung the cloth on top of the others discarded in a basket
under the counter.

For twelve years she'd put it out of her mind. If she
thought of that box at all, it was as some sort of a bad
dream. But now it was back with her, as real as what she
had seen in the shed.

She would go back and find Mary. Try to limit the
damage. Tell her not to mention the bruising on the baby,
say she might have been mistaken.

There was no one in the back bar, just their two abandoned glasses, conspiratorial on the table. But Mary hadn't
gone far – she was in a window seat in the lounge, leaning
forward to talk to a man in a grey suit. Ali walked towards
her, and the man turned in his seat as he saw Mary's attention shift. Ali knew him. It was her mother's friend Seán
O'Loan, a chubby man whose straggly moustache looked
like it was trying to crawl inside his mouth.

Seán showed no surprise to see her there. He stood to
shake her hand and kiss her cheek with a wet tickle.

'Ali, pet. So sorry for what you've been through.'

He put a hand on her shoulder and squeezed. Ali made a mumble of thanks.

'Fate's very cruel. It was the last thing you needed.'

His pouchy eyes were trying to dig into hers. The hand on her shoulder was a clamp. Seán's attention was more than plain sympathy.

'The girl probably needs to get home, Seán,' said Mary.

Ali took her chance to escape. She had no doubt that they'd been discussing her just before she appeared.

# 7

The nun who opened the convent door was dark and nervy. She looked to be in her twenties or early thirties. Swan's eyes moved automatically to her belly. Could you tell if a woman had given birth, just by looking?

The entrance hall that she led T. P. Murphy and himself into was a double-height space with a grand wooden staircase rising up from the centre and dividing in two, so that you had a choice of route to the railed gallery that ran around the upper area. A glass cupola brought in light from above, but it had lost most of its brightness by the time it fell to where they stood. The nun pointed at a row of ecclesiastical chairs against the wall. They were the least comfortable-looking pieces of furniture that Swan had ever seen outside a designer showroom.

'Please, if you wait here,' said the nun, and he sat. T. P. Murphy eased himself onto the adjacent chair with a suppressed groan. The nun clipped away up the stairs, leaving them in the gloom. Like Pavlov's dogs, they were – obedient at the sight of a habit.

Murphy was not Swan's first choice of partner for a case like this, or any case. But he was the only other murder squad detective available. T. P. was not only a lead-swinger and a slipstreamer; he looked a right eejit too, with those sideburns and aviator specs, not to mention the wide tie just hiding the gaps between his strained shirt buttons. The best you could say for T. P. was that he didn't take anything too seriously, not even his mistakes.

Swan stood up, stretched his arms out unnecessarily and strolled about. The walls were crowded with paintings, a variety of saints suffering or beseeching behind layers of amber varnish. Only a few bright details shone out – the flash of angel's wing, the white of an eye rolled heavenwards, the glint of a sword. There were also portraits of nuns sitting at their desks with a Bible in handy reach or praying on their knees, their plain, redoubtable faces framed by elaborate arrangements of stiff white cloth.

He hated this atmosphere, the varnish and cold tile incarceration. Clearing out the attic recently, he had come across a picture of himself in altar boy's vestments. Ten years old. The pious solemnity of his younger face, his small unlined hands pressed together and pointing skywards. Before he understood what he was doing, he'd torn the photograph to confetti.

The first stages of the investigation had turned up nothing so far. All the babies born in hospitals and in registered maternity homes had been accounted for. A few tip-offs were being followed up – a travellers' camp by the Dodder, a hippy commune in some old mansion. Most likely the mother was local and had given birth in secret. That was the simplest explanation, and Swan liked to keep things simple until he was forced to complicate them.

A small, precise cough drew their attention upwards. The nun had returned and was gesturing for them.

They climbed into the light and followed her down a series of corridors featuring the same orange-stained wood everywhere, shiny panelling and rails and doors and benches. They finally stopped at the end of a wide corridor lined on one side with glass cases. Another row of straight-backed chairs stood to the side of a door on which a small card read *Reverend Mother* in crabbed Gothic calligraphy. It was hard not to imagine a line of fretful girls sitting there, awaiting punishment.

The nun took it upon herself to knock and a voice within called, 'Come!'

Swan had been expecting Mother Mary Paul to be alone, so he didn't welcome the sight of her sitting shoulder-to-shoulder behind her desk with a priest. The man was wearing a well-cut black suit and a dog collar. A gold chain with a plain cross added to the elegant effect. He had close-cropped hair at the sides and a polished baldness on top.

'This is Monsignor Kelly,' said Mother Mary Paul. 'The archbishop has been good enough to take a special interest in this tragic event and has sent the monsignor to assist us. Monsignor Kelly is trained in law.'

The priest offered them a thin smile, verifying confidence in his qualifications.

Swan introduced Detective Murphy, and they sat down on their side of the desk. Swan had hoped for an informal, wide-ranging chat. With God's lawyer present, he doubted if there would be much in the way of that. The monsignor already had a pen in his hand, poised over what looked like a typed list of names.

'I think it would help, Detectives, to get us off the ground as it were, if you'd outline the scope of your investigation so far – and perhaps indicate which areas you think we might assist with, and we can take the discussion from there.'

T. P. looked at Swan and crossed his arms.

A knock sounded on the door, and the dark nun entered with a tea tray. No one spoke as she settled the tray on the desk, filled four cups and handed them round.

'Thank you, Sister Dreyfus,' said Reverend Mother as the nun exited backwards, the empty tray held to her chest like a shield.

Once the door closed, Swan looked to the head nun. 'Sister *Dreyfus?*' He had decided to ignore the monsignor.

'It's an unusual name in these parts,' agreed Mother Mary Paul. She dropped her voice and leaned towards him. 'Family came here in the war. Converted.'

'Yes,' said the monsignor, 'perhaps we could—'

'Tell me, Mother,' said Swan, overriding him, 'why is it that some nuns have Christian names after the "Sister" and others have family names?'

Mary Paul stroked her veil as he had seen other women smooth their hair.

'Well, it varies from order to order. In the Sisters of the Annunciation, both apply. Nuns like Sister Dreyfus keep their family names while nuns such as myself and Sister Bernadette, who you've ... erm ... met, were moved to adopt the names of saints or holy people who had particular meaning for them. I took the name of our founder – Blessed Mary Paul Grammaticus.'

'I never realised that.'

'Most interesting,' said Monsignor Kelly without a shred of sincerity. 'I'm eager to know, Detectives, whether you've identified the poor child.'

Swan let T. P. waffle on a bit about the case, how everything that could be done was being done, and so on. He told them the enquiries were concentrating on the community surrounding the convent grounds.

'I wish now that we had put gates across the back lane,' said the nun, 'but we've never been in the habit of locking out the world.'

'That may have to change,' said Monsignor Kelly.

'Gates wouldn't necessarily have prevented this from happening,' said Swan, 'just caused it to happen elsewhere. Unless the baby was already in the convent. In that case, our task might be narrower in scope.'

The monsignor and the Reverend Mother stiffened.

'It's a theory I have to consider.'

'That isn't possible.' Mary Paul was adamant.

'How can you be sure? This is a very large establishment, Mother.' Swan suddenly realised how odd, and somehow disloyal, it felt to be calling an acquaintance *Mother*.

'Out of term, it's a very quiet place. We nuns live together in a community with only a few lay helpers for the grounds. We eat and pray together every day. Not much gets by me.'

'So there's been nothing different?'

'Nothing.'

'I'll bear that in mind when I speak individually to the nuns.'

The monsignor and Mother Mary Paul exchanged a glance.

'Is that necessary at this stage?' asked the monsignor. 'The disruption and anxiety have taken their toll on these women already.'

Mother Mary Paul looked annoyed for an instant, but worked her face into an expression of passivity. Not a woman who cared to be patronised, even by a monsignor.

'I wouldn't be doing my job if I *didn't* interview your community. There is no accusation to be inferred – it's simply procedure.'

Monsignor Kelly sighed, but didn't press the matter further.

'I'll need a list of all the nuns, even if they weren't here on Monday, and also names and telephone numbers of the hired staff that you mentioned.'

Mary Paul jotted down some notes.

'We'll need that today, Mother,' said T. P., 'and it would benefit us if you could include each woman's age?'

The nun looked up. 'Their age?'

Swan's patience vanished. 'Look, we're not suggesting a strip-search,' he said. 'We just need to know the age.'

Swan watched her write 'AGE' and underline it.

'The phones haven't stopped ringing here, and at the diocesan office, since news of this came out,' said Monsignor Kelly. 'Journalists and busybodies. The last thing we want to do is fan the flames of any salacious publicity. The archbishop is concerned the police don't encourage this kind of insinuation by the line of their enquiries.'

And no doubt the archbishop had many friends in

Garda HQ and in the Dáil with whom he was willing to share those concerns.

'There is no insinuation, Monsignor. And for what it's worth, flames get fanned when an investigation can't progress quickly and journalists fall back on their imaginings.'

'It's confidentiality that concerns me – things leaking out.'

'Not from my investigations, they don't.'

Sometimes Swan wondered at his own idiot reflexes.

Monsignor Kelly smiled. 'You haven't seen this morning's papers then.'

Swan looked at T. P., who gave him back a minuscule head-shake. They'd been shut in the case conference earlier, hadn't had the time. But someone would have shown him if there was anything important. Eager to move on, Swan arranged to have the list collected and said they'd set up interviews with all the nuns within the week.

'I realise that it's hard for you – for all the sisters – coming into contact with something like this.'

The look she gave him was fierce.

'Don't make the mistake of thinking we sit in our holy tower arranging flowers and sweeping floors. Some of my nuns work with the least fortunate in the city. They see poverty and degradation and death.'

'Point taken.'

Swan rose to his feet, T. P. followed.

'I just don't want them subjected to suggestions of … promiscuity or whatever. It wouldn't be … fair.' She reached up her sleeve for the wad of tissue. He had wondered when it would reappear.

Monsignor Kelly shifted one hand over so that it lay in front of the Reverend Mother. A restraint.

'The Church will assist in whatever way it can. In fact the Reverend Mother has thoughtfully drawn up a list of girls she thought might be worth talking to, for your purposes.'

The monsignor passed the piece of paper that had been lying on the table to Swan. He sat back down to study it. It was a list of girls' names, divided up into little sections headed 'sixth year', 'fifth year' and 'fourth year'. The second half was divided by year headings: 1983, 1982, 1981. There were about thirty names in all.

'It wasn't necessary to go any younger than the fourth year, I thought.' Mother Mary Paul had recovered herself. 'The others are girls who left in the last few years.'

Swan simply looked at her.

'We thought it would help,' said Monsignor Kelly, 'if you had a list of girls who, their teachers suspected, may have been in intimate contact with boyfriends and the like.'

'How can they tell?' said Swan.

'You can't, for sure,' said Mary Paul, in a reasonable tone. 'But in every year there are always a few who test the limits, and no doubt test their parents too. They're the risk-takers, and sometimes they wind up in trouble. They're all off on holiday or graduated, but I had a feeling a girl in trouble might just seek the shelter of the school she knew and loved.'

'Do you have a reason to believe that any of these girls were pregnant?'

'Only one for certain. Sixth year … Eileen Vaughan.'

Swan found the name on the list.

'She's not the one you're after, though.'

'Oh?'

'She left the school in March. I've enquired and she was delivered back in May.' The nun pressed her lips together.

'I'll need her address. And all these others?'

'Suggestions.'

'Thank you, we'll look into it.'

Swan took the list, folded it and put it in his inside pocket. The hypocrisy of them. It wouldn't be right to mention sex to any of the nuns, but here's a bunch of schoolgirls you might want to grill instead. Again he rose to his feet, and this time the nun and priest rose too. T. P.'s hand was on the doorknob when Mother Mary Paul's grave voice said, 'Perhaps a little prayer for the baby?'

They stood with clasped hands and bowed heads while the nun led them in a Hail Mary linked to some longer bit that Swan only half-recognised. Who was the hypocrite now? He mumbled the 'Amen'.

Monsignor Kelly walked them back through the maze of empty corridors, trying to interest T. P. Murphy in the history of the building. Swan's mind was on the list of girls. Just because their teachers thought them a bit wild didn't make them child murderers. Even if this Eileen Vaughan had been politely disappeared, that only proved the point. Most of these girls would be well taken care of, if they slipped up – a trip down the country for a few months or a shorter trip to England in some cases. Infanticide mainly happened in conditions of ignorance or secrecy. It wasn't the bolshie, confident girls you wanted. It was the quiet, mousy ones with only a vague grasp of the mechanics, or the ones being abused at home, or by a neighbour or friend of the family. Friend of the family – that's how they always referred to some old bastard with his eye on the kids.

Thing was, this time felt different. The other cases Swan knew were plain tragic, drenched with desperation. But this one: three days of food and care, love perhaps, before someone changed their mind. Maybe the mother was being watched by her own mother, say, and had to wait for her chance to do away with her child. Or was it the reverse: the mother had been content with the child, then someone else had discovered its existence?

Outside, Monsignor Kelly stepped into a shining black Mercedes and drove off with a roar.

'Great car,' said T. P. Murphy as it swept out the gate.

'Off to another crime against the faith,' said Swan, 'Do you ever get the feeling there's more than one police force in this town?'

'If it wasn't for the whole celibacy stuff, I'd happily join theirs. They know how to look after their own.'

'I can't quite picture that,' said Swan.

'You'd pass,' said T. P., 'you've a whiff of incense about you, and we've never seen this wife you claim to have.'

Swan glanced back and caught sight of a pale old nun watching their departure from a first-floor window.

A maroon Ford was pulled up beside their brown one. Detective Garda Barrett was propped against it, reading a paper in a slightly studied way. At the opposite end of the car, Detective Sergeant Gina Considine stood with her arms crossed, scanning the convent windows.

Barrett folded the paper back on itself and held it up

in front of his chest like a sign. 'You should look at this, sir.'

Swan took the paper and T. P. pressed in beside him to share it. The pictures registered first: a portrait of Alison Hogan looking like she'd lost her puppy and a shot of the gate to the Rosary Garden, its metal scrolls thinned with rust in a way that looked suddenly sinister. At the top of the page the incongruously smiling face of Mary O'Shea rested on a thick stripe of black, and below it the headline: *Suffer the Little Children: The Tragedy of the Rosary Baby*.

*Shit.*

Less than forty-eight hours since the find and Mary O'Shea was interviewing key witnesses. How had they got hold of that daft girl? He skimmed the article: *Under the petrified gaze of a stone Pietà ... eerie bower ... tiny corpse ... privileged walls.* It was mostly a colour-piece, a lot of breast-beating about the truths behind respectable surfaces – nothing substantial. Then Swan's glance froze on one sentence: *According to witnesses, the baby did not die of exposure, but suffered a violent death at the hands of a person or persons unknown.*

Ali Hogan was quoted extensively, saying although she was shocked by the find, she couldn't find it in herself to condemn: '*This can be a cruel country for girls in trouble.*' The article went on to say that even in a school like this, girls were not immune to mistakes, and that St Brigid's had experienced one schoolgirl pregnancy last year.

*Shit and damn.* This was what the monsignor had meant about leaks. Summer was slow newstime and this was probably just the start. *Give me a nice bank shootout any day*, thought Swan, *where nobody feels they have to talk through the symbolism of it all.*

The article took up a whole half-page. Superintendent Kavanagh was bound to see it and Swan would have to endure a session in the great man's office, laced with anecdotes about how understanding journalists were in the old days.

Swan shook the paper, folded it clumsily and thrust it back at Barrett.

'Why am I only seeing this now?'

'It's the second edition, boss. Wasn't in the first.'

Considine gave Swan a wry look.

'Hope you're not here to mock our troubles, Gina.'

'Just passing, Vincent. But I am on my way to Limerick to take a statement, and a little bird told me you wanted someone to do a bit of poking around in east Clare.'

'Yes, this baby Ali Hogan's supposed to have found twelve years ago. I'm wondering now if she's a fantasist.'

'I could phone the local Guards,' offered Barrett.

'If Considine can do it face to face, so much the better. You've plenty to get on with – have you nothing new from forensics?'

'We've a blood type on the baby, but no post-mortem yet.'

'Jesus. Give me the type.'

Barrett pulled a notepad from his pocket and looked at the last page.

'Blood type A, boss.'

Common as brown hair or blue eyes. He'd hoped for something a little more exotic.

Swan took the list the monsignor had given him from his breast pocket and scanned it quickly. Sure enough, the name *Alison Hogan* appeared in the list under the heading 'sixth year'. Risk-taking, attention-seeking.

'Back to the phones, Barrett. None of this is good. Murphy – you and I should swing by and pay the Hogan girl a visit. Screw the lid on.'

'Wish me luck on my travels,' said Considine.

'Like you need it.' Swan gave her a quick nod. At least Gina was on board now. That could only help.

# 8

A dying note of pipe and fiddle whined from the big monitor hanging in the corner of the green room. The screen showed a close-up of Gay Byrne applauding. Pointing off-camera, he said, 'Ladies and gentlemen, the legendary Chieftains!'

The applause engulfed him briefly before he doused it with an elegant swoop of his hands and moved on to announce the next item on the programme.

The door of the green room opened and the six members of The Chieftains walked in, passing close enough to nod to Ali as they headed to the drinks table, some with instruments still in hand. It was weird, like a photograph in a book suddenly coming to life. Ali clutched the wet neck of her beer bottle and tried to still her nerves.

She would be enjoying it so much if she didn't have to go out that door and be in front of the cameras herself. Mary O'Shea was on the other side of the room, chatting happily to a small curly-haired woman from the North whom Ali had often seen on the *Late Late*. In a corner beyond them, a middle-aged man sat on his own, looking very serious as he flipped through a wedge of papers. He looked familiar too.

*The Late Late Show*. It would be like walking naked down Grafton Street with a neon arrow over her head. Up on the screen, Gay was talking to two men who had rowed around Ireland in a *currach*. They'd been right here just five minutes before, a pair of burly lads debating whether to keep their Aran jumpers on in the stifling heat. Comfort won the argument, and now their pullovers lay discarded on a sofa like a couple of empty sheep.

Mary had phoned Ali at home that morning – her newspaper article had gotten a huge response, she said.

'They want both of us, Ali. On the *Late Late*. And you're not to worry, it's not about the case – they want to talk about girls and sex education, so I told them you'd be good for that: a real girl, for God's sake. It's a great opportunity.'

Ali had let herself imagine it. A sea of blurry faces, all turned to her. Being scared was no reason not to do it, though. She'd been mortified when she'd read Mary's article, all those quotes that made her sound firm and opinionated. But Mary was right. Girls her age never did get the chance to speak. A light would shine on her and she would be tested.

Her mother was mad with pride, and slipped her money for a taxi to the studios. She'd already bought three copies of the newspaper with Mary's article in it.

'It's a lovely photograph,' she said. 'Despite the circumstances.'

Davy had mastered a wicked impersonation of the newspaper photo and would tilt his head to one side and jut out his lower lip each time Ali passed him in the house. Meanwhile, Fitz was mysteriously unavailable whenever she phoned, and Ali worried that she was angry with her, for the reference to Eileen lurking in Mary's column.

Detective Swan had called round with another man on

Wednesday afternoon, angry with her too. The policemen sat in the kitchen, drinking coffee, like they were on a social call between crimes, but then Detective Swan started in on how *personally disappointed* he was. At least her mother had had the grace to take a bit of the blame, passing the buck on to Seán O'Loan, making out that the press had squeezed details out of them against their will. Ali promised there would be no more talk of what she'd seen.

Yet here she was, waiting to go on television.

At the RTÉ studios a skinny-hipped young woman collected her from reception and rushed her up two flights of stairs. She had big earphones hanging around her neck, as if she had recently been unplugged from some important broadcasting machine.

'There,' the girl opened a door on a crowded office. Mary O'Shea was sitting on a desk in the middle, swinging her crossed legs for an audience of two young men in shirt sleeves.

'Ali!' Mary cried when she spotted her, thrusting both arms out as if a hug was expected. The men turned to look at her, appraising. Ali threaded her way towards them through a maze of desks.

'Look at you! Look at your dress – so sweet.'

'Maybe I should have worn something more—'

'No, sweet is fine. Sweet is more than fine. We don't want them thinking you're a hard-nosed old bag like me.' And Mary threw back her head and laughed at the thought. The men joined in.

'I'm worried what to say.'

'Just nerves. By Tuesday you'll be a pro.'

'Tuesday?'

'My radio show. Remember? We'll see how things go tonight and work up a few topics together beforehand – that thing you said the other day about girls not knowing their sexual desires – that could be dynamite.'

The two men looked at Ali with renewed interest. Mary put an arm round her and was saying how fine everything was going to be, when there was a shift in the atmosphere.

A slight figure in a blue suit had entered the room, causing all around to change their behaviour; the loud ones fell silent, the diligent ones lifted their heads from their typewriters and called out for attention.

It was Gay. Gaybo. Mr Byrne. He managed to looked both mild and of consequence, and his charisma was unsullied by a ruff of tissues sticking out from his collar to protect it from the fall of peachy powder that covered his face. He had a certain grace, like a dancing master.

Gay made even Mary look like an ordinary joe. His radio show was bigger, and his TV show was required viewing, as obligatory as mass. *The Late Late Show* had always been there, as long as Ali could remember. You never knew beforehand who would be on – politicians, movie stars, farmers, ventriloquists – and there might just be something remarkable.

Gay waved over in their direction.

'He never talks to guests before the show,' Mary whispered.

Ali watched him now on the green room monitor, swivelling behind his desk and chatting to the *currach* men, taking polite questions from a beaming audience, laughing often. It would be okay. The beer in her mouth tasted of nothing at all, but something like vinegar was swilling around her stomach.

The girl with the snake hips appeared beside her. 'You're next.'

She gathered up Mary O'Shea and the quiet man from the corner and herded the three of them downstairs to stand together in the darkness at the edge of the bright studio.

'... and we'll be back with you after the break.' Gay's voice came from beyond a tangle of cameras and equipment.

The audience chattered while Ali's group was guided forward over cables into a lit arena. They were directed to a curved line of chairs facing the seating bank, full of people. Microphones pointed at them from the low table in front. A hundred lights pressed down, baking the mascara the make-up girl had pasted on Ali's lashes to a tight crust.

Someone called for hush, and Gay walked towards the audience. Ali looked across to Mary for reassurance, and Mary smiled briefly at her before reapplying her eyes to Gay, who had started to speak.

'... we're not going to go over old ground here, so you can put your badges and banners away. What we have here is a human story, a sad story – a story about some things that maybe don't change, even after all the talk. Tonight we have with us a young woman, Alison Hogan, from here in Dublin. You might know from the papers that Alison was the person who found the child now known as the Rosary

Baby. Despite this ordeal, she's gone on to make a public plea for better sex education in schools and for the abolition of illegitimacy as a legal category.'

Ali frowned at his back, not recognising the girl he was describing. He was making it sound like she had held a press conference or something.

'And we're delighted to welcome back journalist and women's rights campaigner Mary O'Shea, who has been collaborating with Ali. We also have with us an expert on sex education in schools and author of the bestselling pamphlets *Life Talks for Boys* and *Life Talks for Girls*, Dr Donald Beasley …'

The audience were clapping politely now, but Ali wasn't looking at them. She had turned to stare at the man who had been in the green room and was now sitting just on the other side of Mary.

How could she not have recognised him? The knitted brow and slightly prissy expression. Dr Beasley was the man who had spent a day with the second-year girls of St Brigid's explaining the romance of the sperm and the egg. His detailing of private parts and monthly cycles had impressed them, because they had never heard anyone speak in that way. She remembered the manic embarrassment of that day, and her class leaving the hall quietly, carrying strange knowledge like a weight.

Before she had time to collect herself, Gay was upon her.

'Alison, we're not here tonight to talk about the Rosary Baby case. The Gardaí are still looking for the mother, and it's all hush-hush for now.'

Ali nodded, not chancing a word.

'I was wondering, though, how have you coped with coming across something like that? A thing no one – let alone a young girl – should see?'

Ali turned her face so that he was the only one in her vision. She would pretend that this was a normal conversation.

She opened her mouth and spoke, realising within a sentence that she had to make a choice between thinking and talking. She started with something her mother had said, about not being able to understand why someone couldn't have handed the child over alive, and let her mouth flow from there, listening in to what she was saying after she had said it. She railed against the hiddenness of things; she raised the issue of contraception. Gay was running out of sympathetic nods, was starting to look a little alarmed. She found the end of a thought and pulled up to a halt. The last thing she said was, '… we don't seem to want these babies that we go on about loving so much.'

Her heart was hammering but maybe it hadn't been so bad after all. She hoped she'd spoken for her generation.

The audience were muttering, shifting in their seats.

'Ah now,' said Gay, 'surely this case is not the normal run of things.'

'I think it happens often.' Her words were defiant, but she spoke quietly, not wanting an argument, not wanting anything now but to go home.

'We'll come back to that,' said Gay.

A few hands poked up rigid among the heads and shoulders in front of her – bids put in with Gay for future notice. He didn't pay them any attention, but turned to the other guests.

'Donald, Alison here seems dissatisfied with the way she was taught the facts of life. Now you're the man who devises those classes – do you think there's a need for a fresh approach?'

'Hello, Alison,' said Dr Beasley with a creeping smile, as if he remembered her well. 'We only aim to supplement the parents' own teachings, you understand, Gay. The home is still the foundation of sexual morals.' He spoke on about the merits, the responsible science, of his own system. Mary jumped in to question whether it wouldn't be better for a woman to be teaching these things to girls. Ali half-listened, but was also trying to replay her own impassioned speech and see if she had said anything stupid. Her eyes ran over the faces in the audience – some sneaking their eyes diagonally upwards to check the monitors and see if their reactions were being broadcast home.

Mary was worked up, plying her outstretched hands as if she was shaking an invisible football. She was angry with Beasley about something, then she turned and pointed to Ali, saying something about St Brigid's. Ali strained to pay proper attention, but her mind was not operating normally, her thoughts like scattered beads.

'That's hardly my fault,' Beasley said.

Gay swivelled to look straight at Ali.

'Do *you* blame the doctor, Ali?'

'For what?'

'For what you told me,' Mary interrupted, 'about the girl in your school that got pregnant and went missing ...'

'Missing?' asked Gay. There was a silence without air, a vacuumed-out pause waiting for her.

'Not missing,' Ali managed to say. 'She left our year, that's all.'

Mary rode away with it. 'You see, it happens again and again – a whole culture of secrecy.'

The audience was simmering, desperate to add their bit. Hands strained towards Gay, patting the air. He finally turned, scanned the rows.

'We can't discuss individual cases, of course – let's go to our audience. Sir!' he said, pointing into the crowd.

A strained-looking man with a side parting stood up.

'I have fourteen children,' he paused, 'and each one is a precious gift from God.'

'Is your wife with you tonight?' Mary called out. A twitch of a smile moved on Gay's lips.

'As it happens, she's at home ...' The sound of female laughter drowned out the rest of his words, and Gay pointed at someone else, leaving the man stranded, with no choice but to sit back down. A woman in a yellow tweed jacket stood up and looked at Ali. She had a tight, excited look about her.

'I have a daughter just your age, and do you know, I'm terrified for her. Terrified. There's so much pressure on her – from the media, from boys, from other girls even. To have sex, I mean. Tell me, as a young one yourself, how do you stand firm?'

Ali was at a loss. She tried to imagine what Mary would say.

'Maybe I don't.' A slight gasp came from the audience, and Gay wheeled around to look at her.

'Promiscuity is hardly a solution!' shouted Beasley.

The woman with the question raised her voice. 'Well, I'm glad my daughter isn't a little slut like you,' she said.

'Ah now! There's no need …' said Gay, but the audience was in uproar again, everyone talking at once, Mary and Dr Beasley leaning forward to speak into their microphones. Ali caught sight of the monitor to one side of the stage and her own face was filling it – stricken eyes, flaming cheeks.

Swan sat in his mother's front room, disbelieving his eyes and ears. His mother was on her knees at the side of his chair, mopping up the tea he'd knocked over when Alison Hogan had appeared on the television screen.

'Leave it!' he said again.

'It's my rug and I'll save it if I want.'

Her grey head bobbed by his elbow. He could either argue or listen to what that little rag was saying about the case, and he should know by now that his mother was immune to argument. The innocence of the Hogan girl's face was amazing, given her lust for the spotlight. Two days ago she'd sworn to him that she wouldn't talk to any more journalists and he'd believed her, and now here she was, opining away about the state of the nation. She was trouble.

Just as well Considine was already looking into the girl's past, that other baby. With any luck it would turn out to be nothing – bad dreams, imagination.

His mother exhaled an *Oof* as she got up and threw the dish-towel over onto the table, where the remains of their dinner still lay.

'I've a lot of time for that Mary O'Shea,' she said, settling back into her chair.

Swan grunted assent. His mother's appreciation was probably of a different flavour from his own. That night he was introduced to her at the theatre, he'd fluffed it. Words had failed him. He was still amazed that someone as elegant at Elizabeth had agreed to marry him; but Mary O'Shea, she was in another league entirely.

The screen was filled with Ali Hogan's face, a glisten of tears in her eyes, the whipped look of her. Hard to fake that.

'She's not getting an easy ride, your girl. Did you see that aul' bitch in the audience go for her?'

'No one made her go on,' said Swan. 'I'm not sure the nuns at her school will appreciate it.'

'Pity about them.' Mrs Swan took up the paper, folded it to the crossword page. 'The spare bed is still made up, if you want to stay. Save you going back to an empty house.'

'Ach, I shouldn't,' said Swan, but his attention had returned to the screen.


Mary was saying how we would do well to listen to young people rather than old men. Dr Beasley got personally offended and started tugging at his tie.

'Eh— eh— eh—' he said, attempting to find a gap in Mary's tirade. Gay held his hands out, one palm facing the audience, the other towards his guests.

'Please.' Silence fell at once.

Out of the corner of her eye, Ali noticed one of the cameras rolling silently towards her.

'Mary, you said back there that no one could understand what Alison had been through, and Alison herself said a curious thing. You said you thought things like this happen often. Last week wasn't the first time you've seen this kind of tragedy, was it? Is that why it matters so much to you?'

Ali looked at Mary, but Mary was just staring back at her, waiting. She remembered Seán O'Loan talking to Mary at the Shelbourne. Her mother must have told Seán what had happened in Buleen. She wouldn't discuss it with her own daughter, but she had told Seán.

'Is there anything you can tell us about that?' Gay was in touching distance now.

The camera moved a little closer. There was a red light beside the lens, like a little warning. She thought of all the people beyond that lens, watching her. Aunt Una and the rest them at the farmhouse.

'I was very young ... I can't really remember.'

But that was a lie. The memories were turning up in force now, pressing their noses against the glass, wanting to be let in.

'God help me, I shouldn't have let her do this.'

'Jesus,' said Davy. 'He's meaning what happened at the farm. Isn't he?'

Ali's shocked face appeared in close-up on the old black-and-white screen at the foot of Deirdre Hogan's bed.

*I was very young ... I can't really remember.* Her voice as thin as wire from the little speaker.

Gay moved the discussion back to Mary O'Shea, then rounded it up without going back to Ali. As the cameras drew back for the endshot, they could see she was looking at her knees, not up at the cameras like the others.

'She was so excited – I should have stopped her.'

'Well, you didn't.' Davy got up from a little armchair draped in clothes and leaned over the end of the bed to reach the set. 'Do you want me to turn it off?'

'No, just turn the sound down.'

'You should never have told that policeman about Buleen,' he said with his face turned from her. He heard her sigh.

'Well, it was just so weird – you know, happening again. You remember it, don't you?'

'Not much …'

'Ach, you were practically a child yourself.'

'I was sixteen.'

Davy left his sister to her regrets and went down to the big sparse room he'd been using as his own. He pulled a suitcase from under the single bed. It was an old case that Una had turned up from somewhere in the farmhouse, made out of cardboardy stuff and reinforced with metal corners and clasps, sandy with corrosion. He dragged a pile of his things out of a corner cupboard, started throwing them into the case.

He surveyed the room, then snapped the clasps shut.

The only thing left in the cupboard was that cheap bottle of whiskey, plenty left. He grabbed it and spun the top off with a swipe of his hand. He remembered that Christmas all right, much better than his sister ever could.

The farmhouse had been full to bursting. Una's four kids were home from school, and Deirdre and Ali were staying with them, ever since Ciaran's funeral. The only peace he could get was late at night. He'd go down to the kitchen, drink a coffee, listen to the big radio. He could tune in to a foreign station and pretend he was somewhere else – somewhere with pavement cafés and jazz clubs, not a bog-hole in the middle of nowhere.

On Christmas Eve, it was, he'd gone downstairs at about two. The light over the range was on, as usual. There were presents for the kids on the table, some wrapped, some not. He didn't even notice her at first. He filled the kettle at the tap and stepped over the dog on the way to the range.

'You get up on the sofa, boy, I'll tell no one.'

But the dog stayed where he was, his eyes fixed on the heap of rugs on the sofa, like he was scared of it, his tail sweeping slowly across the flagstones. The heap gave a groan and Davy nearly jumped out of his skin. A glob of water hopped from the kettle spout and hissed on the hot plate.

He'd felt annoyed. He couldn't have his peace with her sleeping there. Why couldn't she go home? She groaned again – deep, like a cow lowing – and the dog moved a step closer, keeping his belly to the floor.

She must have known he was there, but wouldn't let on, her face turned to the sofa back. When he'd asked her about her condition before, asked her straight, she'd denied it, wearing a big man's jumper to cover it, struggling to bend or rise.

He took the dog by the scruff and led him out to his kennel in the yard. Then he stood by the kitchen window and looked back in at her. She threw the blanket off after a time, and he could see everything: the sweat on her, the strain in her bare legs. It was a cold night and he wasn't dressed for it, but he couldn't go back in. The moon gleamed off the pig-shed roofs and frost whitened the upper field.

Eventually she heaved herself off the sofa and squatted beside it, hanging on to the arm, looking down into herself. She was huffing and grunting, the hair plastered to her skull. Somewhere in the middle of it she turned her head and looked at the window, looked right through him.

He remembered the awful streaks of blood on her haunches as something bulged and slithered from them and onto the heaped blanket she had put beneath her. She was bent over the mite, arse in the air, pulling at the cord that joined them. He saw a puny arm rise from the rug – trembling with anger was what it looked like, shaking its little knot of fist in the air – and he felt exultant, something bursting in his chest, coming from nothing and filling him full.

# 9

When Ali got to the bus stop outside the television studio there was a group of people already gathered there. Several turned to look at her.

'Don't they drop you home in a limo?' said one woman.

They were from the audience. Ali looked at her watch and walked away from the bus stop as if she simply didn't have the time to wait. Maybe there really was a limo – she hadn't stuck around to find out. Now she'd have to walk home.

She could hardly believe how her mouth had run away with her. Imagine talking about sex like she knew what she was on about. She had *had* sex. A couple of times, with the flirtatious brother of a school friend, but it wasn't what she thought it would be; it was clumsy and mystifying.

Ali walked up Eglinton Road, limping in her high heels now, but halfway home. A car drove by slowly and came to a halt in front of her, brake lights glowing. She moved closer to the houses on her left and looked away from the car as she passed it. It slid into motion and kept pace with her for an awful minute before suddenly accelerating off. She remembered the heavy make-up she was still wearing, the heels, no coat – she must look a sight. She stopped and unbuckled the straps of her shoes. Better barefoot than hobbled. She kept her eyes on the pavement ahead for streams of liquid or glints of glass.

Why had her mother never discussed the first baby with her, never tried to explain things, let her believe it was in her head? Her aunt and uncle, they'd seen it too, but no one ever spoke of it. Someone must know who that baby was, where it came from. She suddenly recalled her mother lying in bed all those winter days, crying and crying.

'You okay?'

Ali was standing at the edge of a road crossing. She might have been standing there for some time. A girl had drawn level to wait for the light, hand-in-hand with a sullen man. She craned her neck to look into Ali's face.

'Okay?' she asked again, but her boyfriend tugged her onwards, away from involvement.

'Fine …' Ali managed and trotted across behind them.

She was glad to see the pool of light that fell on the pavement from the all-night shop called The Cottage. Her home was behind the shop. After her father died, Ma sold their little bungalow and bought a tall terraced house full of sitting tenants, and a shop built in the former front garden. It was the practical thing to do, she explained.

Ali walked up the narrow passage beside the shop and through a small yard filled with bread trays and stacks of flattened boxes. The house rose like a cliff in front of her, stone steps leading up to the front door. Above it, her mother's bedroom light shone through the gap in her curtains.

Ali opened and shut the front door quietly. There were no signs of life downstairs, but she could hear the muffled sound of the television above. She went up and knocked as she entered.

Her mother's unerring eye went straight to the shoes in her hand, then took in her grimy bare feet. 'Did you not get a taxi, like I said?'

Ali pretended she hadn't heard.

Her mother's room was large, stretching across the front of the house. It functioned as a workroom as well as a bedroom, now that her mother had taken up mending china as another way to make a bit of money. An old dining table filled one side of the room, covered with broken things – dishes, vases, a massive soup tureen decorated with pink scallop shells, and dozens of ornaments missing vital pieces. Saucers of glue and paint sat along the edge, and jam jars stuffed with wooden sticks and brushes.

On the other side was her mother's ornate bed, hemmed in by draped chairs and small tables toppling with books and lamps. In the middle of this jumble, like a hen on her nest, her hair loose over her shoulders, her mother waited. The awful topic to be broached hanging in the air.

Ali sat on the edge of the bed. A film with subtitles was playing on the TV; a beautiful woman in a tight dress leaned, smoking, against a wall while a man remonstrated with her. Ali promised herself a cigarette once she'd got this over with.

'You watched it, I presume.'

'Your dress looked nice …' said her mother.

'Jesus, my *dress*?'

Ma looked away, blinked quickly. Ali took a breath, tried to keep her voice steady.

'You told Seán O'Loan, didn't you? About what happened in Buleen.'

'I was upset that night. It just came out. I'm sorry. And I should have stopped you going on that.' Her mother pointed at the television.

'You have to explain it to me, Ma.'

'I wasn't even sure you remembered – you never mention it.'

After all these years they were talking about it. The thing that couldn't be spoken had re-entered the world.

'It was your baby, wasn't it?' Ali made her voice soft.

'What? – no!'

'It would have been my brother or sister.'

Her mother put a quick hand to Ali's shoulder. 'Really, it wasn't. God, things were bad enough, but no, not that. I can't believe you thought that.'

Ali looked back at her. 'Then who?'

Ma hesitated. 'It's funny, I never really asked Una about it. It was such an odd time. All I could think about was losing your father – I'd nothing to spare for someone else's troubles. I always presumed it was Joan's. Do you remember Joan?'

She did. Freckle-faced Joan, who did all the cooking at her uncle's farm. She had been timid in company, but sweet and funny when the two of them were alone in that big kitchen. Joan sang her silly songs, and let Ali help hold the big knife to mark the cross on the brown bread before it went into the range.

Her mother reached for the glass on her bedside table. 'She came from an odd family, you know. I'm not sure what went on there. I'd no idea she was pregnant. She still comes to the farm sometimes, Una says, looking for her job back – though she's been in and out of hospital mostly. Damascus House – you know, psychiatric.'

'Because of what happened to her baby?'

'Well, she was always a bit not-there, a bit wandering. I really did think you'd forgotten.'

Ali stood up and wandered over to the work table. 'Some of these things have been here for ever,' said Ali. 'If you can't mend them, you should get rid of them.'

'Hey,' said Ma, 'what's all this about you campaigning for better sex education?'

'That's not what I said.'

'Or more contraception, or something.'

'Don't remind me. I feel such a fool.'

A raucous burst of Italian came from the TV. Ali lifted her eyes. A young man was being chased through a market, but he was laughing as he ran. She wished she could run with him.

'Mary O'Shea wants me to go on her radio show to talk about it again.'

Her mother tilted her head, then quickly shook it. 'I'm not sure that's—'

'I don't *want* to – I'm never leaving this house again.'

'Don't be melodramatic.'

Ali ran her finger down the sharp chalky edge of the broken soup tureen.

'Leave it, please,' said Ma. 'I did buy you that doll, you know.'

'What?'

'The doll you were looking for. Baby Tears or whatever it was called, but I couldn't find it to wrap it for you. I thought I was going mad ... Well, I was going mad, those days.'

'I know.'

'You should go to bed, love. It'll feel better in the morning.'

Ali went over and bent to kiss her mother goodnight. She could hardly bear the intimacy of the smell of her warm bed.

She didn't go up to her room, but crept downstairs to stand outside Davy's door. No light shone from under it. Ali pressed her ear to the yellowed paint of one panel and listened hard. There was a gently whooshing sound that could have been his breathing, deep in sleep, but might just as well have been the sound of her own blood circulating.

'Davy?' She spoke quietly into the crack of the door jamb.

'Yeah?' She jumped as the reply came from behind her. Davy emerged from the dark of the back hall, grinning, a glass in hand.

'You bastard.'

She followed him back to the kitchen and turned on the small light over the cooker. On the table stood a bottle with a yellow label – *Queen Anne Whiskey* emblazoned in garish script.

'What are you doing drinking in the dark?'

'Pull up a pew. I'm having a wake.'

Davy was drinking from the glass with *The Flintstones* drawings on it, one she loved when she was a kid. She fetched a glass from the draining board – a fancy-looking stemmed one from a petrol-station giveaway.

'What are we having a wake for – my reputation?'

'Nobody made you do it.'

'I don't remember half of what I said. It was a nightmare.'

The whiskey was harsh and smelt of disinfectant. She went to the sink and diluted it.

'Some other shite will come along and eclipse it soon enough. That's my philosophy.'

She sat across from him, took her packet of ten out of her dress pocket and lit a cigarette. 'So, what are you celebrating?'

'"Celebrate" is too strong a word,' said Davy, flapping his hand to divert the smoke. 'More of an ending. My family needs me, it seems.'

'You're going back already? We're your family too.'

'I can't go on living off your mother.'

'I do.'

Davy laughed and poured himself another drink, pointed the bottle at her. Ali put her hand over the top of her glass.

'Thanks, but it's disgusting.'

'Two ninety-nine: it *should* be disgusting.' He hit his glass against hers forcefully, a dull *thunk*. 'Brendan's got this business thing' – Davy spun a hand in the air, looking for words – 'gaming machines in pubs. He needs a hand. He'll pay.'

She watched his hand come to rest on the table and thought about touching it.

'Can I come with you?'

'Don't know if you're strong enough; those machines are bloody heavy.'

'Seriously. I'd like to get away from Dublin, Davy, far away from Mary O'Shea.'

'I wouldn't run away from her.' He leered over the rim of his glass.

'Shut up. Will you ask Una if I can come and stay?'

'No need to ask, sure. Her darling niece. You haven't visited them in years …'

She swirled the last of her whiskey and water round the glass. 'I was talking to Ma just now about the time we stayed with you, you know.'

Davy frowned into the depths of his drink.

'Do you remember, Davy?'

When he looked up, his eyes swam with the effort of focusing. Ali left him at the table, kissing the top of his head as she passed and making him promise to go to bed soon.

At the sink in her bedroom she held on to the edge while waiting for the water to run hot. It didn't. She turned it off and went to bed with her make-up on.

# 10

The cat would be raging – it was way past his usual breakfast time. Swan shoved his newspaper and packet of rashers under one arm while he struggled with the front-door mortise lock. It took him a moment to realise it was already unlocked, that's why he couldn't turn the key. He slipped the Yale into the lock above, clicking the door open easily.

Benny was sitting in the middle of the hall, licking himself, a back paw sticking up over his shoulder like a Nazi salute. He'd obviously had his breakfast and was onto the next task of the day. Beside him was Elizabeth's small blue case. The smell of coffee beckoned from the kitchen.

'Vincent?'

His wife didn't sound worried or annoyed, just calmly checking that it was her husband rather than a key-toting stranger. She was sitting at the kitchen table, the garden a blaze of greens behind her.

'I stayed at my mother's,' he said. 'She needed the bit of company. When did you get back?'

'Aunt Bridie was driving up early to the sales. She dropped me off half an hour ago.'

'You should've phoned.'

Elizabeth shrugged. Swan placed the paper in front of her, put the bacon in the fridge and helped himself to coffee from the pot on the table.

'How's Aunt Josie?'

'Oh, you know ... up and down.' Elizabeth was scanning the front of the paper, didn't look at him as she spoke. 'How are things with you?'

'I guess "up and down" would cover it,' said Swan.

They never talked much about his work – a rule she instituted early in their marriage that he had grown to see the wisdom of. She was wearing a pale-lilac jumper he couldn't recall having seen before.

Not for the first time, he wondered whether there was a secret part to her life. He had absolutely no reason to doubt her. Elizabeth had always been close to her posse of Enniscorthy aunts. As they entered their fragile years, frequent health crises naturally pulled their only young relation back to them. But it was hard to judge the urgency of their calls, why they needed her to stay so often.

'It isn't as though I've much to do here,' Elizabeth had said as she packed. Her voice was apologetic, but somewhere in that statement another intention lurked – something dark and pointed.

'That film you wanted to see is on at the Carlton,' she said now, 'the one with the gangsters.'

'I have to go into work for a while – but I should be free in the evening.'

She took her eyes from the paper and studied him. 'They should give you a proper weekend. You look tired.'

'It's been busy.'

The light shifted in her eyes. 'It's not the baby case, is it? Oh, Vincent …'

This was why it was better not to tell her things. Especially on this case. Now she was upsetting herself. *Oh, Vincent* … like he'd brought the corpse home in his briefcase.

'I think we should look at the garden after coffee – talk about that arch-thing you said you wanted.'

Elizabeth produced a patient sigh. 'If you like.'

Swan was changing into his work clothes when the doorbell rang. Elizabeth went to answer it and he heard a woman's voice in the hall. By the time he got downstairs, Gina Considine was sitting at his kitchen table and Elizabeth was asking if she wanted tea or coffee.

Considine was only a bit younger than his wife, but they made such a contrasting pair that he felt like he was looking at women from different eras: Elizabeth subtle and airy in her pale clothes, a vase of garden flowers beside her; Considine with angled cuts in her black hair, shiny leather boots, jacket belted tight against all-comers.

They hardly acknowledged his arrival, caught up in beverage choices and niceties. They'd met before, in passing. Considine often picked him up from the house, but Elizabeth had never asked her in before.

'So where are you living now, Gina?'

The mug that Elizabeth put in front of Considine was sprigged with little pink roses.

'I'm in a flat in Rathgar. Managed to get on the property ladder at last.'

'Not Rathmines?' asked Swan, surprised.

'That was before,' said Considine, taking a quick sip of her tea.

'Are you on your own there?'

'Elizabeth …'

'We're just having a chat. Stop being so uptight.'

Considine's eyes darted between them. 'It's fine. I don't mind. I … I live with a friend. Probably couldn't afford it otherwise.' She fiddled with her watch and stood up. 'Hey-ho.'

'Do you have to rush off?' Elizabeth asked.

'Why don't I meet you in the car?' said Swan.

'Thanks for the tea – it was lovely.'

Considine hurried away. Elizabeth raised an eyebrow as the front door closed. Swan walked across the kitchen to her, drew her close.

'Stop it, nosy.' He kissed her neck.


Swan apologised to Considine as he got into the car. 'My wife can be overly curious.'

'I don't mind at all. Your house is very nice.'

'Thanks, but we don't usually do the personal thing, do we?'

'No, we don't.'

'I'm glad to hear about your flat. Is it a new-build?'

'Shall I tell you about my trip to Clare or not?'

Swan laughed. 'Carry on.'

'Buleen's a cute little town, I suppose. The Garda station's about the size of your kitchen, and the Garda I met had been posted there for decades, which was really helpful. He brought me to see a doctor who knows the family, and the doctor recalled being asked to their house on Christmas Day in 1972. He says the baby was stillborn.'

'The doctor saw it?'

'I think so. He definitely said he examined the mother. She wasn't a member of the Devane family – that's their name – she was a girl who cooked and cleaned for them. Joan Dempsey was her name, but I've written it all up for you. It's on your desk.'

'How did our girl come to find the baby?'

'He couldn't tell me anything about that. I think he was called in afterwards.'

'Did you talk to the family or the mother?'

'I didn't have that much time. I wasn't even supposed to be there. If it's worth looking at, we'd need to do a proper investigation. Can I give you a lift into the office?'

'Seeing as I'm in your car.'

Considine drove fast through the dawdling weekend traffic, nipping into gaps, her hand always on the gearstick.

'Barrett said you got the post-mortem results yesterday,' she said.

'Uh-huh.'

'He said he didn't have time to tell me about them.'

'He's a cocky one. There were no huge surprises. Cause of death was the severing of the spinal cord from a single blow to the nape. The bruising on the back was also caused by trauma from some kind of blunt weapon – a bar or heavy stick. The skin was broken in places.'

She was silent for the rest of the journey. Swan knew

they were both doing the same thing: playing out scenes of violence in their heads, imaginations reaching into the dark for actions that could fit the consequences.

# 11

Ali watched Davy sleep, his cheek vibrating against the train window, his skin the colour of lard. She ate crisps and drank tea from a plastic cup, gazing idly at the hedges and fences scrolling by. In an hour or so she would be at her aunt and uncle's, see her cousins for the first time in years. She had four cousins in Buleen: Roisín, married the year before; Brendan, the eldest, who now worked the farm with his dad; and the twins Michael and Gerard – rowdy boys who teased her when she was small and made her cry. She hadn't seen them enough over the years to think of them as friends now.

A man passing down the aisle turned his head to stare at her, and she wondered whether he recognised her from the telly. There was no way of telling how conspicuous she had become. She kept her eyes on the window as much as she could. After a long time, she shook Davy's arm.

'Hey, we're almost there.'

He stretched and rubbed at his mouth, frowned at the passing view and executing a wailing yawn that gave her a full view of his gullet.

'My, what a big mouth you have.'

'All the better to regurgitate my innards, through,' he said.

'You shouldn't have drunk all that whiskey. Tell me what Una said on the phone. Are you sure it's okay?'

'She said you were more than welcome. She's making up Roisín's old room.'

'Davy?'

'Mmm?'

'I've only ten pounds with me, and I don't know how long I'm staying. I feel I should give her something.'

'Nonsense, she's your aunt. Buy her some Milk Tray. You might need a bit more for drinking money, though. Maybe Brendan will pay me up front and I'll give you a favourable loan.'

'Gee, thanks.'

Her cousin Brendan was leaning against a pillar on the platform at Kinmore. Last time Ali had seen him he was an almost-mute adolescent. He still looked grumpy, still wore glasses, but was as tall as a drainpipe now and, in his narrow black trousers and wrecked denim shirt, somehow more youthful than he had been as a child. She was immediately conscious of wanting him to think well of her.

He greeted Davy with an open-handed blow to his shoulder.

'All right?'

Davy just winced.

'Travel sickness,' said Ali.

'Me arse,' said Brendan, 'looks self-inflicted to me.' He looped his arms around Ali in an awkward hug. 'Saw you on the telly!'

She groaned.

'You're not to mind Mam, if she gets at you for some of the things you said. She's old-fashioned.'

'She'll probably have the priest waiting to exorcise you,' Davy said.

Brendan gave a short laugh. 'Not everyone gets called a slut on the *Late Late*. It's quite an honour for us.'

A faded red van stood outside the station and Brendan urged them to praise it, even though rust frothed at the door corners. He found space for their bags among a collection of bulky gaming machines in the back. Their fake-wood sides made Ali think of coffins.

They sat in a high row behind the windscreen, Ali sandwiched in the middle. Brendan drove fast out of Kinmore and along twisting roads with high hedges heavy with summer's growth and the dust of the road. The Clash sang about Spanish bombs on the tape deck, and Brendan shouted along, thumping the steering wheel. Davy was leaning out the open side window, jaw clenched against nausea.

They turned onto a main road, and Ali could see fields stretching out around her, rising and falling in gentle humps. Between two hills the bright-silver pan of Lough Dreena appeared briefly.

'Why are we going this way?' asked Davy.

'A little side trip, Big D.' Brendan pointed ahead to a large ochre-coloured building. It sat naked on empty ground like a box fallen from the sky. Big red letters made to look like rustic logs spelled out 'Red Rock Saloon' on the gable end.

He pulled the van into the vast car park, executing an unnecessarily tight turn into one of its empty bays. They could feel the machines tip and bang as they bumped to a halt.

'Give us a hand here – I'll run you in gently.'

Davy grunted and climbed out of the van.

Ali followed, standing on the hot tarmac while Brendan hooked a wooden ramp to the back of the van and manoeuvred one of the machines down it on a porter's trolley.

'Get the plug, will ye?'

Davy picked up the trailing flex and walked after Brendan. Ali waited, glad of the stillness and sunshine. A liver-coloured spaniel walked along the side of the road, all on its own. When it spotted Ali it increased its pace, looking over its shoulder as if it didn't want to be associated with the likes of her. Maybe it had seen the *Late Late*. The word *slut* wouldn't leave her ears.

The boys finally appeared again, bickering loudly. Davy had staged some kind of miraculous recovery. His colour was better and he was laughing. Brendan carried a cloth bag in his hand, heavy with coins. When they got back in the van she smelt the beer.

'We had to,' protested Brendan, banging the gearstick into reverse, 'you can't be stand-offish in this business.'

It wasn't long until they came to the grotto on the outskirts of Buleen. Ali craned forward to look at the town. They passed the church first, a big Italian-style basilica the colour of strawberry ice-cream.

'I see God's sticking with pink,' said Ali.

'Man!' said Davy. 'I could sell a machine to Father Philbin to put in a side chapel. That'd bring in the young folk all right.'

'In your arse.'

They drove down the wide village street. Brendan slowed the van and stopped outside a tiny pub with the name *Melody* over the door.

'Won't Auntie Una be waiting for me?'

'No rush,' said Davy, opening the door.

'It's business,' said Brendan. 'I'm trying to persuade them into a CD jukebox. C'mon.'

Ali let them go ahead. She wanted to just look at the place. Buleen hadn't changed much from her last quick visit, down for Granddad's funeral five years before. A little fancier maybe – the hotel had been freshly whitewashed, and frothing hanging baskets flanked the door. A blackboard was propped beside it with a list of dishes that made her mouth water: poached salmon, chicken casserole, lasagne. She'd eaten nothing but a packet of crisps since breakfast.

When she went into Melody's she had to stop for a moment to let her eyes adjust to the dimness. Brendan was at a back table with two pints and a glass of lager. Davy was at the counter, talking with Mr Melody. She went to sit with Brendan.

He put his pint down, adjusted the beer mat under it, cleared his throat with a cough. 'Are you all right? After what happened … are you okay in yourself?'

'Yeah, thanks. I'd rather forget about it, though.'

Brendan nodded, pushed the beer mat again.

Davy was shaking hands with the barman, telling him, 'You won't regret it.'

'I don't fucking believe it,' said Brendan under his breath.

Davy joined them, lifted his pint and gave Brendan a toothy grin.

'You bastard,' said Brendan, 'he's going to take the jukebox?'

'Nothing to it – this is why you need me: persuasion is my particular gift.' Davy sank his lips into the cream of his pint.

'You couldn't manage to get a job for yourself in Dublin,' said Ali, lighting up a fag.

Melody's was not the kind of pub where a jukebox would look at home. Dusty bottles of lime and lemon cordial stood beside a ceramic Johnnie Walker striding out in his top hat and cane, and the lino was studded with decades of cigarette burns. Through the door at the back of the bar you could see tea towels and pillowcases hung to dry over a range in the Melody family kitchen.

'I said he could select his own music from a list of thousands of CDs and I'd give him his own free code, so he could play it to himself whenever he wanted.'

Brendan struggled to keep his voice down. 'Then he'll tell the regulars and we'll make nothing.'

'He won't – he hates giving anything away.'

Ali looked up at the bit of blue sky visible through the clear panes of glass above the window shutters. Brendan was telling Davy about the record decks he'd got cheap, how he was setting up as a DJ on the side. Mr Melody polished the bar surface with a cloth. It was so still that her smoke settled in a thin layer just above their heads.

Davy rippled through it as he went up to get another round.

'Business is going to boom, Bren, now that I'm on board,' he said on his return. 'The old Davy Brennan magic touch.'

'Not so magic in all areas, is it?'

Davy gave his nephew a cool look, took a deep swallow of his pint.

'What?' said Ali. '*What?*'

'Didn't he tell you he's been unlucky in love?'

'Shut the fuck.' Davy turned his face away. He hadn't mentioned anything about a girlfriend, ever.

When Brendan suggested a third drink, she managed to persuade them against it, insisted she needed to eat. The light was already fading when they got outside. She was wondering where she had left her purse, when Davy thrust it into her hands.

'The food in the hotel looks nice,' she said.

'Dunno,' said Brendan, 'never been in – it's just for tourists.'

They climbed back into the van and Brendan steered a fast U-turn, then turned left over the old bridge and out onto the road that gradually swept them a field's distance from the river. She recognised little landmarks along the way – the ruined chapel, the cattle mart, the brutal concrete of the handball alley in front of Glinchy's farm. Dark squares of pine plantation patched the hills over towards Ennisbridge.

In a minute she would be at the farm, Caherbawn, with a bathroom and food and afterwards a bed to lie on. She could make out the white gate posts ahead, but instead of turning up the driveway, Brendan drove past it and pulled into a rough track about a hundred yards beyond.

'You don't want to go to the old folks yet,' said Brendan, 'you want to see Davy's new place first.'

She looked at Davy, but he didn't seem to be paying attention to anything. They bumped up the track and stopped in front of a new bungalow, identical to thousands of others throughout the country, a low grey shoebox with a brown tile roof and nothing to recommend it beyond the cheapness of the build. This one wasn't quite finished. The breezeblock foundations were left bare, and the ground around it was churned mud, baked into ruts by the summer heat. A lone oak tree rose from the wasteland, a couple of its lower limbs roughly lopped. Ali suddenly recognised the site as the place where the farm's stables used to stand, home to an ancient carthorse and her cousin Roisín's envied pony, Skipper.

'So where does Skipper live?' said Ali, confused.

'She's long gone,' said Davy, and Brendan drew a finger across his throat and grinned.

'Dog food. Davy and the twins have supplanted her.'

'Are the twins living here?'

'They were here on sufferance!' said Davy. 'And they can get their own lodgings when they come back.'

'Does it have a toilet?' said Ali.

'It did when I left,' said Davy, 'but God knows.'

It appeared that the construction had been abandoned just before the final push. An open ditch ran around the outside walls, with pipes laid along the bottom. Near the front door a pillow of solidified cement stood on its end, the plastic bag that once contained it blowing in tattered ribbons around its base. The step up to the porch was knee-high.

'Did they not finish the front steps?' asked Davy.

'Nothing to do with me,' said Brendan.

'They're supposed to have done work in exchange for rent,' Davy said as they hauled themselves up onto the doorstep. He opened an elaborate front door with patterned glass panes and held it wide for her, annoyance bringing a dark flush to his face.

Ali thought Davy had come to Dublin to make a new life in the city. It was odd he never mentioned this place. The walls and doors and brass-coloured light switches were all pristine, but the floor was a concrete screed, raked like corduroy. In the front room, an old sofa was complemented by a massive low table made from a sheet of chipboard propped on breezeblocks. The battered television in the corner stood on an empty cable reel.

Davy stopped in the middle of the hall, looking dazed, as if he hardly knew the place.

'Toilet?' said Ali.

'Second door on the right,' said Brendan, bringing up the rear.

She passed a bedroom furnished only with a mattress on the floor and glamorous mirror-fronted wardrobes built into the walls. The bathroom had a new suite but no toilet seat. The edge of the bath still had paper tape on it. Ali hovered over the cold porcelain to pee and hoped that no one would try the lockless door.

Brendan was in the corridor, waiting, when she came out.

'Y'all right?'

'Shouldn't I go down to the farm?'

'Don't be fretting.' He went into the bathroom and shut the door.

In the front room Davy was pulling out bottles from a six-pack of beer that must have come from Melody's. He had an unlit cigarette in his hand.

'You don't smoke,' she said.

He looked at it for a moment, wondering, put it behind his ear.

'Sometimes I do, but it's horrible.'

Ali sat beside him on the sofa, retrieved the fag from his ear and lit it herself.

'Where *are* the twins?'

'They got a job in a pea factory in England. Seasonal work. That's why Brendan needs a hand.'

'A pee factory? Is that a joke?'

'A *pea* factory – P-E-A – little green yokes, canning them, eh, Brendan?'

Brendan edged around the table to join them on the sofa.

'Give us a bottle there. D'you want one, Ali?'

'I'm okay, thanks.'

'But we only got Smithwick's cos you like it.'

Davy put a bottle in her hand and gave another to Brendan.

Ali slumped into the couch and the boys talked over her, Brendan giving wandering updates about the local team and minor village scandals. They weren't going to mention the baby. They weren't going to mention the *Late Late*. It was good to come here, to escape it all. She leaned her head against Davy's shoulder.

A sharp rapping shocked her awake. There was a strange

figure pressing against the window, in a darkness that had gathered from nowhere. He wore a mackintosh and a cap; she couldn't see his face. The boys exchanged guilty glances. Davy motioned the figure to come inside.

Her Uncle Joe had aged a good deal since she had last seen him, and his open mac framed an impressive dome of belly. He was wearing a vexed expression.

'Una had dinner ready an hour ago. Did ye not think to bring her down? Hello, Ali.'

'Sorry, Da,' said Brendan, 'lost track of the time.'

Joe looked pointedly at the bottles and the butt-strewn saucer. With a push from Davy, Ali got to her feet and went over to kiss her uncle on the cheek.

'I'm sorry, Uncle Joe. I'll come down with you now.'

'You coming too?' he asked the boys.

'Later. Few things to sort out here – about the business, like,' Davy said.

Joe gave a little snort and lifted Ali's rucksack lightly onto his shoulder. She followed him out, stepping carefully off the front porch into the darkness.

They followed a path through trees that widened into a dirt drive. She could sense the bulk of the barn looming to her right – darker and heavier than the gloom about. Up the hill on the left, she saw the roofs of the pig sheds, a dull gleam of iron. They walked around the corner of the barn and the lights of the farmhouse appeared, the kitchen window spilling a buttery glow into the dimness.

Ali caught her breath. She could see the corner of the big range, the table with its faded oilcloth, the dresser stacked with delft. Caherbawn. Nothing had changed; it was like stepping out of the dark and into the past. Sensing her pause, Joe stopped too and for a moment they stood wordlessly, looking on as Aunt Una appeared like a figure on a stage, passing through the lit square with a stack of plates in her hand.

'I'm sorry' were Ali's first words of greeting to her aunt.

She wondered if there would ever be a time in her life when there would be no need to apologise. Una stood with her back to the range, a thinner, more worn-away version of her own mother. Her face was plain, and her short bobbed hair was pushed firmly behind her ears. It was a lighter colour than Ali recalled, a kind of faded blonde. Una came forward to press her dry cheek to her niece's.

'Your dinner's in the range.'

'She was kidnapped,' said Joe.

'Is Davy not with you?'

'He's up in the bungalow with Brendan,' said Ali.

'Talking *business*,' said Joe, taking off his coat and cap in the scullery, 'like a pair of Nelson Rockefellers.'

Ali sat at the kitchen table, and Una put a big plate of stew in front of her, yellow domes of boiled potatoes rising from a brown pool of gravy that had lost its shine. Una said that she and Joe were going through to watch *Tenko* and Ali could come and sit with them when she had finished.

'You don't mind, do you?'

'Not at all,' said Ali.

'We'll talk properly tomorrow, eh?'

'Sure.'

If discussion could be put off once, it was more likely to

be put off again. Ali mashed her potatoes into the stew and started to bolt it down, but by the time she was halfway through she felt stuffed.

She didn't want to seem ungrateful, so she took her plate through the scullery to the back door and surrendered it to the yard cats. Five creatures ran to her – skinny black-and-white cats, some with splodges of tabby brown. They hissed and swiped at each other as they fought for position around the plate.

She remembered a kitten she fell in love with that December, a little black one with a white front paw. She smuggled it upstairs to sleep in her bed, but woke in the dark to find the kitten curled tightly around her neck, making it hard to breathe. She moved the kitten away, but it kept trying to be at her neck. Every time she removed it, the kitten would mew, showing its tiny needle-teeth. She grew scared of those teeth next to her neck. She couldn't make it understand. Finally, in exhausted tears, she snuck downstairs and put it out the back door into the freezing night.

There wasn't a speck of stew left on the plate, but two cats still worried away at the glazed surface with rasping tongues. Ali lifted the plate and stepped back into the kitchen. As she closed the door, she remembered something else. That long-ago night, taking this very same route from yard to kitchen, a groggy voice had called to her from the sofa in the corner. She had nearly jumped out of her skin with fright. But it was only Joan, sleeping under a pile of blankets. Telling her to go back to bed.

Only Joan. Joan's face filled her mind, the paleness under the freckles, the wary look she often wore as if she was hiding inside herself. The cloud of hated curls. Ali remembered taking the chance to pat those curls one morning, when Joan was crying over a lamb that hadn't made it through the night. Joan seemed so much older than her then, a woman like Aunt Una, but was probably only the age that Ali was now, only a grown girl.

The old sofa was still here, dressed in a flowered slip-cover now. It was strange to realise how many scenes from her past this house contained, ready to spring into life. She had hardly given the place a thought in years. But the farm and her family were here all that time, waiting for her.

# 12

When Sister O'Dwyer appeared in the doorway of the convent parlour, her frailty made Swan and Barrett jump automatically to their feet. The old nun might have been all of five foot if she was able to stand up straight, but gravity or curvature of the spine had bent her towards the ground so that she now cleared no more than four. Barrett rushed forward to support her arm during the last leg of her journey across the room. Her other hand clutched the knob of a varnished blackthorn stick that she poked into the carpet in little hops. But Sister O'Dwyer's frailty was only physical, Swan noted. As she took her seat she tipped her face up to look at him eagerly, berry-eyed, apparently delighted to engage with a couple of policemen.

Swan smiled warmly at her.

'I'll assume you know why we're here – what happened in the Rosary Garden – but I've been hearing that some girls call it Sister O'Dwyer's Garden.'

'Well, I've been nominally in charge of the place for thirty years now, so the girls associate it with me. It's only called the Rosary Garden because of the Rosary Walk beside it. It has no religious use of its own. In fact some would say it's quite a pagan place.'

'Why would they say that?'

'You mustn't take me too seriously. All I mean is that the girls who use it don't necessarily have God on their minds. Gossip, sweets and the odd cigarette are their main devotions. Oh, and the occasional bit of forced labour with a rake.' She gave him a dry smile.

'It's a credit to you.'

'I wouldn't go that far. Even if I had the knowledge, I don't think you could make a decent kind of garden in that spot. Too shady, too dry. But gardening's not really the point.'

'It isn't?'

The nun leaned forward, her face aglow, light through parchment. Swan sensed Barrett shift beside him, impatient at this circuitous talk.

'Are you familiar with the term *sanctuary*?' said the nun.

'Of course.'

'It has religious connotations: the sepulchre, the place of something precious. But I'm an admirer of St Francis, Detective, and when I think of the word "sanctuary", I think of a bird sanctuary. That is what my garden is – in a literal sense because of all the nests in those hedges – but, really, it's a *girl* sanctuary!' And she clapped her hands together and wheezed a laugh.

Barrett was doodling on the page in front of him, drawing a man's face, bland, square-jawed. *You wish*, thought Swan and gave Barrett's leg a little kick. She had something about her, this old bird, and Barrett should do her the courtesy of looking like he was listening.

'That seems a wonderfully liberal approach, Sister. Can I ask, when were you last in the garden?'

Her face clouded. 'On Monday, after they found the mite.'

'And before that?'

The nun looked down at the carpet beside her chair, as if the answer might lie in its pattern. 'Sometime in spring. I seem to remember crocuses.'

'I thought you ran the gardening club.'

She looked up at him and frowned. 'Perhaps you're trying to flatter me. As you can see, I don't get about like I did. My supervision has been at a distance, but someone else will be running the club soon.'

'Another nun?'

Barrett was jiggling his leg now, sending vibrations up Swan's chair.

'Yes, Sister Bernadette, a wonderful young woman. She'll pull it back into shape, I know.'

'She seems very cool-headed all right,' said Swan.

'I forget you've met. She's far more than that – Bernadette is worth ten of me to our little community. She knows nursing, she did a course in social work, she leads all of our city initiatives … she has such energy.'

'Sister – I need to ask you – if your girls thought of the garden as their sanctuary, is it so unlikely that one of them might bring their baby there?'

'I don't think any of them were in that kind of trouble. And none of them would murder a child.'

'How can you know for sure? You weren't around much.'

'I know it in my heart.'

It was difficult to argue with that kind of defence, but Swan pressed on.

'Could the child have been born to anyone in the convent?'

He expected immediate rebuttal, but Sister O'Dwyer appeared to think it over, as if running through an album of people in her mind.

'We would have known.'

'So what do you think happened? Indulge me. I can see you're a woman with a decent imagination.'

Sister O'Dwyer smiled slightly at her clasped hands, and strained her face up to meet his eye once more. 'Do you know cats, Detective?' she said.

'I have one that abuses my hospitality, yes.' He thought of Benny, curled tight as a snail on Elizabeth's side of the bed, even when it was empty of her.

'Well, you'll know how they sneak away to a dark place when they're sick or giving birth. My garden is a place like that. I think it was a local girl or woman who sought it out by instinct.'

'Is the shed ever locked?'

'No. Though Bernadette says we must do that, from now on.'

'Sounds like Sister Bernadette might be a bit stricter than you.'

'I don't like expecting the worst of people. Not that Bernadette does – that's not what I'm saying. She's out in the world more than I am. It's a different perspective.'

'We'll be talking to Sister Bernadette later,' said Barrett.

'Oh, I thought she'd be at St Jude's; it's a Saturday today, isn't it?'

Barrett drew himself up in his chair, moved a sleeve over

his doodle. 'We stipulated that all the nuns be here today to talk to us, Sister. I believe Sister Bernadette has agreed to that demand.'

Sister O'Dwyer raised her eyebrows and gave one slow nod of her head to Barrett, acknowledging or perhaps mocking his great power.

'What's St Jude's?' asked Swan. He should be winding this up; they had more nuns to see.

'It was where I trained as a novice, Inspector, before the order moved out here to the suburbs. A lovely house by the canal, on Percy Place. It was once the home of a famous writer – now was it Gogarty or Synge? Are you fond of reading?'

'Enormously. What is the house used for now?'

'Oh ...' The nun looked confused for a moment, losing focus, 'I believe it's a ... *community project.*' She said the phrase triumphantly, as if she had retrieved it against the odds. But the light drained from her suddenly and she looked even smaller than when she came in. Swan tried to calculate her age, as Barrett went through the rigmarole of giving her a card and asking her to get in touch, if anything ... et cetera. More than eighty, certainly. Possibly in her nineties. She asked Barrett to ring a bell beside the fireplace. Within moments, young Sister Dreyfus appeared to help Sister O'Dwyer out of her chair and guide her to wherever she spent her daytime hours. Swan hoped it was somewhere comfortable, light-filled.

Swan asked Sister Dreyfus to send Sister Bernadette to them.

As they waited, Swan sneaked a look at the day's

*Independent*. The public hand-wringing went on. The Rosary Baby was being dragged into expositions on the family, the decline of religion, the promiscuity and ignorance of the young. There was no editorial that couldn't be spiced up with an innocent dying for society's many sins. Only the banal or brutal truth would put an end to it. Kavanagh was pressing him for results, but all the Technical Bureau and most of the murder squad had been diverted to work on an armed robbery at a creamery outside Dundalk, where a woman office worker and an off-duty Garda had been shot dead. What kind of cheapjack set-up was it when the country could only deal with one murder at a time?

'Shall I get us a coffee, boss?' asked Barrett.

'Yeah, see if you can whistle up a cup.'

Barrett was gone only a minute when the parlour door opened and Sister Bernadette walked in. She wore a veil that reached just past her shoulders and what looked like a black pinafore over a longish black dress. She reminded Swan somehow of that picture of Alice in Wonderland after she had drunk the bottle that made her grow. She was so long and pale and had an odd way of stretching her neck up when she looked at you.

'Please sit down. I know we talked at the station, but now we're building a fuller picture of events.'

'I see.'

'And you'll have had time to gather your thoughts.'

Sister Bernadette walked over to the table, pulled the chair back and sat in front of him. The action was compliant, the face wasn't. It was the face of someone willing to endure something unpleasant.

'My colleague's gone to fetch coffee. We'll have to wait for him to get back.'

She acknowledged his statement with only a bat of her pale lashes. There was no question that she was a striking woman, even in that get-up and with the veil covering her hair. Red hair, it was; he could see peeks of it at her temples. But she wasn't freckled at all. She had this amazing pale skin, like a lily, he thought, before catching himself. She's a nun, *jaysus, man*. But he kept looking: the violet shadows under her eyes intrigued him. Had they been there on Monday?

Sister Bernadette kept her gaze averted, to all appearances fascinated by the view out the window. He remembered a film he'd seen at the IFT, something arty that Elizabeth had dragged him to. Arty? Debauched more like, with Vanessa Redgrave as a nun and Oliver Reed as a priest – I ask you – and all of them rutting away, rolling their eyes. But that was all made-up stuff, wasn't it? He once attended a raid on an illegal sauna near the quays, where they found two nuns' habits among the French-maid and nurse outfits that the girls wore. Irish solutions to Irish problems.

This silence was becoming uncomfortable.

'We're grateful you could spare the time for us. Sister O'Dwyer said you usually spend weekends at St Jude's, was it?'

The hazel eyes flicked to his instantly, then away. He had only been making conversation, but had somehow hit a nerve.

'What sort of place is that, now?'

'It's one of our projects. Community work.'

Her voice was stiff and two pink spots were emerging

through the paleness of her cheeks. She had that kind of complexion. Volatile.

'That's interesting. What do you do there exactly?'

'Oh … I do some admin, help with maintenance, boring stuff. We have many different projects around Dublin – we help run a nursery in Sheriff Street, you know.'

He loved this. He wasn't sure what she was trying to hide, but he was going to have it.

'I hear a famous writer once lived there – in the Percy Place house.' She met his eye, offering nothing. 'This famous writer, do you think he'd be happy about his home being turned into a … a …' He circled his hand at her lightly, cueing her to supply the missing word.

The door banged open and Barrett appeared with a tray, looking flustered. Swan lifted his hand from the table to signal him to wait, but Barrett barged across the carpet, his tray dripping at one corner. The nun was immediately out of her chair, ushering him over to a side table, helping to mop the spill with a lacy cloth.

Swan kept his seat as the two of them fussed about. When Sister Bernadette finally handed him a cup and saucer, he said 'Thank you' with a deliberate evenness to convey that he had lost none of his focus during Barrett's comedy entrance.

When Barrett sat down, Swan resumed.

'Sister Bernadette here has been telling me about some of her community work. You have to excuse my ignorance of these things, Sister, but who is it that you're serving at St Jude's – is it, like, an old folks' home?'

'No'

'What is it?'

'It's … a drop-in centre.'

'For women?'

She nodded, looked down at her lap. She had a rope of wooden rosary beads attached to her belt, and was spinning one of the beads between forefinger and thumb.

'Is it for battered women – domestic stuff?'

She raised her head, something firm in the set of her jaw. 'We try to help all women in need. My focus is on the working women in the area.'

Swan's mother, who was into any left-wing cause, had told him about radical nuns. He'd seen a few on CND marches, their faces painted white as skulls, but he hadn't yet come across the ones that she claimed were working with street prostitutes along the canal, giving them food and check-ups and running the risk of the Church's wrath by – it was rumoured – ensuring they used condoms.

That would account for Sister Bernadette's discomfort.

'I think you probably do a great deal of good out there. It's a dangerous scene now, with the drugs.'

'Fair play to you, Sister,' said Barrett.

She received their praise indifferently, running the beads through her hands, then dropping them abruptly.

'I thought you had further questions about the child,' she said.

Swan drew out a sheaf of papers from his folder. 'A few things came up from your statement … Can you confirm that, when you came upon it, the child was naked inside a paper bag?'

'Is that what I said?'

127

'It is.'

'Well, then …'

'Not a white cloth?'

'… I don't recall one.' She sounded less certain than her statement.

'We found a piece of white clothing in the shed, Sister, and one of the other witnesses said the baby was wrapped in white, when she saw it.'

'Are you asking me to change my statement, for the sake of neatness?'

'It's a curious anomaly, that's all.'

'I can't swear I noticed the exact nature of the wrappings; it was the child I was thinking of – the possibility that something could be done.'

If Ali Hogan was telling the truth, someone had removed the white wrapping and tried to hide it in the sling of the deckchair. Both girls said they hadn't touched the baby, so either Sister Bernadette was that person or someone else was on the scene.

'You were walking in the grounds for some time – I think you said ten minutes – before the girls found you. Thinking back now, did you see anyone else about during that time? Or anyone in the garden?'

'You asked me that before.'

Swan was getting irritated with the ice-queen act. 'Yes or no?'

She gave him a look of forced patience. 'No. I saw no one in the grounds.'

They went over a few more details, but Sister Bernadette would give them nothing useful or new.

As he waited for Barrett to bring in the next nun, Swan looked out of the parlour window at the mountains rising hazily beyond the empty hockey pitches, beyond the avenue of horse chestnuts that curved up from the main road. For all their talk of community projects, these rich acres were lying unused, while inner-city kids played in the summer traffic. Withholding – that's what they were good at. Even if one of these holy women had seen something, he was not convinced they would tell him.

# 13

The bell jingled, a cue to kneel; on either side of Ali, Aunt
Una and Uncle Joe pulled themselves forward onto the
padded kneeler. Ali never went to mass in Dublin. She
wondered whether to stay sitting, to separate herself from
the rigmarole. People were kneeling close behind her –
she could feel someone's breath on her neck. She moved
forward onto her knees and Una gave a tiny satisfied hum
as Ali drew level.

She had been woken early by her aunt, with a mug of
tea and a slice of fruit bread, flicking the curtains open and
saying that it would be a good thing if Ali came with her to
ten o'clock mass. People could get a good look at her, Una
said and, having seen her, wouldn't be bothering the family
with nosy questions. Ali still felt guilty about being late for
dinner. Una said they'd be leaving in fifteen minutes.

A clinking of coins at the end of the aisle announced the
collection, and a couple of gaunt men supervised the safe
passage of baskets through the congregation. Una brought
her handbag to her knee and pulled out a pre-folded note.
Ali passed the wicker bowl across her lap, a weighty nest of
money. The organist filled the hiatus with a swirling noise
that suggested a tune might emerge by and by. Against
this wash of sound, individual noises rose to the curved

roof – someone at the back suppressing a chesty cough, a toddler whining, the occasional jackpot jangle as the collectors poured the takings into the large wooden box being trolleyed up the centre aisle.

After mass, the congregation milled around in the bright morning, a busy crush between railings and church front. Car engines revved as the road was filled with a sudden traffic jam. Up the street, some people were heading into pubs for an après-mass pint. A striking man with thick white hair and glasses moved in front of Ali and held a hand out for her to shake. Was it her imagination, or was the crowd thicker around them than in other parts of the churchyard?

'You remember Dr Nolan,' said Una as Ali surrendered her hand. She recognised him, but his hair had been dark back then. He asked politely after her mother and her own prospects. A picture of him from long ago bloomed in her head – Dr Nolan standing in the doorway of the living room, holding a gift wrapped in shining red paper. He had visited that Christmas Day – yes. With some children.

Dr Nolan turned to talk to her aunt. A finger tapped hard on Ali's shoulder. She looked round to find a large, florid-faced man smiling at her.

'I saw ye on the *Late Late*,' he said, as if claiming kinship. 'I thought ye were great.'

'Thanks very much.'

'And that Mary O'Shea, she's great too, though I wouldn't want to be married to her.' He laughed, and two other young men who had drifted over to flank him joined in. Ali was distracted by a glint on the big man's lapel. A familiar gold badge – two metal beans each topped by five pinhead dots: the footprints of a foetus, the tiny soles of the endangered womb-dweller. It was a badge to signal that its wearer was a dedicated pro-lifer, a man unashamed to defend theoretical babies.

'Would you like to come for a drink with us sometime?' His companions exchanged a delighted glance.

'Go on with you, Cathal,' said Uncle Joe, appearing beside her.

'No harm, Mr Devane. Just being welcoming.' The three men sloped off in the direction of Melody's.

A small woman with a headscarf scooted forward and pressed something into Ali's hand and muttered that she would pray for her.

'Thank you,' said Ali to the woman's departing back. 'Do you think we can go back to the car now, Uncle Joe?'

'We're waiting for Roisín.'

'We are?'

She opened her hand to see what the woman had given her. It was a medal, light as a feather, the metal thin and chalky, a jellied pool of blue glaze on the front holding a scene of the Adoration at Lourdes. Or that's what she presumed – the medal was so crudely made that the figures looked like stalagmites in a cave. Ali slipped it into the back pocket of her jeans, her fingers brushing against Mary O'Shea's business card.

'Who's that woman in the headscarf?'

'She's a religious nut. Don't mind her.' It seemed that, in Uncle Joe's mind, there was a subtle but important barrier between the nuts and the very devout. 'Maeve Dempsey,' he added.

'Anything to Joan Dempsey?'

'You've a good memory. Her mother.'

There had been a passing likeness between them – the slightness and quickness of Joan turned to a kind of bony agitation in the mother.

'And is Joan about?' She tried to make the question casual, just a polite addition to what went before.

Joe glanced past her, cupped his hands to his mouth and shouted, 'Roisín!'

Over by the railings, two young woman were talking, small children churning around their legs. One turned at the sound of Joe's voice. Her cousin was still beautiful, Ali thought, lean like a tennis player, her fair hair now cut into a little crop, sensible, brisk. Roisín ran over to give Ali a hug.

'God, it's been years! I'll bring her over to mine, Dad, and have her back to you later.' Ali had no choice in the matter, it seemed. Like the evening before, she felt like a parcel passed from hand to hand.

Roisín talked non-stop on the way to her car, pointing out sights that Ali already knew, asserting her old bossiness. Her cousin had four years' head-start on her, a gap that presumed Ali would always be trailing behind, in sophistication and experience. That was the deal between them. Roisín had recently upped the stakes by marrying a handsome GAA captain, Colman Carroll, and soon after, baby Emer arrived.

As they drove, Roisín kept going on about how it was a mobile home – not a caravan – that they were living in, and how comfortable and convenient it was. Ali always thought

Roisín wasn't bothered about what anyone thought of her, but something had changed.

The caravan site that Colman managed was half a mile outside the village, where the river ran into Lough Dreena. Roisín turned down a narrow boreen, no more than a rutted lane between high hedges. Fuchsia branches skittered against the car windows. The road crossed a metal bridge and carried on over the brow of an open field where, all at once, the white oblongs of caravans came into view, clustered like giant cattle under the lakeshore trees. The nearest caravan was larger than the rest and was surrounded by a knee-high wooden fence. A rotary washing line trembled beside it in the breeze.

As Roisín stopped the car, the caravan door swung open and a well-built man with a bush of sandy hair came down the steps towards them, his face clenched.

'Rowsh! I told you I had to get to the grounds by eleven. Out!'

'Colman. Darlin'. This is my cousin Ali.'

He spared Ali a quick once-over while snatching the car keys from Roisín's hand.

'You the famous one?'

'I wouldn't say that.'

'Well, you're famous here,' he said and reversed the car off in a wide curve.

'Don't mind him,' said Roisín. 'Bear with a sore head. Where's he left the child?'

In the middle of the tiny living room was a playpen that reminded Ali of a lobster pot. Sitting inside it, a tiny Buddha among soft toys, was Emer. The baby's mouth dropped open in awe at the sight of a stranger. Then a wriggle of delight convulsed her and she lifted her chubby arms in celebration. Roisín plucked the baby up into the air, spun her around once and brought her to rest on her hip, babbling loving nonsense all the while.

She took Ali on a brief tour of her new home. Ali nodded at the two bedrooms, feigned amazement at the plumbed-in bathroom with its tiny pink bath. She said that it was a lot better than Davy's house, and Roisín laughed.

'They're no better than apes, those boys.'

'I didn't even know Davy had a house.'

'Well – I think he's a bit embarrassed by it …'

'Why?'

'He thought he was going to be setting up a little home, didn't he, but nothing came of it, of course.'

'A little home with who?' she managed to keep her voice conversational.

'You wouldn't know her. Girl called Valerie. She only moved here a couple of years ago.'

'Oh.' Ali walked away to look at a picture of a football team over the decorative mantelpiece. It made her feel foolish not to know something so important about Davy's life. It made her feel like she hadn't been paying proper attention.

'I'll make us coffee. You go to Ali, Emer.' Roisín handed her the baby and went to busy herself in the kitchen area.

Ali held Emer at arm's length for a moment, unsure of herself. The baby looked unsure of her too. Her brow started to pucker, so Ali brought her into her chest for a cuddle. Emer capitulated, slipping one plump fist into the opening of Ali's blouse to come to rest stickily against her collarbone, just above her heart. Then she laid her cheek on the curve of Ali's shoulder, stuffed her thumb in her mouth and sucked on it reflectively. Ali walked away to the front of the caravan, where a wide window brought in the view of the lake.

The baby was limp in her arms. Ali hummed a made-up tune and stroked the hot little back, her palm tickled by the intricate pattern of her cardigan. The fingers under Ali's shirt flexed and curled in time with the thumb-sucking. Emer's hair was pale and fine, growing here and there in curls on her shell-pink scalp. With a jolt, Ali realised what it was she was holding – this was what was lost, this.

Her stomach gave an awful lurch. She wanted to sit down, but all her concentration was needed for holding onto the baby.

She must have made some kind of sound, because Roisín was hurrying towards her.

'Are you okay?'

Ali nodded, but it felt like the child could slip through her arms. She looked down. Emer gazed up at her, steady and accusatory. Roisín was by her side now, the baby being taken from her grip.

'I'm sorry,' said Roisín, 'I didn't think. It's upset you.'

Ali wanted to protest that she was fine – fine – but no words would come out. She went to sit on the sofa while Roisín put Emer back into her playpen.

They drank the coffee and Ali asked her cousin normal, boring questions, about her job, about the wedding, about Colman. But Roisín was incapable of finishing a whole sentence without her eyes sliding over to Emer, her conversation fragmented with little bursts of baby-talk directed at the lobster pot.

'An odd woman came up to me after mass today,' said Ali, 'gave me a medal. Your dad said it was Joan's mother – Joan Dempsey.'

'Oh yeah? Seemed like they were all gawping at you.'

'I didn't see Joan there.'

'Well, you wouldn't,' Roisín said. 'She's in the hospital – that mental place in Kinmore: the big building on the road into town.'

'Yeah, my mother told me. That's awful. I remember her well from the time we stayed with you.'

Emer started to whinge, bored with her incarceration.

'Yeah, well, the less said, the better,' said Roisín. 'My mother's got a real thing against Joan, so don't go reminiscing to her.'

She went over and lifted Emer into her arms just as a woman passed outside the window.

'Shite,' said Roisín. A knock came on the glass door. She put the baby on her hip and went to open it.

'Peggy!' she said, like she was surprised.

At first glance, Ali had the impression that the woman who entered was middle-aged, but soon she realised it was merely the heavy set of her body and her old-fashioned coat – a blue mac down past her knees, not right for the day. Her broad face was young, with full downturned lips, and her thick auburn hair waved backwards from her face, as if she were standing in a breeze. Ali wouldn't have recognised her if she passed her on a Dublin street, but now

138

– with the prompt of a name and this place – she knew her, could see the trace of the young girl she'd been. Dr Nolan had brought two daughters with him that Christmas, that's right; neat girls in white socks and matching coats sitting side-by-side on the big sofa.

'You remember Peggy, Dr Nolan's daughter? This is my cousin, Ali.'

'Yeah, hiya,' said Peggy, unsmiling.

Roisín's behaviour with her was careful, kind. She coaxed the ugly coat from Peggy and got her sitting on the sofa. Ali offered to make more coffee.

'You haven't seen the baby for a while, Peggy, hasn't she grown?'

'Uh-huh.'

Ali prepared the coffee as slowly as she could, leaving the two of them to talk. By the time she brought the mugs over, Peggy was haltingly relating a shopping trip to Limerick. Her eyes were on Emer, though, as were Roisín's. Conversation sputtered between them, then converged on the baby. Emer wriggled on the carpet, and they sipped from their mugs and watched, calling out praise for every fat handclap or tumble. Ali could feel the energy draining from her.

She got to her feet and walked into the kitchen area, rinsed her mug under the tap.

'Ro – I better be getting back up to town,' she called over her shoulder.

'If I had the car, I'd drive you,' said Roisín, taking the opportunity to get up and move about. 'But this one needs her nap anyway. Peggy, would you mind walking Ali up to the town for me?'

Ali started to protest, but Roisín gave her such a fierce look that she shut up. She already had Peggy's coat out of the slim cabinet that served as a cloakroom.

'Oh, Ali, I've got that thing for you. In the bedroom, I forgot.'

'What thing?'

'The thing I told you about.' Her eyes were insistent. When they got to the bedroom, Roisín hissed, 'There is no thing, ya eejit. I needed to tell you something.'

'What?' Ali was sure they could be heard.

'Since you're here on your own, you should pal round with Peggy a bit. She's lonely. You could cheer her up.'

'I doubt it.'

Roisín pushed her towards the door. Peggy was already outside the little fence, staring back at the caravan. There was something unnervingly still about her, like a post or a stone.

Ali and Peggy walked up the field in silence until they reached the bridge.

'I remember you,' Peggy said, 'you wouldn't let me play with you.'

'What?'

'It was a Christmas. You had a cookery set – was it? – and you wouldn't speak to anyone or let them join you.'

It was hard to tell whether Peggy was annoyed or just teasing.

'Sorry, I don't remember that. I do remember the fancy coat you had on, though. Pale green, with a black velvet collar. You matched your big sister. I was jealous of those coats.'

Peggy stopped and smiled. 'Brown velvet collars,' she corrected, 'and velvet buttons too.' She looked down at her raincoat. 'Wish I had it still. This thing's horrible – my mother bought it for me.'

'Take it off. It's too hot for a coat.'

Peggy looked up at the blue sky for verification. 'You'll be thinking I've some kind of mad coat-fixation.' But she unbuttoned the white plastic buttons, removed the coat and draped it over her arm.

Ali could see the end of the boreen ahead. They would be back in town soon; she could make her excuses and get away.

'Where's your sister now?' Ali said.

'Dublin.'

'Does she like it?'

'Suppose so.'

It made Ali wonder what her life would have been like if her mother had decided to stay on in Buleen. Would she have had the gumption to escape to Dublin, or turned out strange and morose like Peggy? She might even have gone mad, like Joan.

'Sorry,' said Peggy suddenly. 'I'm not myself these days.'

'Could be the sun,' said Ali lamely.

Peggy managed a smile. 'Could be.'

'What do you do yourself?'

'I do reception at Dad's surgery some days, but that's just for now.'

Ali couldn't find anything else to ask and they walked on in silence. They reached the junction with the main road. Ali looked up towards the shops and spotted a familiar figure leaning against the phone box.

'How's your Uncle Davy?' asked Peggy.

Ali looked up towards the phone box again. Davy had vanished.

'He's good,' said Ali. 'We came down yesterday in the train.'

'Right. I'll go this way,' said Peggy, pointing at the road out of the village.

'Okay. See you then, Peggy.' Ali watched her walk away. Funny how people turned out. When you were a child, other kids were all of the same tribe; you could all get on together. Then they grew up and became really hard to talk to.

She started up the main street. Just past the phone box, Davy jumped out at her from a laneway.

'Boo!'

'Are you really older than me?' said Ali. He drooped an arm over her shoulder and carried on up the street with her.

'What were you doing with Peggy Nolan?'

'I met her down in Roisín's.'

'Roisín's too soft. How's about a little libation for the Sabbath?' He drew out some crumpled notes and a cluster of change from his pocket.

'Maybe one. I don't want it to turn out like yesterday.'

Cathal, the man with the baby-feet badge, was sitting on Melody's windowsill with another guy, watching the world go by. The friend was tall, fierce-looking and fair as a Viking. Davy took his arm off her shoulder and walked ahead into the pub.

'Are you needing some company, Ali?' Cathal wheedled.

She flicked them the V-sign.

'Ooo-ooo,' they chorused, the mocking note swooping after her as she stepped into the dark.

# 14

Chief Superintendent Francis Kavanagh was big in every direction. He looked like the kind of man who should be out in the open air, striding the hills of Kerry with a sheep across his shoulders or a maiden in his arms. Even his hair was vigorous, a sprinkling of grey giving sparks to his straw-coloured crop. Yet Swan had never known Kavanagh to take exercise or leave the confines of a building or car unnecessarily. His rosy complexion was probably due more to a combination of bluster and drink than the wind coming in from the Blaskets.

When Swan walked into Kavanagh's office on Monday morning he found his boss sitting behind the desk in a vest, revealing gouts of chest hair, shoulder freckles and the outline of nipples under thin ribbed cotton. It was all Swan could do not to raise his palms in front of his eyes.

'Do you want to me to come back later?'

'Get that prissy look off your puss, Swan. I spilled coffee down my shirt. Could happen to anyone. I asked Considine if she could wash it out, and the look she gave me would freeze a waterfall in spate. Your man Barrett stepped in, thank God; says he knows a laundry and he'll have it back by noon. I've a lunch at the Castle today, the Dutch prime minister ... or is it Belgian?'

Kavanagh searched his desk for the invitation card, distracted by the possibility of a diplomatic faux pas. The current commissioner wasn't much of a man for canapés and glad-handing, so it fell to his deputies to represent the force on ambassadorial occasions. It was a task that fitted Kavanagh well, with his man-of-the-people bonhomie and rampant ambition.

He waved a stiff card at Swan. 'Belgian! – Brussels, mussels, pissing statues. Right. Let's get on with it.'

'Well, our enquiries are continuing on two fronts. We're looking closely at the people on the spot: the religious community, former and current pupils—'

'The nuns – have you won their trust?'

'It's been slow enough. They're very resistant to any suggestion that anyone in their community might be implicated. Problem is, they think they're above the law, or answering to a different law, and I can't have that.'

'You *can't have that*? Careful, Vincent, a little softness doesn't go amiss – you don't want to get into one of your intellectual struggles about what is Caesar's and what is God's, eh? Let's concentrate on finding the mother.'

There was a knock on the door and Barrett swooped in with a pale-blue shirt on a hanger, draped in a gloss of polythene.

'Good man,' said Kavanagh, rising from his desk to grab the shirt. He tore off the plastic cover, threw the hanger in the corner and started to battle with the buttons. Barrett stood holding out the superintendent's jacket by its shoulders, waiting to help him on with it, like some shop assistant.

Swan continued with his report.

'We checked out the pupil who left the school earlier this year. Eileen Vaughan.'

'She's back with her parents in Terenure,' offered Barrett.

'Maybe you should tell the chief what we found?'

Barrett beamed for an instant, then Kavanagh turned towards him and grabbed the jacket from his hands, giving him a suspicious look. With a flick of his hand he directed Barrett back to the public side of the desk. Barrett took his place beside Swan and recited, in a flattened voice, 'The girl was delivered of an infant six weeks ago in a refuge in Arklow …' He stopped to dig out his notebook.

'You're not in court, Barrett – just talk,' said Swan.

Barrett kept flipping through pages, so Swan took up the tale, sensing that Kavanagh's growing agitation wasn't solely to do with buttoning his cuffs.

'We talked with the mother and girl yesterday. The baby was put up for adoption.'

Swan had given up his Sunday morning to visiting the girl at her home. The smell of frying lingered in their kitchen, making his stomach mourn for his own missed breakfast. The mother had refused to let them speak to Eileen alone, and kept answering the questions herself. The girl seemed monosyllabic with misery, a baggy grey sweatshirt pulled over her still-heavy stomach, her lank hair curtaining a face that wore a look of protracted shock.

'And the baby?'

'Yes. The agency that handled it gave us the details of the adoptive family, and Barrett went for a visit yesterday.'

'He's been keeping you busy.'

Barrett shrugged modestly.

'No problem, Chief. It was a big house out in Sutton. The husband is a banker, the wife was too. They're all thrilled to bits. I'd say the little chap is very lucky.'

'So what's your second line?' Kavanagh addressed Swan. 'Pardon?'

'You said you had a second line of enquiry – come on.'

'It's very possible that the baby's mother would go to her doctor for some medical attention afterwards. T. P. Murphy's leading a small team talking to all doctors' surgeries in the area, all Dublin hospitals too.'

Kavanagh was buttoning his jacket now. Looking around for his cap. Swan told him how they had identified a couple of families in the Dodder Vale area known to the social work department: one where a daughter already had an illegitimate daughter living in the home, the other where there had been two suicide attempts in the family in the past six months. There was no evidence of a baby in either case.

'Murphy can tell you more. I thought he would be here.'

'Ah yes. Meant to say – I've sent Murphy to assist with the Dundalk shooting; there's a lot of pressure on that one, and the usual cross-border shenanigans.'

Swan's first feeling was one of relief. He never could hit it off with T. P. and now he could coordinate things as he liked. But if they didn't find the woman – if things didn't work out – it would be entirely his responsibility. He carried on as confidently as he could.

'Forensics have identified two types of fibre found on the baby's body. There are carpet fibres, blue, woollen twist, good-quality; and there are also white polyester fibres, which Dr Flynn has identified as a type used in a looped stretch cloth, consistent with coming from a Babygro or other towelling item. She's working on finding matches to specific manufacturers, but in the meantime it does point to the baby being kept in a domestic situation for some of the time that it lived.'

'So what's your theory?'

'Something different from the usual panicked cover-up. Girl delivers baby at home, possibly with help. Things go normally for a day or two, baby fed and clothed, then either a change of heart or its existence is discovered by someone hostile to the child.'

'You think it's not the mother.'

'Most likely it is, but the extent of the violence isn't typical.'

A knock at the door announced that the superintendent's car was ready. He ushered them out alongside him.

'So you'll have something for me soon?' The boss liked to demand unfounded reassurance.

'We're still waiting on more technical reports. If Gina Considine could come in to replace Murphy, that would help a lot.'

'Don't be making too much of a favourite of her, now – her head's big enough. You can have her if you promise me I won't see another of your witnesses on national television. What was that girl at?'

'She's young. She won't be doing it again.'

'You make sure of it. What's the story about her finding a baby before?'

'We checked it out: something of a sad coincidence. A stillbirth at a relative's house.'

Kavanagh grimaced, dismissed them with a salute and headed down the corridor alone.

'Have a good lunch, sir,' Barrett called after him.

Barrett was getting on Swan's nerves. And Murphy seemed to have got nowhere with his social work contacts. They really needed a break.

If they could find a realistic suspect, the forensics could probably do the rest. Otherwise they were going to be reduced to sampling every blue carpet in south Dublin or seeking permission to do physical check-ups on likely women. Starting with the two unfortunate families in Dodder Vale, then the girls of the gardening club and the younger nuns. But they couldn't go round palpating women without solid reason. He could just imagine what Mary O'Shea would do with that.

'Boss?' Barrett interrupted his thoughts. 'I forgot to say your wife rang. She been called away to her aunt's.'

'Oh. Thanks.' Why did she have to go and do that? She could have just left a note at home, didn't need to talk to anyone here about anything.

'I hope everything's all right,' said Barrett.

'What do you mean?'

'With her aunt, Boss. I hope it's not serious with her aunt.'

# 15

Ali had come to have a look, that was all, just to see what kind of place Joan was held in. The mental hospital, that's what they used to call it. The nuthouse. A long grey building at the top of a grass bank. The bars on the windows were painted white, blending tastefully with the multi-paned windows behind. She imagined Joan appearing at a window, dishevelled in a nightdress, pale fingers raking at the pane.

The big gates to the grounds were open, and as she watched, a couple walked out through them, chatting in an ordinary way, not hurrying or throwing fearful glances over their shoulders. The driveway climbed steeply up the bank and ran level along the front of the building. Maybe she would take a closer look, now that she had come all this way.

There was a glass entrance porch with a niche above it, where a statue of Mary opened her arms to all comers. Ali walked slowly towards it.

'Excuse me!'

A woman pushed past her from behind, carrying a cone of yellow flowers, clacking her way into Damascus House on stubby heels. So they allowed visitors. She might check if there was a notice saying what the hours were. Mary

O'Shea would never be this timid. Mary O'Shea would have phoned, demanded information, be sitting on Joan's bed by now.

But Ali didn't even know what questions to ask, even if Joan was capable of answering them. She wanted someone to make a separation between facts and nightmares. She wanted an explanation. Then the thing could be put to rest. Ali brushed her hands over her hair, pulled her ponytail tighter and opened the door.

There were no details about visiting hours inside the porch. Beyond a second set of glass doors, a man sat at a reception desk. He looked up and beckoned her.

The inevitable smell of chemical pines threaded through blousy heat. The man at the desk was filling in some paperwork. When Ali got close, she realised it was only a newspaper crossword.

'Can you help me?' she said.

'Only if you can help me,' he replied, sucking on the end of his Biro. 'Five letters, second one O, last one S – *Weaver appears mistily.*'

'Sorry?'

He pushed the paper towards her and pointed at the last blank squares on his crossword puzzle. Ali shook her head.

'You should get into it. Keeps the old brain together ...' His eyes drifted up towards the ceiling. 'Looms!' He scribbled the letters in, quick heavy strokes. 'Got ya!'

He flung the paper aside and gave her his full attention.

'I was wondering if it was possible for me to visit Joan Dempsey sometime?'

'And you are?'

'A friend.'

'*I've* never seen you before.'

'An old friend. I don't live round here.'

He leaned forward over the desk and pointed. 'Down the corridor, up the end stairs, turn right and she should be somewhere around the west wing.'

'Is there a room number or something?'

'Well, she won't be in it. She busies herself about the place. A busy bee.' He looked down at the empty desk in front of him. 'Don't know what I'm going to do now,' he said pleasantly.

Ali walked down the wide corridor, her sandals chirping on the vinyl. There were doors on either side, all identical, with small windows of gridded glass beside each handle. One door was open and as she passed she caught sight of someone lying on a bed, an arm flung over her eyes, body covered with a flowery duvet.

As she climbed the stairs, she grew fearful again. It was very likely that Joan wouldn't know her, or wouldn't welcome her if she did. A woman in a white overall banged through the fire doors at the top of the stairs, her head tilted to one side to see past an armload of sheets. She passed Ali without acknowledgement. Ali went through the doors and found herself looking down another corridor. On either side were large wards where people sat on beds or circulated slowly in dressing gowns. It looked like an ordinary hospital. She wanted to ask someone where to go, but the only official person she could see was a woman mopping the corridor ahead.

The woman was facing away from her, wearing ordinary

clothes: pale tight jeans and a baggy jumper. She was humming a song, something just beyond naming, but familiar.

Maybe it was the tune, or something in the way she moved, or the way her curly hair piled together in defiance of gravity, but before she was within ten feet of her, Ali experienced a rush of recognition, like a blast of hot water from her heart. She stood still and watched the woman move the mop to create shining figures-of-eight across the sea-green linoleum.

'Joan?'

The mop turned first, skimming round in a semicircle, Joan turning neatly behind it as if executing some kind of dance step.

'It's you.' Joan smiled and fine lines radiated from the sides of her eyes and bracketed her thin mouth. Otherwise she seemed not much changed. Smaller, certainly. Ali was more than a head taller than her now.

'I didn't think you'd know me.'

'Didn't I see you the other night?'

'You haven't seen me in years …'

'You were with that man – Gay Byrne.' Joan's smile faded and her eyes grew wide. 'Oh God.'

'What is it?'

'Something bad happened to you. I forgot.'

'You saw me on the telly – is that it?'

'The telly. Yes.'

'I'm visiting Buleen, so I thought I'd come and see you. Is that all right?'

'I suppose I can finish this later.'

Joan put the bucket and mop away in a cupboard, and led Ali to a large room full of vinyl armchairs and smoke, occupied by half a dozen people. A woman was lying on the floor. Sleeping, Ali presumed, since no one seemed concerned about her. Two men in shirt sleeves were hunched over a card game. Joan proudly showed Ali a big television that was set into a cabinet in the corner.

'That's what I saw you on.'

'I'm still amazed you knew me. It's been so many years.'

'She's on the telly!' Joan announced to the room at large. Heads turned to them and quickly away. The woman on the floor slept on.

The lounge felt like a cross between a youth club and an old folks' home. There was a pool table on one side of the room, but no sign of any cues or balls. Instead, the surface was covered with boxes of jigsaws and piles of scuffed magazines.

'Do you have a job here, Joan?'

'I like to help out.'

'But you stay here all the time, do you? As a ...' Ali searched for the right word. *Patient* or *inmate* seemed too direct.

'Oh yes, full-time.' Then, in a low voice, looking round as if worried the others would hear, 'They take care of me.'

'So you do want to be here?'

Joan ignored her. 'What's Gay like? Is he very short?'

'He's normal-sized, I guess, and very like himself.'

'He looks short on the telly. Have you got cigarettes?'

Ali reached into her jeans pocket and pulled out her packet of Silk Cut. 'I don't think I have a light.'

155

'I can get you a light,' said a voice behind her. She looked round to see that a young man with a straight fringe had crept up on them. *Weaver appears mistily*, she thought. Other faces had perked up hopefully around the room. More impressive to have cigarettes than to be on the telly. She gave the boy a cigarette, then one to Joan and took another for herself. The boy walked over to the card game.

'Tony, can I have a light?'

Tony took a lighter from his jeans pocket and, as he did so, Ali noticed the bunch of keys hooked to his belt. He winked at her as he struck the flame.

Over by the window, a girl her own age with a bad complexion was staring. Ali waved the packet of cigarettes in her direction and the girl approached with all the brash confidence of a woodland creature. They lit their cigarettes one by one from the boy's fag, drawing in deeply to make the glow catch across. The timid girl pressed the lit cigarette to her own so hard that the tip of the lit one became unhinged. The boy grabbed it from her, cursing.

'Watch it, Peter,' said Tony, never lifting his eyes from the cards. The boy shuffled off to sulk in a corner, holding the cigarette pointed to the ceiling. The timid girl sat in the chair beside Ali, a little smile on her face. Ali smiled back awkwardly.

Joan leaned across and poked the girl's knee. 'Go on with you.'

The girl moved away, and Joan leaned closer to Ali.

'You've gotten very tall. Have you heels on?'

Ali showed her the flat soles of her sandals. 'My dad was tall.'

Joan bit her lip and put her hand to her chest. 'Your poor daddy. God, I remember you coming to Caherbawn with your mammy, and the tears still wet on your cheeks.' She looked as though she would cry herself.

'You weren't too happy either, were you, Joan?'

Joan shot a look around, settling on the card players.

'I have to be careful. They rely on me to be cheerful.'

Joan picked up an ashtray and motioned to the window with a jog of her head, and they strolled over with exaggerated nonchalance. Outside, the sun beat down on a brutish tarmac yard stretching away from the back of the hospital. Cars were parked along its far edge, where it butted up to a field dotted with black cattle.

'Do you remember me finding something that Christmas Day?' ventured Ali.

Joan shook her head, looked out at the hot cars.

Ali moved an inch closer. 'There was a baby. It wasn't alive. It was in a box, up in the back bedroom. And I wondered, was it yours?'

'You found a baby in Dublin. I've never even been to Dublin.' Joan wouldn't look at her. As she lifted her cigarette to her mouth, Ali noticed a tremor in her hand.

'I'm talking about before.'

'Boxes. Bedrooms. I don't know what you're on about.'

'You *were* expecting, weren't you?'

There was a tiny flicker from Joan, a tightening of the corner of her mouth.

''Twas a miscarriage.' She hissed the word out.

Ali looked out the window. What she had seen couldn't be a miscarriage, could it? A miscarriage would be unformed, would look like something from that abortion film the nuns had shown them, with the bin full of discarded foetuses; a red galaxy swirling with the soft outlines of frog legs and newt palms among nameless clots of matter. Girls had fled the assembly hall, retching as they went.

Joan flicked rhythmically at the cigarette butt with her fingernail. Ash flakes sprinkled the windowsill.

'The baby was wrapped in a towel,' Ali persisted. 'It was a small baby, but it looked perfect.'

On the word *perfect*, Joan froze. She addressed the windowpane.

'Not a miscarriage, the other thing. When it doesn't live. A stone birth – I mean *still* birth – that's what they call it. Your aunt said that there would be other babies. But she was wrong; I tried and no others came. I gave myself to men I didn't even like.' Joan's voice grew unsteady. 'Sometimes I think God must hate me. He just hates me.' She put her forehead against the windowpane.

Ali wished she hadn't mentioned the baby. She had prised open a whole world of upset. What right had she to come here, bothering Joan? If the people who ran this place knew what she was at, they would keep *her* in – her and her dead babies. And Tony would wink at her as he tucked her up in her narrow bed, keys jingling at his hip.

'I'm sorry, Joan. Nobody ever explained what happened. I'm just trying to make sense of it.'

'You said it was perfect. Was it really?'

Ali nodded, put an arm round Joan's waist. 'I'm sorry.'

'What did your aunt tell you?'

'I didn't ask her.'

Ali had never sung songs with Una, never run her hands through Una's hair. She couldn't ever remember speaking to her aunt when there weren't other people present.

Joan turned away from the window, smoothed out her cheeks with her palms.

'You used to drag that black kitten about – remember?' said Joan. 'Carried it all over the place with you like a dolly, never mind the fleas on it. You had bites all over your arms.'

Ali smiled. 'You put calamine lotion on them.' Chalky streaks of it, crackling when it dried.

So odd to think of this tiny woman taking care of her; the substantial presence of her then compared to now. Joan had been queen of the kitchen, the heart of the house for Ali, but she had just been passing through, had owned nothing but her labour.

A woman wheeled in a trolley of blue cups and handed strong, sugary tea to everyone, Ali included. She and Joan sat in chairs near the window. The boy with the fringe turned on the television, and everyone looked at the screen for a while, supping their tea. Onscreen, a man in yellow dungarees was talking to a red-haired puppet. The card players took a break from their game. It was sort of cosy.

'I went to visit, but your aunt shooed me off. They won't give me my job back.'

'It was a long time ago, Joan. More than ten years.'

'Well, she used to be very good to me. And then she wasn't.'

'When you were pregnant?'

Joan frowned and checked that no one had heard. The

159

card players were talking. The sleeper on the floor slept on, a cup of cooling tea by her head.

'You and your mammy were as bad.'

'What did we do?'

'You passed me on the road – me and my brother – like we were too dirty to pick up, like we were tinkers.'

As Joan said it, Ali had a vague memory of being in her mother's new car, starting the trip back up to Dublin, and Joan on the grass verge of the road, holding a yellow-haired boy close in to her body as their car drove past them.

'Did you leave Caherbawn the same day as us?'

'Thrown out, more like.' Joan screwed the butt of her cigarette into the ashtray, mashing it.

'You know, there really isn't much of a job to do any more. There's hardly anyone to cook for,' said Ali.

'How d'you mean?'

'Roisín, the twins and Davy are gone. They have their own homes. There don't seem to be any farmhands, either. It's only my aunt and uncle there now. And Brendan.'

All the anger drained from Joan's expression, to be replaced with confusion. Ali got out of her chair and stooped down in front of her, catching Joan's small hands together in her own. She looked over at Tony, but he didn't seem to notice Joan's distress. Only the shy girl was watching, scratching her cheek rhythmically.

'You were very good to me,' Ali said, searching out eye contact. 'I remember that. You were kind.'

Joan wouldn't look at her.

'You sang me the farting song that Auntie Una banned. You let me plait your hair, and you made me show you my

Irish dancing, up on the kitchen table, and clapped out the beat for me. Do you remember?' Joan nodded, a suggestion of a smile on her face now. 'I didn't come to trouble you, Joan. I'm sorry if I have.'

'I can't believe where the time goes,' said Joan. 'I lose track.'

'Why are you in here, Joan?'

She looked around the room and back at Ali. 'I needed to feel safe. And then they needed me.'

'Things can change.'

'Will you do something for me?'

'Sure,' said Ali.

'Take me out.'

That wasn't what Ali had been expecting. 'I don't know if … I wouldn't be allowed.'

'It is. We could go on a jaunt – just for an afternoon.'

'Okay. If they let me.'

Joan's smile was broad now, and she brushed Ali's hands away from her. 'We'll have a picnic.'

'Let me ask at the desk if that'll be okay, first, Joan.'

'It will, it will.'

'All right. If it's allowed.'

Tony was on the reception desk when she came down, and he said it would be fine for Ali to take Joan out on Thursday. For however long she wanted. It all seemed rather casual. It wasn't that Ali was scared of Joan, but she wasn't sure she wanted to be responsible for her. It served her right for walking back into her life.

# 16

Swan drove along the north quays, then headed over the river towards Ranelagh. He wanted to drop in on the Hogan girl again, make sure she'd no more media appearances planned. Perhaps she'd still have that mortified look about her, the one she wore so well on the *Late Late*. That slimy doctor who spent his time teaching twelve-year-olds the facts of life – something creepy about that. If he ever had a daughter, he wouldn't want her taught by him. A daughter. Elizabeth's voice cut into his thoughts: *If we don't try again, we'll never know.*

He braked as the car in front of him slowed. The traffic looked knotted all the way up Camden Street. The radio news was talking about the recession and unemployment, but it didn't seem to stop people buying cars.

Eventually he parked on Sandford Road and walked up the narrow passage to the Hogans' front door. He'd been taken aback on his previous visit by the scruffiness of the place, forced to revise his notions about St Brigid's girls and their cushy backgrounds.

It was the kind of house he often had cause to visit: tall old terraces divided up badly into bedsits, usually home to the young and the transient. A line of plastic doorbells hung to the side of the door, the names in the little plastic

163

windows faded to sepia scratchings, cut wires hanging below. He knocked on the blistered paint and waited some time before he heard approaching steps.

'Who is it?'

He recognised Deirdre Hogan's voice. As soon as he announced himself, she opened it, all smiles.

'You've good timing. Coffee's on.'

He followed her down to the kitchen. She seemed to still be dressed in nightclothes, but she'd mentioned before that she was some kind of artist, so perhaps she wafted around like that all day.

'Is Ali at home?'

'She's not,' she said, leaning into a cupboard for mugs, 'but I'm sure I can help you with whatever you want.'

Swan took a seat at the big table. Mrs Hogan reached over his shoulder to put the coffee down and a layer of silk brushed his cheek. Sometimes he found the attentions of women uncomfortable, like now – the way Deirdre Hogan was smiling at him, her head tilted away while her eyes slid back to find him. She took a chair directly opposite and leaned forward on the table so that her crossed arms framed her cleavage. It would be easy to misread the situation.

The coffee was strong and slightly gritty.

'I can guess why you're here – it's the *Late Late*, isn't it? I'd be annoyed if I were you. I told her so, but she was determined to go on.'

'I take it you tried to discourage her.'

'What powers have I against Mary O'Shea? Ali's only young. Think of the excitement, the attention.'

'She didn't seem too excited by the end of it.'

Deirdre Hogan looked uncomfortable. 'Well, you don't have to worry about it any more. She's had enough attention to last her for years.'

'I thought she might. Where is she?'

Mrs Hogan opened her mouth to speak, closed it again and smiled. She gave him a look that seemed to convey a great intimacy, as if the two of them were beyond simple whys and wheres.

'You know, when Ali's dad died, my life fell apart. A heart attack. He was playing rugby at the time, only forty-two. How could you expect something like that? My sister down in Buleen took us in and I stayed there, licking my wounds, for quite a few weeks. I was so wrapped up in my own grief, I couldn't see what Ali was going through. She was only six – she acted normally, played, laughed; I thought she hadn't taken it in. But now I see it wasn't the right place for her.'

'I don't understand what you're getting at.'

'Well, a farm is a harsh place, you know ... Ailing lambs by the cooker, crows strung up on the barbed wire, baby pigs rolled flat by their sow. More dying.' Mrs Hogan wiped a single tear away with the side of her palm. 'And then that bloody box. It had to be her that found it.' She sighed. 'Ach, I'm indulging my own guilt, Detective.'

'I just needed to have a word with her.'

'That's what I'm getting at: she's gone down to stay with my sister.'

'Right now? We're in the middle of an investigation.'

'She's refused to go back to the farm for twelve years,

wouldn't even go into the house after her granddad's funeral, made me drive straight back to Dublin. Now she's somehow found the strength, and that could be a good thing. Sure, didn't you want her out of the limelight?'

The mother had a point. Surely the girl would cause less trouble down there. He took down the address and phone number. Caherbawn Farm, Buleen, near Kinmore. He'd need to look it up on a map – he didn't know his own country as well as he should. His visit had been a bit of a waste. Then he thought of something Mrs Hogan could do for him.

'While I'm here … could I borrow one of Ali's school blouses? One was found in the convent gardens, and we're trying to gather a few comparisons. I'd be obliged.'

He followed Mrs Hogan – *call me Deirdre, please* – up two flights of bare stairs to the top of the house and into the girl's bedroom, while she flung apologies over her shoulder about the state of the place.

The room looked like someone had stolen half the furniture, then exploded a basket of clothing, kitchenware and toiletries over the remains. Painted floorboards were visible here and there through the wreckage. The lilac walls were decorated with posters and leftover blobs of Blu-tack.

Deirdre Hogan rifled through a chest of drawers and emptied out a dirty clothes basket. While she searched, he examined the pictures of pop stars on the wall, their young faces twisted in sneers and dumb, malevolent stares. He wouldn't be young again, for anything. All that pretending you didn't care. He winced at the ramshackle shower cubicle festooned with clothes and the old sink unit in the corner. On the floor under the sink an electric kettle shared a tray with some mugs and a jar of instant coffee. This room had been a bedsit – a complete home to someone. He looked at the door and saw there was a lock still on it. A tingle ran up the back of his skull.

Was it possible for a girl to deliver a baby on her own and conceal that fact for some time? If she had a lock on the door, didn't have to share a bathroom, it would help a great deal. But could she be as cool as Ali Hogan was, after the fact? That would take some acting. He recalled the first sight of her: the clownish clothes, her eagerness to help. But now he was remembering other things. That baggy dress she had on. He'd seen other girls in dresses like that. He knew it was the fashion, but it could serve another purpose entirely.

For those two or three days that constituted its brief life – its only life – the baby could have been kept somewhere like this, out of sight, out of hearing.

Mrs Hogan was picking up clothes at random from the floor, stirring some larger piles with her foot. There was no carpet here, though, no blue carpet fibres. Although a rug would be easy enough to roll up and remove.

'I give up. There might be one in the laundry room.'

Swan followed Ali's mother down the stairs. When they got to a landing, he asked where her own bedroom was. He wanted to judge the distance between the two.

She stopped still and gave him an amused, searching look. 'Just down here at the front.'

'And this laundry room?' he asked quickly.

'By the kitchen.'

She led him to a narrow room under the stairs that was made even more constricted by the heaps of newspapers massed against the walls and shelves stacked with useless-looking stuff –washed yoghurt cartons, jars, bags full of more bags and folded wrapping paper. There was an old ceramic sink, so big you could stand a child in it, and Mrs Hogan started to sort through one of several plastic laundry baskets massed on the metal counter beside it.

'Where's the one with the ironing?' she asked herself. 'Things are always going missing on me … Ah!'

She pulled out a crumple of white from a tumble of towels.

'We got there at last.' She handed the shirt to Swan, showing her dimples. 'How about some more coffee?'

'You're very kind. May I take one of these bags?'

He pulled a yellow bag from a clutch of plastic bags stuffed into a cardboard tube and put the blouse inside it.

As Deirdre Hogan made the coffee, he asked more about the house, how long they'd been there and who else shared it.

'The lodgers are all gone now,' she said. 'Just the separate basement flat rented out. I bought it after Gareth died, and it did keep us afloat. I practically evicted the last tenant a year ago, but do you know, now they're gone, I don't know where to start with it. Ali and I rattle about. Maybe I'll get lucky and she'll marry a builder.'

Swan stirred his coffee. Pretending concern for Ali's state of mind, he got Mrs Hogan to go through her daughter's movements before the finding of the baby. She was happy to talk. She said she was away with friends on the Sunday – the day before Ali found the baby, the day the pathologist determined it was killed. Ali had been home when she got home, Mrs Hogan thought, but that was late. She said Ali had been hanging around the house mostly, since school ended.

'She complains she has no money, but does nothing about finding a job. My young brother's the same.'

There was nothing in what the mother said to contradict Swan's tenuous new theory. For all her warmth, Deirdre Hogan didn't keep very close tabs on her daughter. Ali had the means to conceal a baby, she wore baggy clothes and she was on the spot when the child was found. Was that because she had recently concealed it? Guilt drawing her back? He remembered the large patchwork bag of hers they had taken from the shed. The one she tried to get back from them. Big enough for a child. The convent was just round the corner from here. Maybe the attention-seeking was part of it, some twisted form of remorse.

Deirdre Hogan released her hair from its metal clasp and started to twist it into some new arrangement at the back of her head. As she held her arms up, her wide sleeves fell down to her shoulders, revealing plump, pale arms.

'And what about yourself – any children?'

He recoiled inside. He didn't want to tell her about his personal circumstances, nor did he want to take her upstairs to some sagging clutter-draped bed. Not in this life. He tried to imagine Elizabeth in a dressing gown, entertaining some caller with a glimpse of her breasts over burnt coffee. Never.

Deirdre Hogan took his silence to be an admission of romantic failure.

'I'm sorry,' she said. 'If you don't want to talk about it, that's fine.'

His disdain vanished. What was the good of having such an admirable wife when she was rarely at home, and hardly spoke to him when she was. They had a chasm between them. That's what it was getting like, a black pit with no crossing place.

'Tell me, Deirdre ...'

She smiled at the intimacy of her name.

'What would you do if your daughter came to you and said she was pregnant?'

'Oh God, is that your trouble?'

'No, it's just a question. I don't have any children.'

*If we don't try again, we'll never know.*

'Well, I always say to Ali, she should come straight to me if anything like that happens; and, God, it can happen so easily, but I would never kick her out.'

He was inclined to believe her good intentions, but a parent's intentions didn't always impact on reality. He had a feeling the mother didn't know her daughter as well as she thought.

# 17

Butterflies skittered about the purple thistle heads rising here and there above the grass and the frothy meadowsweet of the field. The sun suddenly broke through the clouds and Joan looked around and smiled. Beyond her curly head Ali could see the line of trees that marked the edge of the river.

Ali looked back towards the road. She could make out the whole top floor of Caherbawn above its surrounding hedges. She wished Joan hadn't been so insistent that they come here for their picnic, so close to her aunt's. She walked on, following in Joan's tracks until they reached a bend in the river, screened by saplings.

A tongue of butterscotch-coloured sand jutted into the slow, dark water. The opposite bank was undercut, a ledge of rough grass hanging over a mud wall pocked with holes and burrows above the waterline. In the shadows of the trees, midges swirled like sparks.

Ali kicked off her sandals and bundled up the skirt of her dress, tying it in a knot in front, so that it hung in a baggy puff above her knees. Joan sat cross-legged on the river sand, beside the bag she had brought with her, squinting up, smiling.

'It must be nice for you to be out in the open air.'

'I've been out loads,' said Joan. 'My mother takes me shopping on Fridays, and I've been home for a few Christmases. I've even tried to stay out a few times, but something always happens.'

'Like what?'

'I lose the run of myself. I get panicky, and they take me back.' She shrugged, then flicked her chin up. 'Hey, do you see that?'

Ali turned to where Joan indicated. A frazzled grey rope hung over the water from a nearby branch.

'That was your cousins' swing. They'd stay down here for whole days in the summer, and me minding them, if your aunt could spare me. *Make sure they don't drown*, she'd say. I hadn't the nerve to tell her I couldn't swim meself. But sure, they all grew up, didn't they, though the twins had me terrified. Savages, they were.'

'I remember Roisín talking about the river,' said Ali. 'But I never came down here.'

'Were you never here in the summer?'

'No, this is the first time I've stayed with them since, you know, my dad ...'

Ali stepped into the water. It was the colour of strong tea, giving her legs an orange cast. Muddy sand oozed between her toes. She walked back and forth, calf-deep.

'Are you coming for a paddle?'

But Joan was off on more memories, suddenly streaming with talk after her silence on the bus – things that the twins did to scare her, Brendan's fishing exploits and how, if Roisín got splashed, she would squeal in a way that would make you deaf.

'Did Davy not come down?'

'Too grown-up he was. Or thought he was.'

Ali's feet had numbed, so she came out of the water and sat down to unpack their picnic onto the fringed scarf she had brought to serve as a rug. Joan talked on. Two boiled eggs. Ham sandwiches that she had made behind her aunt's back and wrapped in a bread packet. A bottle of lemonade and a yellow brick of Battenberg cake she had bought from the shop. Nothing looked as nice as she thought it would.

'I'm famished. Have something, Joan.'

'I need to tell you something.'

'Oh?' Ali rearranged the food and waited.

'It wasn't until I saw you. Standing in that corridor, tall as a woman – I realised how much time had passed. And now that it's sunk in, it's all different.'

'How do you mean?'

'You saying there was no job at Caherbawn for me. I was waiting to get back to it all this time, waiting for your aunt to give in, waiting to get better. I've spent years up in Damascus House thinking they'd get me right, to take up my life again. But there's no life to take up. Everything's changed except me.'

Joan got up and started pacing, hands dug into her jeans pockets.

Ali watched her walk to the water's edge. 'Was it the baby … Was it that that put you in the hospital?'

Joan stooped to pick up a stone and flung it into the water. 'It's not a hospital, you know. It's a residential facility.'

'Sorry. You do seem pretty normal to me.'

'I'm not well.' Joan turned to look at her directly. 'After the baby and losing the job, things were hard. I fell out with my family. I lived wild.'

She dropped down to settle on the other side of the picnic cloth, hugging her knees tightly to her chest, squinting at the light that flashed from the river.

'I didn't know the baby was coming. My monthlies were never regular. Then there was the pains, and I was trying to keep quiet.'

'Was this in Caherbawn?'

'In the kitchen. I was scared I would die.'

'Oh, Joan. Did no one know?'

'The dog was there for the first bit. Looking at me.'

'What?'

'That old dog, Brownie. I was scared he would eat it.'

'Jesus! Why didn't you get some help?'

'I shouldn't have been staying there.'

'Didn't you go to the hospital?'

'It was too late for that.'

'Why did you hide it?'

'I didn't – they took it away.'

'But I found it in a box. In the back bedroom.'

'You can't have.'

'I did! And my ma knew, and Una, and Joe, I think, he was there too—'

'Shut your mouth, you.'

'I just need to get it straight in my head.'

'Don't bother yourself.'

Joan took a sandwich, tore at it with her teeth. Ali tried to look like she wasn't scared of her. She lifted one of the boiled eggs and rolled it against a flat stone, the shell crackling to mosaic.

They stayed for a while in silence. Ali concentrated on peeling the egg, bit by bit, revealing the shine. Joan threw a hard end of crust in the water. Immediately there was a 'plop' and a flash of silver. Joan and Ali looked at each other and rushed to the river's edge.

Three dark torpedo shapes moved in the depths. Joan was suddenly gleeful – clenching and unclenching her hands as if she wanted to clap, urging Ali to go in and try to catch one. Ali laughed and shook her head, but to please Joan she bundled up her skirt in one hand and tiptoed back into the water, trying to move her feet as smoothly as possible. As her shadow fell over the trout, they shot off down-river, scarcely moving a fin to do so. They were there, and then they were gone. But the mood had lightened, and they returned to their picnic as if starting over.

Ali had forgotten to bring a knife, so they squashed the pink-and-yellow cake into slices with a thin driftwood stick. They passed the bottle of lemonade between them. Joan told proud stories about her three brothers – how they could tickle trout with their hands, how the youngest had tamed a crow to sit on his shoulder.

Every so often, Joan would interrupt herself to ask what time it was.

'What does it matter?' Ali said finally. 'The doors don't close until eight, you said.'

'No, really, what time is it?'

'Quarter to three.'

'I've got to go.'

Joan went over to get her jacket and the sports bag that she had brought with her. When Ali had gone to pick her up from Damascus House she was sitting in the foyer with the bag between her feet. It was suspiciously large, but Ali reasoned that Joan might have brought some picnic things of her own. Not that she had opened it yet. Now Joan put the jacket on, picked up the bag and headed off through the field. Ali shouted after her, but she kept on going, leaving Ali to bundle the picnic things into her basket and buckle her sandals on, before setting off in pursuit. As she hurried towards the road, she thought she saw something moving behind one of the bedroom windows at Caherbawn, but when she stopped to look properly there was nothing there, just darkness.

She caught up with Joan at the field gate.

'Wait for me!'

'You don't need to come with me – I'm not going back,' Joan said.

'But the people at the hospital … I signed my name in the book!'

Joan laughed and reached up to touch Ali's hair. 'You're awful chicken for such a big girl.'

She crossed the road and walked along the verge, past the entrance to Davy's bungalow and on towards the forestry road. Ali didn't want to shout after her, for fear of someone hearing, so she was forced to follow.

Joan had disappeared into the trees. Entering their shade, Ali immediately felt chilly. She could see Joan ahead on the yellow clay track and tried to think of ways to talk her round, to get her back to Kinmore. Little stones kept flicking into her sandals, and she had to stop and shake them out while Joan increased the distance between them. One time she looked up and Joan was gone.

Ali called her name and listened to the shout die in the trees. There was only the creaking of boughs and the dull wave of a car engine passing on the road behind. It was tempting to go back, to leave Joan in the woods, but the moment Ali thought it she felt ashamed. She hurried on towards the spot where she had last seen Joan.

The trees thinned on one side of the track and tyre marks led off into what looked like a clearing. She could see far ahead on the forestry road, and it was empty. Joan must have turned off here. Ali followed the tyre ruts, passing a tumbled wall of mossy stones. She entered a clearing where a ruined, roofless cottage stood among rusting bracken. She could hear someone talking inside the ruin – Joan's voice. There was a blue van parked at the back of the building. Sunshine still caught on the tops of the trees, but at ground level the air was shaded, almost foggy.

As Ali stepped through the cottage entrance her eyes took in several things at once: that there was an odd little corrugated shelter at one end of the enclosure, and that Joan was not alone and raving, but chatting happily to a young man who was sitting on the sill of a gaping window, a can of lager in his hand.

'Ivor wouldn't mind a sandwich, if you have one left,' said Joan.

The boy nodded at her. She'd seen him before, outside Melody's on Sunday; the one she thought looked like a Viking. Joan had been talking about Ivor at the river. The little brother who had tamed the crow was now six feet tall, incongruously large beside his sister. Ali unwrapped a sandwich for him and handed it over, not knowing what to say.

He offered her a drink from his can. She shook her head.

'I'll have some,' said Joan.

'You won't,' said Ivor. 'God knows what kind of drugs they've been giving you up in that place.'

Joan looked delighted at his bossiness. Ali took out the lemonade and passed it to her.

'I'm going to stay with Ivor.'

'You can't stay in this place,' said Ali, looking at the rusting patchwork of the lean-to hut.

Joan gawked at her, like Ali was the one who was crazy.

'No, in the village! Ivor's got a flat above the garage. I'm going to look after it for him and cook.'

'Do you think I look like I live in this dump?' said Ivor.

Ali stuttered. 'Sorry. No offence.'

'It's true we used to stay here the odd night when we were young. This was our granddad's place, before the Forestry bought the land.'

'Ivor was only ten when he put that shelter together,' said Joan. 'He was always good with his hands.'

'When times got a bit wild up at our house, Joanie would take me down here. *Going camping*, she'd call it.'

He smiled then, a brief wave of sunshine across the dour plains of his face, revealing one gold incisor among the white of his teeth.

Ali wanted to see him smile again, just to see the flash of gold. She talked about their picnic at the river, making a fool of her own attempts at paddling and swinging, claiming she had stolen the picnic food from under her aunt's nose. Every time he smiled, she felt she had won something.

Ivor finished the last swig of his can and threw it in the old hearth, where it joined a heap of other cans and a mess of ash and twisted wire. Ali noticed that Joan looked exhausted, and had been quiet for some time.

'Sorry. You'll be wanting to get on, and I've been prattling.'

Joan came over and hugged her, the top of her head bumping off Ali's chin.

'You were good to take me out. I couldn't have done it on my own, and Ivor won't go near the place.'

'They might keep me in,' he said.

'I said to myself you coming was like a sign.'

'I'm sorry I upset you,' said Ali.

Joan's eyes shifted briefly to Ivor, then back. 'We'll not mention it again,' she said, then lifted her voice. 'There's a marquee dance on by the school tomorrow night, Ivor says. Maybe I'll go. Maybe I'll see you there.'

'Oh, I'll be there all right,' said Ali. 'Brendan's doing the disco.'

Ivor rose from the windowsill and brushed invisible crumbs from the front of his thighs. He gave his sister a little smile and she returned it and lifted her sports bag. Now that Ali realised it held all that Joan had packed for her new life, it seemed terribly small.

At the doorway Ivor hesitated, waited till Joan went on, then came back to stand in front of Ali. The blazing sky cast him in silhouette, the edges of his crinkly hair on fire, his face unreadable.

'Who's taking you to the dance?' he demanded.

'I'm taking myself to the dance. It's the twentieth century.'

He looked at her for a moment, not saying anything. She held up a hand to shade her eyes, to try and read his expression, but he was already leaving.

She listened to the van fire up and drive away, wondering why he'd been so nosy.

The lean-to was a strange little construction, a bit like a metal tent. She strolled over to an open end and saw an old mattress lying inside, smeared with mud on top, with a blue bloom of damp rising up its sides. Some animal had been chewing at a corner. She hoped it had been nicer back when Joan and Ivor used to camp here.

Ali threaded her way back to the forestry track, glad that Joan would be living in the world again, but worried about her own name lying in the register at Damascus House.

As she walked on, she found herself wondering what Joan meant when she said *they took her baby away*. Did she mean after its time in the box? Why did she deny that she hid it?

A gust of wind nudged her and Ali walked faster, forcing herself forward, back to Caherbawn. Crows argued above her. She told herself to stop fretting at it. It was a long time ago, and memories often differed.

# 18

The security guard at the back gate of Trinity College examined Swan's ID carefully before waving them through. The university controlled the most desirable car park in the city centre, but did they have to be quite so up themselves? Those college porters with their stupid frock coats and riding hats, like they were off to a hunt, when they were from the same plebeian stock as himself. Never so much as sniffed a horse, except for the ones that pulled the knacker's carts.

'Boss?' said Considine.

Swan realised he'd been muttering. He pulled into a parking space near the cricket pavilion. Sports fields spread out in front of them and, beyond, the stately quadrangles and cobbles that featured in a hundred thousand postcards.

'Why weren't we born to this, Gina?'

'Did you apply, boss?'

'Did I, biffo. My parents wouldn't hear of such a thing, and the bishop's ban was still in force. I hear its mostly southside types now, the cream of young Ireland.'

'I got in. Did a year of economic and social studies. Loved it.'

Swan carried on as smoothly as he could manage. 'Why didn't you graduate, so?'

Considine shrugged, looked at her watch. 'Circumstances. The need to get a job.'

'You're full of surprises.'

A rustle of far-off applause greeted them as they got out of the car. Young ones sat about on the steps of the pavilion, drinking, watching lean boys in whites play cricket. They couldn't even play an Irish game here, loping around like *Brideshead* aristocrats with their little red ball. God, he was getting like his father – disgust as a first resort.

They passed behind the pavilion and entered a nondescript building that was part of the science department. Four flights up was the office of the chief pathologist, a man who combined an academic career with intimate examination of the country's dead. He was a well-known figure throughout Ireland, striding across newspaper photographs – out of court, into court or entering a tented area in some newly blighted place.

The room they entered hummed with fridges, freezers and extractor fans, and the whiff of formalin brought Swan's nostrils to attention. The muddle of the place reminded him of Deirdre Hogan's house, but here the clutter was elevated to a professional level. Slide carousels, files, shelves of reference books, microscopes and other precise-looking instruments he couldn't put a name to crammed the room. Stacks of Tupperware boxes filtered the light from the attic windows. Of course it probably had a different name when put to scientific use – *plasticeptacle* or *polyquarinator* or something.

Among this attic of delights stood the Edwardian figure of the pathologist, leaning on his knuckles over one of the island counters that sliced the room, half-moon glasses balanced mid-nose as he stared at something in a white plastic box in front of him. His open lab coat revealed a tweed suit, check shirt and knit tie. He looked like a man who might go and shoot some grouse when the office day ended.

As they approached, he pulled a lid onto the box and pushed it to one side. While they made pleasantries, Swan's eyes kept wandering towards it, imagining lurid contents – a severed body part or some naked, quivering organ.

'Vincent, do you bring me news or are you wanting something from me?'

'I had a question,' said Swan. 'It's going to sound a bit naïve.'

The pathologist folded his arms and leaned back in readiness. 'It's the simple ones that are the tough ones,' he said. '*Who made the world?* and all that.'

'How can you tell if a woman has carried a child? Internally, I mean.'

Swan got a smile for his effort.

'Hmm … pregnancy shifts the pelvic girdle, widening and loosening the joints to a certain degree. It also stretches the womb, naturally enough, and even though it contracts again, you can tell the difference at post-mortem if the deceased is still of child-bearing age. After the menopause it's a bit more difficult. Of course in cases where there was a subsequent hysterectomy, the difficulty is obvious – just the bone girdle to go by.'

'What if the woman is still alive?'

'I don't get you.'

'If she's walking about saying that she hasn't had a baby at all, can you prove she has?'

'There would commonly be signs from such a major event, of course: trauma … scarring from tears likely – a lot depends on how much time had passed between delivery and examination.'

The pathologist reached over and pulled the plastic box an inch towards his body, then poked it so it lay exactly parallel to the desk edge. Swan felt the silence between them like a great fog of uncertainty.

The pathologist looked at Considine. 'Any insight you would care to offer?'

Gina's face darkened and she flashed a quick look at Swan. 'I've never been pregnant.'

'I think you should be talking to an obstetrician about this,' said the pathologist, addressing Swan once more. 'But I imagine the accessible signs to look for are stretching of the skin, scar tissue from tearing at the mouth of the vagina and changes in the os.'

'The what?'

'The os. The opening in the cervix – it becomes distended into a line rather than a dot. And a scan would probably reveal womb changes.'

Considine had pulled out her notebook, was writing 'OZ?' on a blank page, head bent.

'What about the psychological effect? Do you think it would be possible for a woman or girl to deliver a baby and then sort of forget about it? Or not really forget about it, in the ordinary sense, but blank it, act as if nothing at all had happened. Even tell herself that nothing had happened?'

The pathologist pulled over a stool and sat down. 'Psychology's not my field. But I remember a case in England, about eight years ago, still sticks with me. A young guest at a wedding delivered herself in a toilet cubicle during the reception, then placed the baby and the afterbirth in the sanitary bin and re-joined the party. People were coming and going all the time, and one witness saw the girl retouch her make-up before leaving the Ladies. And none of her friends or even her boyfriend admitted to noticing she was pregnant.'

'Complete denial?'

'Yes, or at least a sense of putting things back to how they should be, *sans* baby.'

'And just carry on normally.'

'Exactly. Unless you've come across yet another dead infant, I presume we are still discussing your Rosary Baby?'

Swan nodded.

'In cases of denial, you don't take the time to wash, feed and clothe your baby before killing it. Quite the contrary.'

'Yes, that's what doesn't fit. Given those few days that it lived – do you think it's possible for a girl to deliver and look after a baby on her own, to keep its existence from anyone else?'

'I'm flattered that you seek my opinion on such a wide range of things.'

'Have a go—'

'Probably. Maybe. Women have delivered on their own throughout history. I'm sure they still do, though few would actually choose to. There's a good man at Holles Street I can recommend for all this stuff.'

Considine wrote the good man's name in her book. The pathologist reached out for his plastic box again, pulling it directly in front of him and pausing to look at them with his thumbs hooked under the lip of the lid. Swan braced himself. The pathologist flipped the lid off to reveal a stack of white sandwiches, then smiled a wicked smile.

They said their thanks and goodbyes quickly. In the stairwell, Considine put her hand on his sleeve, and Swan stopped.

'Why did you bring me here?' she asked.

'Because you're working the case with me.'

'Well, you could have told me what it was about.'

'You can't afford to be that sensitive.'

'What's going on in your head? Is it the Hogan girl? The blouse you gave me for forensics, it was from her house, wasn't it?'

Swan didn't answer, just led the way back to the car. They stood on either side of it, looking at each other across the roof.

'Say it was her, how could she act so cool?' Swan asked.

'Cool all right,' said Considine. 'Garda O'Malley said she asked for a last look at the baby when they were taking it from the garden. Did you know that?'

'I didn't … That bag of hers that was in the shed – bring it up to forensics for a check on the inside. And get in touch with her friend again, Carmen Fitzgerald. Have a little chat.'

# 19

Their footsteps boomed on the wooden floor of the empty marquee. Davy did a little crouching run around the pillars with the loaded trolley; *brumpa-brumpa-brumpa* across the boards. Ali thought this was hilarious and probably would have been pretty funny even without the cans of cider they had shared in the van.

'Watch out for the whirly light-cupboard thing,' she said.

'Oh, we wouldn't drop the whirly light cupboard,' Brendan said from the empty stage, and Ali bent over on a wave of giggling that was almost annoying in its intensity, like being tickled by someone who wouldn't stop. Brendan jumped down and patted her head in passing, dislodging one of the combs that held her hair in a whirl on top of her head. A hank of it fell over one eye. She cursed, he laughed.

Father Philbin appeared at the marquee entrance and squinted across the gloom at them.

'Are you not set up yet, lads? The band's due for the sound check.'

Not waiting for their answer, he crossed the floor and disappeared into the side tent, where refreshments would be sold. Brendan and Davy quietened and started to connect their speakers and decks. The wall of the tent behind them lifted at the bottom and a thin man in a boiler suit and flat cap crawled through, holding a cable and plug board, which he handed to Brendan.

'Good man!' Davy called after him. From outside came the wheeze and splutter of an engine cord being pulled. A low thrum started, followed by a click, and the tent was cheered with light from the strings of coloured bulbs that hung across the space.

'Hey, Ali – here's your whirlies!' Brendan had the light box working, kaleidoscope patterns pulsing across its square screen like fast-blooming flowers. An insistent beat burst from the speakers and Ali started to move. The bass was so loud she could feel it vibrate in her kidneys. She shut her eyes and danced. She hadn't felt this good since … she couldn't remember. When the last bars faded away, the music seemed to drain through the floor.

She opened her eyes to find five men in matching jackets staring at her. One of them started to clap slowly.

'You the floor-show?' said another.

'Just, ah, testing the boards.' She stomped her heels in a little tattoo, looking down at her feet to hide her embarrassment.

The one who had clapped stepped forward. He had ink-black hair in a style that could only be described as a pageboy. The oldest pageboy in the kingdom – close up, he looked about fifty.

'We're The Corvettes,' he said with a smile and held out his hand. He couldn't be prouder if he was saying, 'We're Roxy Music.'

More sockets and wires were brought in for The

Corvettes to do their sound check. Brendan and Davy were sorting out their record boxes, so Ali stood against a pillar and watched the band run through a few numbers. What they lacked in originality, The Corvettes made up for in versatility. They raced through versions of 'Karma Chameleon' and 'The Hucklebuck', before the singer produced a *bodhrán* and someone else got out a fiddle and they were whooping up a jig and a reel. Two of them never even moved the fags from their lips.

The man with the pageboy whispered closely into the mike, 'And this one is for the be-yootiful girl in the tight red trousers', and they swung into 'Three Times a Lady', before deliberately fluffing it and breaking down into a tumble a few bars in, the bass drum whacking alone into the empty tent like an amplified heart.

Some women came in carrying crates of teacups and an urn the size of a rubbish bin. Drink wasn't allowed at the dance, which was why Davy was now pulling Ali outside – so they could get a pint in at the Red Rock Saloon before things got busy. Brendan left a cassette of party music playing, just to fill the space.

'The machine plays both sides, so we've got sixty minutes and counting,' he announced, gunning the accelerator in the van.

By those calculations, the tape ran out ten minutes before they made it back to the marquee. A dozen quite elderly people sat on the benches that lined the edge of the tent, while two children practised their spinning on the empty boards.

Brendan hopped up on the stage, mumbling words of welcome and apology into the microphone, while shaking a twelve-inch single from its sleeve.

'Here's one I *know* you're going to like.' Bouncy electro-pop streamed out of the speakers.

Ali sat on the side of the stage. It was good to have a pseudo-occupation, to pass the occasional record up for Davy to pass to Brendan. Around eleven the marquee started to fill up in earnest, people drifting in, the men bowed by the weight of bottles in their jacket pockets, the girls carrying clinking shoulder bags. Ali noticed tight huddles where she could just glimpse something being added to the bottles of Fanta and Coke that everyone clutched.

Four girls drifted out into the middle of the floor and started to dance, smiling only at each other or down at their shoes, pretending not to be aware of the crowd that now ringed the hall, three or four deep as closing pubs swelled the numbers. Brendan turned up the music to rise over the sound of the talking. In response, people raised their voices, yelling conversations into their neighbour's ears. Ali looked round to see who she recognised; there was Roisín's husband Colman, roaring drunk and hugging an equally red-faced buddy by the neck – Cathal, the arsehole with the foetus-feet badge. Roisín must be home with the baby. More girls were dancing now, sedate little shimmies set against the wild gestures and stumbles of the roiling crowd ringing the floor. It was either going to be a brilliant night or a riot.

Davy hopped off the stage and grabbed her wrist, pulling

Ali out into the centre of the sparsely occupied floor. He was the first man up, and what he lacked in rhythm he made up for in enthusiasm, twirling her about, playing various invisible instruments, winking at the other dancers. They danced for four songs, by which time the floor was packed. Brendan gave them a thumbs-up from the stage.

'Want a mineral?' said Ali. 'I'm parched.'

Davy signalled that he had another source of drink up by the decks, so she threaded her way to the refreshment tent on her own, squeezing her fingers into her pockets to find the fiver she'd stowed earlier.

Things were quieter in the side tent. Women poured tea and offered Club biscuits or packets of crisps from big tin boxes. As she stood in line for her lemonade Ali spotted Joan standing with a couple of older women. After she bought her bottle, she wandered over, noticing as she drew close that Joan wasn't doing any of the talking, was in fact smiling past the women's heads at the blank wall of the tent, jiggling her head from side to side. The women eyed Ali with suspicion.

'All right?' she called to Joan. Joan didn't seem to hear, so Ali tapped her on the back. She swung round quick as a flash, something like fear widening her eyes, then settling into pleasure as she recognised Ali.

'Look at you – and that hair: you've mad style.'

'I wouldn't get looked at twice in Dublin, but here ... Anyway, how are you settling in at Ivor's?'

'Yeah, yeah, it's good,' said Joan, dismissing the question. Her eyes raked the crowd beyond Ali's shoulder. 'Is your aunt not coming?'

'She's a bit old for this, eh? Not much of a groover, Aunt Una.'

'I need to talk to her.'

'Tell me, I'll pass it on.'

'Nope,' said Joan and turned back to the whispering women. Ali headed back into the main hall. She hoped it wasn't her old job that Joan wanted to ask Una for. She thought they had got past all that.

She found a quiet spot by the marquee wall and took the combs out of her hair, shaking it down and raking it through with her fingers. 'Mad style' was not the look she'd been aiming at.

She looked up and saw Peggy Nolan standing alone in a rose-printed dress at the edge of the light, watching the dancers. Her expression was as miserable as her frock was merry. Some people could make you feel guilty just by breathing. Perhaps she would go and talk to her. But then Ali saw a hand reach out and touch Peggy's shoulder from behind. Peggy turned round to the man on the end of the tapping hand, her dull expression unchanging. But the man must have read some consent in her eyes, because he guided her out into the swarm of dancers, an arm firmly round her middle. Ali moved to the little gap Peggy had vacated. Davy was close by on the floor, dancing slowly with a tall girl Ali hadn't seen before – elegant, with dark sleepy eyes and high cheekbones, like a girl in a magazine. Davy was talking close into her ear, but the girl hardly seemed to listen, looked bored.

Ali squeezed her way back to the stage and asked Brendan to top up her lemonade with the Bacardi she'd seen him buy at the Red Rock.

'The lovely Valerie,' he said when she pointed to Davy's dance partner. 'And he's still trying to get her back, poor sucker.'

So this was the girl Davy had built a house for. Ali found it hard to believe anyone would turn down Davy, even a girl who looked like that.

Then The Corvettes took to the stage and the marquee skipped and sweated to a ceilidh set. Davy reappeared to persuade her up for 'The Walls of Limerick'. Ali hadn't ceilidh-danced since she was thirteen and spent three unhappy weeks down in Irish college in Spiddal. They hopped and they spun, passing under the facing couple's steepled arms after each bout, to meet a new pair to repeat the moves with. Halfway round the hall they ducked under and came face-to-face with Ivor Dempsey, holding hands with a small busty girl who seemed to be unable to dance without holding her mouth open in a delighted silent scream.

'Theresa, darlin',' said Davy and kissed her hand as he sidestepped her away.

Ivor looked either furious or embarrassed as he offered his hand, it was hard to tell which. Why had she acted like such a stuck-up tit yesterday? It had taken her until now to realise that he'd perhaps been asking her out.

'Howya?'

'I'm grand, Ivor,' said Ali and gave his hand a little squeeze.

He stood still for a moment and looked at her. Everyone around them was spinning, and he belatedly caught her elbow and whirled her so hard that her feet lifted up from the ground. He laughed and brought them to a sudden stop. Her head kept twirling, even as Davy danced her on to the next pair.

'Lively girl, that,' said Ali.

'Oh, yeah, Theresa's a panic.'

'Does she go out with Ivor?'

The steel-haired woman that Ali now faced grabbed her by the waist and whisked her around grimly, prompting another bout of dizziness. She hoped Davy would remember the question.

They came together again and held their hands high for the pair of women to pass under.

'That big galoot? I doubt it.'

The jig squealed to an end, but most people stayed in their places for the next one to kick off. Ali dragged Davy away from the floor, needing air. They went out the front entrance of the tent, where a man stamped the back of their hands with an indecipherable blotch.

Figures milled in the dark. You could see the street lights of the town away to the left, but here in the school grounds there were just a couple of floodlights over the playground, lighting empty tarmac beneath and making the surrounding darkness blacker. The marquee itself glowed a dim yellow through the grimy canvas. Over to the right, a line of girls was queuing for the three Portaloos. Men were pissing against the yard wall beyond that, legs spread for balance, chatting. The field across the road was full of cars and vans now, where there were none earlier. Dozens of bicycles leaned in the ditch.

Ali took out a flattened fag packet and removed an oval cigarette.

'That your idea of fresh air?' asked Davy.

They stood in silence watching people come and go, disappearing into the dark or looming suddenly back into the orbit of the marquee. Ali asked about the girl he'd been dancing with earlier. Davy pretended not to know which girl she was talking about.

'Brendan said you used to go out with her.'

'Brendan's got a loose gob.'

'C'mon, tell.'

'Nothin' to tell. My own fault, that's all. Got caught looking the other way. Nobody does that to her ladyship.'

'God, she sounds a nightmare.'

A man was shouting beyond the circle of light, up the road or in fields beyond. Hard to tell if it was serious or just tomfoolery.

'What's it to you?' His voice was teasing.

In Dublin they had spent a lot of time together, out in the balmy garden nights, with candles and moths and strange drinks. Just the two of them – no Valeries, no tragedies. Ali wanted that feeling back.

'Remember that night you made us Harvey Wallbangers?'

'Ah, now.'

'I can't remember a thing after the second drink.'

'That's convenient,' said Davy, and there was something hard in his voice, no teasing now.

Ali gave a weak laugh and stepped away from him, confused. She truly didn't remember. A car drove past slowly and came to a stop near the school building.

'Back in a minute,' said Davy and went over to the car, leaning in the passenger window to talk. The queue to the

Portaloos was getting shorter; she might as well join it. Ali called out to Davy, to point out where she was heading, but he didn't seem to hear. The car engine was revving loudly, the smoke from the exhaust drifting up against the brightness of a broken brake light. Everyone drove wrecks around here. She took her place behind two girls. To one side of the queue, a metal stand held a spotlight pointing right at the toilet doors, dazzling all who exited.

When Ali came out of the toilet, Joan was in the queue.

'Joanie!' said Ali, enfolding her in a hug.

'Stop it, stop it.' Joan pushed her off and glanced round to check who was looking at them.

'I'm only being friendly.'

'Well, I'm tired. I should be in bed by now, you know.'

'You've got to tell me one thing, though – honestly.' Ali waved ahead the person behind Joan in the queue.

'I don't want to talk about that.'

'No, not *that*. You've got to tell me: do you think I look like a freak?'

Joan said no, but Ali told her how everyone kept staring at her clothes. She was stroking Joan's arm to get her to listen. Joan suddenly slapped her hand away.

'You know nothing about being looked at funny. You know nothing about nothing.'

'Don't be like that.'

Someone called Joan's name then, and she pushed past Ali, swallowed up by the dark after just a few strides. Ali looked round and noticed the women in the queue staring at her.

'Is it the red trousers?' she asked.

*

Inside the marquee the band was taking a break, and Brendan was dancing behind his record decks, urging people to keep going. *Too shy shy, hush-hush, eye to eye, Too shy shy, hush-hush, eye to eye.* Ali waved and did a little imitation of his moves. Laughing, he held a hand up at the side of his face to block out the sight of her.

She decided not to drink any more. For one thing, she didn't want to have to visit those loos again. Brendan put on a slow song, and she went up to sit on the edge of the stage, in front of him. All the couples who had been flinging their arms and legs about suddenly fell on each other, as if delighted to have something to lean on. One couple stood stock-still, French-kissing studiously, like they were working their way into each other's mouths. Ali's view of the floor was blocked by some idiot standing in right front of her. She tilted to one side, before realising that the idiot was Ivor Dempsey and that he was holding a hand down towards her.

She met his eyes and slipped her hand into his, to see how it would feel to touch him again. Then she was on her feet and Ivor's arm was around her, drawing her out into the middle of the shuffling dancers. She rested one hand on his shoulder. His shirt seemed such a thin barrier to the body beneath. He pulled her close and she moved her hand to the back of his neck. His hair touched her cheek. She felt him inhale, his nose just behind her ear, and she hoped there was something pleasant to smell there, not the reek of smoke and booze. He smelt lovely, sharp. She was allowing herself to relax into it when there was a scraping shriek across the record and some manic Madness track kicked in, leaving the dancers as disorientated as if someone had flung a bucket of water on them. Ali looked up to the stage and saw Brendan grinning, looking straight at her.

She tried to guide Ivor to the back of the marquee, but he had seen.

'They're great jokers, your family,' he said, and his face was like granite. He put his hand against the curve of her spine and steered her towards the refreshment tent. She wasn't sure if he was angry with her too, but they could have a sit down in the annex and maybe sort it out. But just where one tent led into another, Ivor drew aside a flap of canvas and pushed her out into the darkness. She stumbled over the muddy grass, his hand still pressing against her waistband. It was quiet behind the tent, though she was aware of huddled, possibly embracing figures here and there in the shadows. She stopped walking and turned to face him, put her hand flat against his chest. She could feel the pump of his heart under her palm.

'I don't want to be rolling around in some ditch,' she said. He put his hand out and rubbed his fingertips slowly across her lower lip.

'Would a van do?'

A moment went by, and then she said yes.

They drove a mile or two out along the road, turned down a lane and parked. He collapsed the back of the bench seat so that it formed a kind of cushioned recline for them. He did it in such a practised way that Ali flickered with doubt, thinking of other girls in this same place. Ivor brushed a hand over the surface and smiled at her.

Everybody thought she was a slut already. Even Davy.

She didn't want to try to remember what it was that Davy had been hinting at. She wanted to be only her body, not thoughts or memories. She took off her top and sat before Ivor in her bra. There was only one thing.

'Do you have something?'

He smiled and patted his shirt pocket, then reached for the button of her trousers.

They wrestled each other out of their clothes, laughing and straining. The image of a smiling, approving Mary O'Shea came into Ali's head and she pushed it away as Ivor pushed into her.

Sometime later she was on her hands and knees and he was covering her. There was a slick of sweat between his chest and her back. He reached a hand round to touch her, and pressed his teeth against her neck. Her body shook, her arms suddenly unable to support her. Ivor groaned and collapsed onto her.

'Fucking hell,' he muttered and rolled onto his back, one hand fumbling at his groin, taking care of the condom. She nuzzled into his side, trying to keep the feeling going, sneaking looks at his body through half-closed eyes, the dim light barred by shadows of branches around them. He looked like he was sleeping, but his fingers moved slowly back and forth through her hair, keeping her quiet. Owls called in the woods.

The marquee was still alight when they got back. Ali wasn't sure how much time had passed. They parted outside the van.

'I need to find Joan,' he said.

She slipped back in the way they had snuck out. All the refreshments were packed up. Sleepers and snogging couples occupied the benches. Half the dancers had gone home. The Corvettes were playing 'Spancilhill', and a scattering of people were lurching around the floor to it. A circle of six men, including Roisín's husband, rotated drunkenly at one end of the floor, arms around each other's shoulders like a rugby scrum.

Brendan was putting the records away.

'Where's Davy?'

'Fucked off somewhere. Just like you did. I wouldn't mind some help with this lot.' He wouldn't look at her.

'I met some girls outside,' said Ali, acting more pissed than she was.

'Did you now?'

'They were such a laugh. I lost track of time.'

'And which one of those charming ladies gave you that big hickey?'

Ali clamped her hand to her neck.

'Other side.'

She wrapped both hands round her neck.

'Must have got your head stuck in a tent flap,' he said, but he wasn't smiling, and wouldn't speak to her on the way home.

# 20

Joan came over when Davy called her name, but refused to get in the car. He'd told Una she wouldn't want to, but Una never listened. He hadn't set eyes on Joan for years, but she was exactly the same: shy, her animal wariness alert to entrapment.

'Just a quick chat,' he said, 'in private, like. You *said* you wanted to talk to Una. Well, here she is.' The chug of dance music started up again in the marquee behind them.

'She can talk to me up there.' Joan pointed up the road to where the village started, sodium light falling on darkened house fronts and empty pavements.

She walked away, up the middle of the road, towards the lights. Davy got into the car with Una.

'What's she playing at?' Una asked.

'I don't know. Maybe she's drunk.'

'You're pretty well on yourself. She shouldn't be out of Damascus House. I told Peter Nolan, they should keep her in. She's not right, she's been making threats.'

Joan was a smoky flicker in the darkness. Una started the engine and eased the car along the road in her wake. She didn't turn the lights on.

'What threats?'

'Letters in the post, most days.'

'Is she saying she'll tell on you?'

Una gave him a disgusted look. 'Tell on *me*?'

Joan looked back over her shoulder. Davy rolled down the window and stuck his head out.

'Come here for a minute, eh? Just – come on,' he called.

A wash of light fanned through the car as a vehicle appeared behind. Una pulled into the side and ducked her head low. Davy copied her, not really knowing why they were playing this game. The other car swooped past, then braked hard as it lit up Joan in the centre of the road. She scrambled to the side with one hand shading her face.

'Maybe you should do this another time,' said Davy.

'I don't want her coming to ours, for Joe to get wind of it. I need her alone.'

'I've an idea. You drive on past her and let me out. I'll talk to Joan, take her to Olohan's Lane. You come join us. It'll be quiet there.'

'She mightn't be so easily charmed.'

'Leave it with me.'

He found her standing at the little triangle, the one with the tub of flowers and the signpost on it. She was looking down towards the bridge. He stuck his hands in his pockets and sauntered over.

'Nice night for it,' he said.

'Is your sister coming?'

He slid his hands out of his pockets and transferred them gently, sliding, over her shoulders.

'Joanie. How are you doing?' He purred it. She met his eye only briefly. She was such a little thing. Big trouble in a small package. 'Come away to the lane with me.'

She examined his face as if trying to remember something about him that wasn't coming back to her.

'No,' she said, and his hands tightened.

Down by the old bridge a figure appeared and stood watching them. But it was only Una, come round the back way. Davy put his arm firmly around Joan's shoulders and marched her down to the bridge. When they got near Una, he gave her a little push and backed off. He'd got them together, he could go back to the dance now, but he hesitated, curious to see how Una would handle her.

'What do you think you're playing at?' said Una in her familiar scold.

Joan walked slowly to the centre of the bridge. 'I want to show you something,' she said. Davy could only just catch her words over the sound of the river rush. He moved with Una to flank her. Joan pointed over at the crumbling bulk of the old chapel ruins. 'Do you know what's there?'

'What's there?' asked Una tightly.

'It's the *cilleanach*,' said Joan. 'My mother told me about it. It's where the unbaptised babies go.' Davy shifted to see exactly where she was pointing. It wasn't the chapel, it was the little walled plot beside it, frothing with brambles and bracken.

'It's not used any more, Joan – it's only stories,' said Una.

'That's where he should be … my baby.' She sagged as she spoke. 'I'm very tired.' She turned so that her back was against the wide bridge wall and tried to push herself up to sit on it.

'Why don't you and me talk about it,' Una said. 'Davy doesn't understand about these things.'

That was so typical of her. Make him help when she needed him, then try and wave him off, like he was still a boy. Next she'd be saying it was women's things, women's business. Well, he wasn't going anywhere. He stepped in and put his hands under Joan's arms, gave her a hoosh up so that she could sit on the wall. Now she was at an even height to Una, eye to eye. This would be interesting, he thought.

'Your child's at peace, Joan. You need to understand that,' said Una.

'You told me he went to limbo. Someone at the hospital told me there was no limbo any more,' said Joan. 'I hate to think he might be floating alone in the dark, the cold.' Davy made a small, involuntary sound. Una shot him a fierce look, put her hand to Joan's arm.

'Don't talk like that.'

'You said there would be other babies, but none came.'

'You've been unlucky.'

'If his remains were in the right place, he'd rest. Maybe another child could come to me then.'

'That's a bit morbid now,' said Davy, trying to lighten things, but Una gestured him to shut up, no appreciation for his efforts. Well, all right then, she could handle it herself. He turned from them, ran his eye over the backs of the houses. Dark windows, everyone asleep or at the dance.

'He *is* at rest,' Una was saying. 'On the farm.'

Joan started wailing then. 'I'm not asking much of you, missus. I just want you to move him to the graveyard.'

'Keep your voice down—'

He was vaguely aware of Una reaching for the girl, then

a flurry of fast movement in the corner of his eye. Una knocked into him, holding her jaw, and Joan – Joan was gone.

He threw himself across the width of the stone wall, looked down into the dark. He could make out nothing, only some smears of river foam scrolling by.

'Jesusgodnojesusno …' Una's voice ran out over the flowing water.

'What have you done?'

'She kicked me! She flung her leg out and kicked me!'

'Did you push her?'

'Of course I didn't. She toppled herself!'

Una grabbed his hand and pulled him after her, over to the chapel and down the riverbank, sliding on the muddy grass. She hadn't held his hand since he was a child. It was so strange, like a game. He was aware of wanting to laugh, to scream with laughing. They were feeling their way along the outside of the bridge, down to the arch, the stone damp and gritty under his fingertips. He kept looking at the surface of the water, its even drift. No splashing, nothing moving in it.

'Are you sure she fell in?'

'Don't be a bloody simpleton,' Una said.

'I can't see a thing.'

'She's probably hiding. Call her name, would you? Quietly.'

'Jo-an?' His voice was tentative.

They stood and listened; there was only the river's steady flow.

Una shook his hand off, drew herself up and stepped off

the bank, into the water. It was waist-deep at the edge, and her coat floated out around her, like a lily pad.

'She'll be hiding,' she said, and waded her way under the arch.

Davy looked at her stiff posture as she disappeared into the shadow, her awful determination. What had just happened could not have happened.

He scrambled back up the bank. Far off on the main street, a pair of drunk women were singing, holding each other up as they walked along.

He started to run, away from the town, the bridge, the lights. He clambered over the first gate he came to and ran up two fields before he let himself stop. Lungs sore, he flung his body down in the lee of an old wall. A cow wheezed nearby and he jumped with fright. It was a wonder his nerves still worked at all. He remembered the naggin of rum in his jacket pocket. It hadn't broken. He clamped it to his lips. Una would be wondering where he had got to, but he didn't care. It wasn't his fault this time.

# 21

It was pathetic to admit it, but Swan quite enjoyed Saturdays in the office. The drive into work was clear, and a sunnier air was discernible among his colleagues – dress code loosened by one button. The overtime helped, of course. A packet of chocolate biscuits lay open beside the coffee machine. He took two and balanced them on a saucer on top of his coffee cup. Breakfast.

Half of the others were in already, and Considine's jacket was on the back of her chair. Barrett scooted across the aisle to pass him a sheaf of messages. The top one said Dr Flynn from the Technical Bureau wanted him to call. The number was an internal extension, not the one for the state lab at Abbotsford, so he guessed she was upstairs. He felt invigorated; things were starting to move. Hopefully Goretti could provide another piece of the jigsaw.

Dr Goretti Flynn's office was crisp and organised, as was the woman herself. Her hair bothered him – a perfect dome of it floating about her skull as if it had never met the resistance of a headrest or pillow. He imagined her sitting bolt upright in bed in a frilly nightdress, fast asleep. He was once tempted to comment on the hair, but stopped himself in time. It was hard enough to get forensics results through at the best of times.

Goretti was at her desk, a china cup in one hand and a pen in the other, making marks in a grid on a large sheet of paper. Swan rapped gently on the glass door and she looked up and smiled. As he entered, she put her cup down and wiped her fingers on a tissue from a box on her desk.

'I've something to show you,' she said.

She unlocked the door of the small lab behind and brought him over to a counter where three fat paper bags lay.

'These are three school blouses – the one on the right is from the crime scene, the one on the left Declan Barrett got from the convent laundry, the one in the middle you brought in a few days ago. The blouse from the convent has a name tag sewn in at the neck, and Declan said all boarders' shirts are required to have the same. Neither of the other two blouses has a name tag or signs that one was ever attached.'

Goretti was on a roll. She had that tight quality to her voice that usually boded well.

'So, taking the name-tagged blouse out of the equation for the moment, I compared these two. If you washed out the fluid stain, you would be hard put to tell them apart. Identical material, identical size and, as far as I can tell, identical wear and tear.'

'This type of blouse is made in Birmingham and imported by one Irish wholesaler. It's sold in places like Arnotts, Clerys and Roches Stores. Since it's a standard piece of school kit, the wholesaler estimates they shift thirty thousand units a year. But that's predominantly at primary-school level, in smaller sizes, so there's only about one thousand sold per year in this size.'

'*Only* a thousand? That's a lot of blouse.'

'Yes – were it not for two things. Now neither is conclusive, but put them together and they are … well, quite the coincidence.'

She shook both blouses out of their bags and showed him the right cuffs – both were frayed along the edge in exactly the same way, in exactly the same place.

'Probably from rubbing against an edge or surface while writing, but interesting how the wear is identical.'

'A common thing, though.'

'Okay, but look at this.' Goretti swung a lamp out over the counter and switched it on. 'Look closely – just above the pockets.'

On both blouses there were several holes pierced through the fabric in the same position on the right breast, the tight weave of the polyester pulled open at minute entry-points. Something had been pinned there.

'Could be from some badge or religious medal the girls all have.'

'Not in St Brigid's they don't. Prefects wear a sash, and only one medal or cross on a chain around the neck is allowed. All else is considered jewellery, and Sister Mary Paul would kill you if she found it.'

'Your research is formidable.'

'Sure they drilled it into me.'

'Ah, for God's sake, why didn't you mention it?'

She shrugged. 'It's not important. Let's just say my days at St Brigid's weren't the happiest of my life. I'm sure whatever was attached to the shirt would have been hidden by the tunic bib that covers it – so it was something clandestine.'

'So, badges or brooches aren't allowed, but Ali Hogan wore some under her uniform, as did the owner of the shirt in the shed.'

'Or they're both Ali Hogan's.'

'Do y'know, that's a possibility that's looking stronger by the minute. Did you have time to look at that bag she left in the shed?'

'That's why I'm in here on a lovely morning and not on the golf course.'

Ali's patchwork bag was on the central table, pulled inside out on a sheet of white card, so that only its black cotton lining showed.

'You wanted a check for blood?'

As he walked towards it, Swan could see that the lining looked spotless, except for some deposits of lint in the corners.

'Nothing?'

Dr Flynn nodded, not breaking eye contact.

Perhaps a stain of bloody fluid in the bag, to match the one on the shirt and paper bag, would be too neat. The baby could have been wrapped in some other layer that they hadn't located, or she brought the baby to the garden in just the paper carrier at an earlier time. The misty woman or girl in his imaginary scenarios now wore Ali Hogan's face.

There were no leads yet from the towelling or blue carpet fibres, but they could come if they found a location to match them to. He urged Goretti Flynn to get out and grab what was left of the weekend.

'If I served only you, Vincent, I'd be happy to, but there are others in line. Thanks anyway.'

Considine was waiting for him outside the door.

'Managed to track down Carmen Fitzgerald,' she said. 'Her mother had taken her on holiday – South of France, no less. She brought her in this morning.'

'I told her to tell Rathmines if she left the city.'

'Do you want to hear this or not?'

'Anything good?'

'Well, Carmen says she's shocked at the idea that Alison might have been pregnant. Says she didn't have a boy-friend; they told each other everything and shared rooms in each other's houses, so she would have noticed if she had a bump.'

'Is she plausible?'

Considine shrugged. 'I think so, but then she told me something very interesting. You can hear it from her.' She jigged her head towards the corridor of interview rooms and Swan followed her.

Carmen Fitzgerald lit up the dreary room with her red jacket and electrocuted yellow hair, but her face was ashen.

'Tell him what you told me,' said Considine, 'about the night before you found the baby.'

'Can I go home if I do?'

Considine looked to Swan. He nodded at the girl.

'We were at the school that night – near the hockey pitch. We go there sometimes ... to drink. It's just round the back of Ali's house.'

'What time was this at?'

'Dunno. About nine or ten. We met two blokes we knew from Rathgar College, and we had some drink. But we weren't near the Rosary Garden.'

'She says they didn't see anyone else,' said Considine. 'That they drank some beer and went home by eleven.'

'And Ali was with you all the time?'

Carmen chewed her bottom lip into a small sideways loop.

'She went off for a little while with Ronan – they didn't go far away.'

'And you were involved with the other boy.'

'God, no! Bobby Kinsella, you must be joking.'

'I thought you said Ali didn't have a boyfriend.'

'She doesn't – that was just, y'know, a little bit of messing. Ali always had a soft spot for Ronan. He used to go out with Eleanor Glenn.'

She spoke as if Swan would have foreknowledge of her social scene, of the repulsiveness of Bobby and the cachet of Eleanor Glenn.

'Was Ali a virgin, do you know?'

Carmen blushed as red as her jacket. 'I don't know!'

'I'm sure you talk about those kinds of things.'

'I don't know,' she insisted.

They let the girl re-join her mother, but asked them to stay to have a statement taken and give details of the boys.

Considine and Swan regrouped in the corridor. Carmen's hotly claimed ignorance of Ali's sexual experience wasn't particularly convincing. And the fact that they'd been in the grounds of St Brigid's around the time of the child's death was impossible to ignore.

Swan reminded Considine of the pathologist's anecdote, about the girl whose boyfriend didn't even notice she was pregnant. Wasn't it possible that a best friend mightn't notice, either?

Considine ticked off the known facts on her fingers. 'Ali was there that night, she had the means to conceal it, the blouse found at the scene is probably hers.'

'We're going to have to move this forward, fast. I'll get Barrett to track down the two boys this morning, but more importantly we need to recruit an expert, a thingummy – gynaecologist – can you take care of that?'

# 22

Ali had slept badly. Her mind had kept startling awake to thoughts of Ivor and what had happened in his van. The shame and the wonder of it. How different it felt compared to every fumbling misadventure she'd tried before. But on the way back to the marquee they'd found nothing to say to each other. Maybe they never would. It was only a one-night stand, she told herself, trying out the phrase she knew from magazines, flicking it away.

Ali swung her feet to the floor. This swoony feeling was just exhaustion, not emotion. She had slept naked and now peeled the sheet from her body, pulled on her pyjamas and an old jumper, and went downstairs.

The house was strangely silent, the kitchen empty. Toast crumbs littered the oilcloth and the teapot felt warm. She checked the immersion was switched on for a bath, and went to the scullery to get milk for cornflakes from the big jug there. It was so fresh from the cows that it was still lukewarm and frothy. She changed her mind about eating.

As she filled the kettle she wondered if Davy was up and about in the bungalow. Maybe she could bring coffee up to him, try to get back their normal jokiness, after the strange mood they parted with last night.

The love-bite. She tried to see it in the small rectangle

of mirror that hung over the sink. It was hardly anything, just a purple smear. If she remembered not to push her hair back, it would stay hidden. She met her eyes. She could go out for a walk later. Down through the village maybe. Joan said Ivor's flat was above the garage.

There was a sudden movement in the background of her reflection. Someone had passed by the window and was opening the door in the scullery. She heard rustling among the coats hung there.

'Hello?' she called.

Brendan appeared in the doorway. He looked shattered, and she smiled at him, thinking of a joke to make about hangovers. But he didn't smile back, just stared at her like he wasn't sure who she was or what she was doing there, and hurried up the hall to the front door. Something wasn't right.

By the time she got to the front of the house, Brendan was halfway down the drive, running. Two Garda cars were parked in the road, their blue lights spinning silently. There was a tractor in the field, and a couple of Gardaí were trying to connect a flatbed trailer to it. She could see there were more people down by the river. They were right beside the bright curve of sand where she and Joan had picnicked. You could see it so clearly from here.

Joe and Una were standing down by the gate, looking over at the cars. When Brendan reached them, he stopped briefly and pointed back up at her, at the house. Joe turned, started to make his way up the drive.

Brendan reached the tractor and pushed past the Guards to quickly finish hooking the trailer to it, using something he had brought from the house. He got into the tractor cab and drove off to the river with both Guards sitting on the back edge of the trailer, feet dangling like children. A car passing on the road slowed right down to have a look.

Her uncle stood below her on the path.

'Something's happened,' he said, and Ali's first instinct was to laugh, but nothing came out of her mouth. She had a sensation that the inside of her body was completely hollow, light as a balloon.

'Kevin Lawlor, from next door. He was out walking his dog. He found someone in the river. Drowned. Dear God!'

A response seemed to be called for. 'Who?' she asked.

'Do you remember Joan, who used to work for us? I didn't even know she was let out, but he recognised her straight away. She was caught on a branch in the shallows, lying on her back, you see. Not a mark on her.'

Ali put her hand out to clutch the door jamb, and the sharp corner of wood became the only solid thing in the whole world, an axis around which everything spun. Joe caught her by the waist and steadied her.

'It can't be Joan – she was at the dance last night. We were talking.'

'She shouldn't have been out of that hospital, let alone at a dance. You go inside while they bring her up.'

'Bring her up?' Ali had an image of Joan rising through dark waters, a rope wrapped around her waist. None of it made sense. The memory of Joan pushing past her in the dark outside the marquee, just hours ago, angry with her, telling her she knew nothing. What was it she didn't know?

Down in the field the tractor was returning, heading for

217

the road, the two Gardaí jogging along behind, hands on their batons. She couldn't see what was on the trailer; it was hidden by the cab of the tractor. Joe turned to look.

The tractor steered out of the field and into the road, revealing a long blanketed shape on the trailer. An ambulance had appeared from nowhere and waited on the roadside behind the police cars. Another car drew up to join the line of vehicles. Father Philbin got out from one side, wearing his black raincoat. He took a rolled-up length of green material out of his pocket and hung it over his shoulders, hurrying to the shape on the trailer. Dr Nolan emerged from the other side of the car, and Aunt Una turned quickly and started to walk back towards the house.

Joe had an arm round Ali's shoulders, was trying to turn her round and get her into the house. The last thing she saw was Dr Nolan lifting one end of the blankets, revealing a flash of Joan's face, white and sharp-nosed, nesting in brown curls. Father Philbin was making the sign of the cross in the air above her. Joe gave Ali a final nudge into the hallway and pulled the door closed between them.

She swayed in the middle of the hall, a strange ringing in her ears. Maybe she would lie down here on the tiles, the diamonds of red and black that were so familiar. She folded herself down to the floor. The tiles were so cold. She shifted so that her back was against a wall.

Here was where the box had lain. Ma had taken it from her arms and bent down to put it right here. Ali moved her hand over the tiles as if they retained the print of it.

*What have you got here, love?* Ma in a crouch, lifting the

lid. Ma putting her hand to the grubby towel, then falling back like she'd been bitten, thumping her back against the stair post. Aunt Una coming up the kitchen passage, bearing down on her like a storm. So fierce that Ali had covered her face against the blows she thought were coming. Feeling the spittle on her hands as Una shouted close to her head: *What in Christ's name have you done?* Everybody looking at her; Una grabbing her wrist in her iron fingers, pulling at her. Nobody stopping her doing it. Ma looking away. Ashamed, it seemed.

The shifting guilt that always lurked inside her. This was the place it had come from. The front door opened and Joe came to stand over her, reached down his hand.

'Get up now, we'll go and have a drop of tea.'

Brendan was already sitting at the table, still as a statue. Ali took a chair opposite. His eyes were red-rimmed, but dry. Joe ran the tap, rinsed out the teapot and mugs, bustling and clattering.

'Did you see her at the dance?' Ali kept her voice low.

Brendan shook his head.

They heard the front door open and Una came down to the kitchen. She looked as if she had somehow lost weight since the day before, a scrawny, strained look to her face and neck. She went to the scullery to take her jacket off, still in Ali's line of sight.

'Father Philbin and Kevin are coming here for a cup of tea,' she said. 'Maybe some of the Guards too.'

She wiped down the table, brought out good cups. Ali watched her and thought of the terrifying aunt of her memory. Una was solemn and frail in the wake of this horror; hard to believe she ever spat curses or lifted a hand to anyone.

Father Philbin blessed the air as he entered the kitchen. Kevin Lawlor, the neighbour, was behind him, cap in hand, his expression caught between embarrassment and woe, but also, Ali could see, the edge of excitement too. He was the man of the hour, the one with the story to tell. He met their eyes boldly, even as he received commiserations from Una.

The tea cooled while Father Philbin led them in a series of prayers – an 'Our Father', the Confiteor and one she didn't recognise that began: *Out of the depths I cry to thee, O Lord* ... Out of the depths, where Joan had been.

The others blessed themselves as he finished, and Una passed round a plate of biscuits.

'Take some sugar in your tea, Kevin,' she said, 'for the shock.'

It was all the cue he needed.

'I don't know how I'll ever get over it, missus. The dog was whingeing to get out, and I couldn't sleep for her noise. So I took her out the back of the house and felt a bit brighter myself for the morning air, so we went on along to the river. It was a beautiful morning.'

He shook his head, took a sup from his cup.

'It was a rag of pink I thought I saw, just near the bank. But when I got up close I could see it was a woman in a pink blouse, lying stretched out by the side of the water. Her curls were blowing in the wind. The sun must've dried them.

'When I was about ten yards away I recognised who it

was and, God forgive me, my first thought was that it was typical mad behaviour to be sunbathing half in, half out of the water. At that hour. But she didn't wake when I shouted at her, and when I got as close as we are now, there was no mistaking the life had gone from her. Her shoulders had caught on a branch under the surface. She didn't look too bad, though. Not bloated or anything ...'

'Jesus . . .' said Brendan.

'You know, I don't think the sight of it will ever leave me. The Gardaí said she was probably carried down the river from the town, or even as far up as Ennisbridge.'

Ali clamped her jaw against the confession that rose in her throat, that wanted to surge from her mouth, spilling her guilt across the cherries printed on the old oilcloth. Joan was her responsibility. She had signed the book at Damascus House for her. People would know that soon enough.

The back door slammed and Davy came in. His hair was tousled and the collar of his pyjamas stuck out of the neck of his jumper.

'A Garda came to the bungalow and told me. Why didn't you come and get me? It's mad, isn't it?' And he gave a little high laugh. 'Unreal, man.'

'Say hello to Father Philbin, Davy,' said Una.

'Father. Kevin. Unreal, eh?'

''Twas me that found her,' said Kevin. 'She looked very peaceful – like your one – Ophelia.' Kevin spread his hands wide on the table. Davy shook his head quickly, like he was trying to flick something out of his hair. Ali wondered if he was still drunk.

Father Philbin said he needed to go to Ennisbridge, to comfort Joan's parents, and that Kevin should come with him. He turned in the doorway to give Brendan a hard look and said that perhaps the marquee dances had got out of hand. Brendan didn't bother to answer.

'Sit down and have some tea,' Una said to Davy, but he ignored her and leaned against the sink, twisting a tea towel between his hands. Uncle Joe sighed loudly several times.

Ali thought of Ivor. He was looking for Joan when they parted. Maybe he had never found her. Not only had she made Joan angry, she had taken away the person who protected her.

Joe and Brendan started to swap theories. Joan had been drunk. Joan had been suicidal. Joan had been unlucky, tripped and fell.

'Do you remember,' Joe said to Una, 'when those two boys from Galway drowned in Lough Dreena. Went for a midnight swim. Both of them drunk, as it turned out. Drink makes you think strange things of yourself, gives you the inclination for adventures, but takes away your judgement.'

'Joan wouldn't have gone for a swim,' said Ali. 'She didn't know how.'

Everyone looked at her.

'You barely know her,' said Una.

'I saw her at the dance. I don't think she was drunk, either.'

'Don't say you met her at the dance,' said Una, 'or the police will want to talk to you. You've had enough of that, surely.'

'Una,' said Davy, flicking his towel in her direction, 'don't work yourself up. She was a depressive – cracked, you used to say. At least she won't be bothering you any more, eh?'

'Steady on,' said Joe.

'You should have more respect,' said Una, her colour rising with her voice.

'Should I?'

The look that passed between Davy and Una struck Ali as being very strange, part of some larger falling-out that she hadn't noticed.

The doorbell trilled, breaking the tension. Joe went to answer it. Una got up to put the kettle on once more. It shook in her grip. They heard mumbled voices, and Joe returned.

'There are a couple of Gardaí here.'

Una banged the kettle onto the range. 'Show them down.'

'They want to talk to Ali.'

It was going to come out now. How she had taken Joan out of the hospital, stirred up the past and abandoned her.

A tall Garda dipped his head as he entered the kitchen, removed his hat. Ali was confused. It was one of the Guards from Rathmines. She had met him in the Rosary Garden. How could he be investigating Joan's death?

'We can give you a few minutes to pack a bag, but we have to hurry,' he said. 'We need to get back to Dublin before teatime.'

'You can't take her away,' said Joe. 'Something happened here this morning – she's very upset.'

223

'I'm afraid our thing trumps yours for the moment, Mr Devane, we need her in Dublin.' He turned to Ali. 'You're not under arrest, but Detective Swan would be obliged if you'd come back with us to help with our enquiries.'

'Is it the baby?'

The Guard's expression changed, shifting from formality to a kind of regretful softness.

'Yes, Ali,' he said gently, 'it's the baby.'

As they drove away from Buleen, she asked the policeman if they had arrested somebody, but he said he couldn't tell her anything. He suggested she take a nap meanwhile, and Ali obediently curled up on the back seat, her seething head cushioned on her hastily packed rucksack.

'This is where I was told to bring you.'

The evening sun glinted off lines of parked cars and spread a mellow light across the old stone of St Enda's hospital. Ali had woken up as the car stopped. Her tongue felt sticky and she had a headache.

'But it's a hospital.'

She thought they would take her back to the station at Rathmines, or maybe home.

'This is where Detective Swan said. He's probably inside.'

He helped her out of the car and shoved the rucksack under his arm. A bunch of nurses smoking by the hospital entrance gawked. Inside the panelled foyer a young woman in a belted mac stood waiting. Beyond, through glass doors, Ali could see the over-lit glare of the hospital, trolleys and oxygen tanks parked against the walls of a long corridor.

The woman nodded at the Garda. She had short black hair and quick expressions. She smiled at Ali.

'I'm Detective Sergeant Gina Considine. DI Swan asked me to meet you. Good trip? Everything okay?'

Ali nodded back automatically, though nothing was okay.

The woman's handshake was strong, not exactly a shake, but a steady, held grip as if she was trying to communicate trustworthiness through her skin.

'I'm sorry about all this,' she said. 'There's no other way to be sure.'

'Be sure of what?'

Detective Considine glanced at the policeman, who gave a brief shake of his head in response.

'Thanks, Liam,' she said. 'I'll take it from here.'

She took Ali's arm in a firm hold and led her into the hospital.

'I'm sorry nobody explained things. It's a bit sensitive.'

Ali wanted to explain about Joan, to blurt out everything that had happened, to make this woman understand that she wasn't up to whatever it was she was asking.

'We've got to a stage in our investigation where we need to clear certain people from our enquiries. The only way to do that is to ask them to give a blood sample and have a quick examination.'

'Right. But why do you need me?'

'You're someone we need to clear,' said the detective, looking at her intently, something like a warning in her eyes.

A yelp jumped from Ali's mouth. 'It wasn't *my* baby!'

The detective held her gaze, let a moment pass before speaking. 'I'm sure that's what the doctor will say.'

'Someone I know killed herself last night.'

Considine frowned. 'Well – I'm sorry to hear that. We can't force you to cooperate right now, but if you don't, we'll have to bring you here again tomorrow. It will happen, Ali, so easier just to get it over with, eh?'

She glanced past Ali, as if waiting for someone to appear in the corridor.

'Is my mother here?'

'No, though I did speak to her this morning,' said Considine. 'The thing is – your mother says she doesn't know where you were at the time of the child's murder. Your friend Carmen has told us you were in the convent grounds. And you managed to discover the body in a place that you had no real business being in.'

'I didn't – Fitz did.'

'There's other things too.'

It was only the two of them in the big hallway, but Ali felt crowded. She hadn't had the chance to have that bath. The sweat and alcohol and smoke fumes of the night before would still be clinging to her skin. She was in no state to be peered at, or poked at or whatever. Despite the sleep in the car she felt frayed, like she might cry if someone said 'Boo' to her. She needed to be home; she needed to be clean and alone, and have a think about what had happened to Joan.

'I can see you're upset,' said Considine.

Ali bit the inside of her cheek hard to stop the tears from coming.

'Would it be you that examines me?' she asked.

'No, we have a proper doctor for that.'

Ali didn't recall saying yes, but neither did she say no, and so she found herself in a cold room, sitting on a paper sheet on an examination bench while a nurse in a plastic apron opened cupboards and set out implements. She had been told to take off her 'lower things', so she removed her jeans and pants and then her socks, because they looked odd on their own. She was glad that her T-shirt was long, and pulled at the hem of it with both hands until it was tented over her knees.

The nurse approached with a syringe and asked Ali to look over at the door. The detective's face hovered there, framed in a small glass window. Ali felt the prick on the inside of her elbow, and the sensation of a needle stretching the underside of her skin. She started to feel wobbly, and was aware that the nurse kept shooting her hard little looks. Once, she heard her click her tongue against her teeth.

'Sorry?' said Ali.

'Nothing. Doctor's on his way.'

Ali was staring at a metal bin, fixing on it as a still point that would save her from nausea, when the door swung open and the doctor from *The Late Late Show* walked in, Dr Beasley, a determined smile on his face. This couldn't be right, thought Ali, her queasiness banished by the shock of seeing him here, the dawning realisation of what an examination might entail. She reached out for her folded clothes, but the nurse was already carrying them to the far side of the room.

'Hello, Alison. Quite a different setting we meet in

this evening.' He pulled on some thin rubber gloves that the nurse handed him. 'Did you enjoy your television experience?'

She remembered him stuttering and irritable, under Mary's barrage.

'Not really.'

He worked the gloves down between his fingers. 'I'm surprised. If you would be so good as to lie back and relax?'

'Wait,' said Ali. 'I need to talk to that policewoman.' But Considine had vanished from the doorway.

'It's seven o'clock in the evening, I'm sure we'd all like to go home soon.'

'I don't think I want to do this right now. I don't feel well.'

'It won't take long. The Gardaí need the information to do their job, that's all. Nothing personal.' He pulled over a curtain, blocking out her view of the door.

She was lying back now, following the nurse's orders to put her feet flat on the bench, to bend her knees. She felt her will give way, a falling sensation.

Beasley stood to one side of the bench, level with her waist. He kneaded her stomach and asked her about sex. How often she had it. Not if.

'Not often. Three times is all.' Beasley raised his eyebrows and waited, as if another answer might follow. Ali said nothing.

'Okay, so when was the last time you had sex?'

A flash of herself rolling around in the van, Ivor laughing and reaching for her hips. She couldn't say *last night*.

'A while ago – a few months ago.'

'Hmm.'

He moved down the bench, asked her to part her legs a bit. She felt his cold rubber fingers on her, poking. She looked right into the bulb of the big lamp that hung over her until black blobs obscured her vision. The nurse handed him something metallic. As he put it inside her, she felt it as angular, cold as ice. The blood drained from her head and saliva pooled in her mouth. Then he did something that made it push her apart inside. It wasn't sore exactly, but it felt wrong, like something that happens just before something very painful. Her whole body felt tense as bone. The stretch became an ache.

She glanced down and saw that he was leaning right over her with a torch, looking inside her, his brows clamped in concentration. Minutes seemed to pass.

'Please ...' Ali said.

In answer, he raised one rubber-clad finger, indicating she should wait a moment, never taking his eyes from his task.

Ali looked beyond the light to the white tiles that covered the ceiling, the galaxy of tiny holes that perforated each of them. She imagined she could float up and crawl into one of those small holes, hide away in the darkness there.

She was aware of something scraping her inside, of sticks and swabs being dropped into plastic bags and vials.

'What are you doing?' Her voice came out shaky.

Dr Beasley sighed elaborately. 'Alison, if I do a full range of tests now, the police will have all they need and you won't have to come back to me.'

They left her lying there, a cold draught across her naked

thighs, while they went to the other side of the room and muttered together with their backs turned.

At last he came back, released the pressure and took the instrument out of her. He dropped it into a dish on a trolley beside him.

'You shouldn't be let near anyone.' Her words were brave, but her voice still wavered.

The nurse came over to the bench as Beasley retreated.

'The doctor is just doing his job. If you don't like it, you should have thought of that before you did what you did.'

This woman knew nothing about her, nothing. Ali stood up, inches from her.

'What is it you think I did, you stupid cow?'

The nurse looked round, but Beasley had left. She flared her nostrils and clamped her mouth, gathering the roll of paper towelling from the bench.

'That's for the Guards to decide, darlin',' she said finally, stepping on the pedal of the bin so hard that the lid clanged against the wall.

# 23

Swan set off for the hospital the minute Considine phoned. He met his wife coming up the garden path, her blue overnight case in her hand.

'Better?' he asked.

'So-so,' said Elizabeth and bent away from him to tickle the cat who was lying on the hot dirt of the flowerbed.

As he started the car he realised she might have been referring to herself, not Aunt Josie. But there wasn't time to go back and check.

The hospital was strangely deserted, fluorescent light falling in the empty corridors, dusk pressing at the windows. At last he spotted Considine looking through a door into a room beyond. He called her to him.

'The gynaecologist's in with her,' she said.

'Did you get the one the pathologist recommended?'

'No. Goretti Flynn gave me a name, says he's very well regarded – Donald Beasley.'

'Beasley. The name's familiar all right. Well done.'

'The staff said we could make use of an office down here.'

She led the way to a side room. The lighting tubes rat-tatted on, revealing two Formica tables and a scatter of chairs. Health-service posters lined the walls: a smiling skeleton with a red heart hovering in its ribcage; an old man sitting beside an electric fire with a Thermos flask on his blanketed lap. Dominating one corner was a human-sized cardboard cutout of Postman Pat.

'How's our girl?'

'Looking a bit shook – she said something about a friend committing suicide. I didn't know whether to believe her.'

'But she agreed to be examined,' said Swan.

'Well, I persuaded her. But I'm not sure now if—'

There was a knock on the open door and Swan turned to see an oddly familiar face.

'I've completed the examination. Do you want me to run through the initial findings?'

'Yes, please,' said Considine.

'Eh. Just give us a minute,' said Swan.

Dr Beasley agreed to come back shortly.

'Jesus, Gina!' Swan hissed, once the doctor was out of earshot. 'Him! Did you not see that *Late Late*?'

Considine stood silent and thin-lipped, while Swan ranted about how it could compromise the evidence, the bastarding smallness of Dublin and their generally atrocious luck on this case.

'Flynn said he was the top man,' she said. 'Done dozens of expert-witness slots for the force – I'm sure his evidence will stand up in any case. How was I to know the girl made him look a tit on the telly?'

Beasley reappeared with a camel-coloured coat over one arm and a snappy, un-doctorly attaché case.

Swan invited him to sit at the table with them and talk through his findings.

'There are certain signs to support your theory – extra weight carried on the abdomen, slight swelling of the uterus, the evidence of recent abrasion at the mouth of the vagina. Also, I'm sure that she lied to me about her sex life. She's certainly no virgin.'

'Her virginity wasn't the question. We just need to know if she was recently pregnant,' said Swan.

'Well, it's difficult to be definitive on this. As I say, she's young, very healthy. Things can return to normal quite quickly. There's little research to measure it against, so I don't want to rule anything out.'

'What about the cervix?' asked Considine.

Beasley's eyebrows crawled up his forehead. 'What *about* the cervix?'

'I believe it changes, or the womb entrance does – something about a slit, not a dot.'

Beasley brushed the back of his hand over the table, as if wiping away her question. 'It's really not as simple as that.'

'Okay, Doctor,' said Swan, 'this is what it sounds like you're telling me. There's no evidence that she was recently pregnant, but at the same time you won't rule it out. Is that it?'

'What I'm actually telling you is that I will prepare a full report, as requested, and I'm happy to testify in court that a pregnancy can't be ruled out. If that's what you're after. I'll write up my notes tonight and telex you a copy. And I'll send the invoice to the finance office.'

Top man, indeed. The baby was born only a couple of weeks past. Surely that would do something to a woman's insides that you'd notice. Swan was a great admirer of the resilience of women, but Christ, that would be some bounce-back.

'What about a scan?'

'Yes, a scan, as I said, would be helpful, but the machine operator won't be in until Tuesday, unfortunately. If you would like to bring the suspect back then ...'

'We'll let you know,' said Considine and showed him to the door. Swan stared at the innocent face of Postman Pat across the room.

'What do you think, Gina? From a woman's point of view?'

'I think he's a prick.'

'I mean about her being pregnant.'

'He says he can't rule it out. And there's all the other stuff – the blouse, the fact of her being on the spot. But you'd think a doctor could tell.'

'You would,' said Swan.

'Are we going to get her scanned?'

'I think what we need is another doctor.'

'Sorry.'

'Sorry for biting your head off.'


Swan found Ali alone in the examination room, sitting stiff-backed on a chair behind the door, a pair of socks in her hands, tears wet on her pale face. He squatted down in front of her, wondering if it was Beasley that had upset her.

'Can I go home?' she asked, her voice polite but strained.

'Detective Considine told you why we had to do this.'

'What did he say? Did he say I had a baby?'

'Did you?'

'No! Is that what he said? He hates me.'

'He'll do a report for us. Is there anything you want to tell me?'

Ali shook her head vigorously. As her dark hair swung back he spotted a mark on her neck – a smudge of bruising with a dotted crimson centre. The mocking voice of Beasley came back to him. *She's no virgin.* Well, she mightn't be a virgin, but it didn't mean she was a mother. There was no real evidence for it. He felt that familiar deflation of a neat theory beginning to disintegrate.

'Am I under arrest?'

'No. I'll get a car to bring you home. We'll have a chat tomorrow.'

The girl bent forward to put on her socks with shaking hands. Pink socks, dotted with little hearts.

# 24

Swan caught himself smiling at some children in their mass clothes outside Rathmines church. He was sitting in traffic, waiting for the lights to turn, and a tiny girl with a ponytail sticking up from the top of her head raised a little hand and wiggled her fingers at him. Without thinking, he grinned like a cretin and waved back. A bigger boy behind her put a protective hand on his sister's shoulder and flicked a V-sign at Swan. That was more like it. He laughed and drove on.

By the time he'd got home from the hospital last night, Elizabeth had made the house cosy again, in a way he never managed to. Table lamps glowed, Benny purred on a fringed cushion. They didn't discuss his work and they didn't discuss her time in Enniscorthy with her aunts. Their sparse chat was about what was on the radio, how well the garden looked. The stuff of strangers at a bus stop. How had this happened to them? It was only when she sat at the piano, at his urging, and music flowed about them that he felt joined to her, emotional, speechlessly close.

He drove on to Ranelagh and parked outside Hogans'. Considine was standing by the gate. Before they reached the front door, it opened and Deirdre Hogan appeared, dishevelled in that fancy dressing gown again, then drew him in by the sleeve, leaning close to whisper that Ali wasn't herself, would hardly budge from her room.

Swan refused her offer of coffee.

'We'll just go on up to her room, if that's okay.' As they walked through the hall, he noticed that the receiver was dangling down from the payphone in the hall. He looked at Considine, and she nodded to say she'd noticed it too.

The bare steps creaked and bowed as they climbed the curved staircase. It could be such a lovely house. He imagined the home that Elizabeth would make of it.

Ali was standing in the doorway of her bedroom, wearing men's striped pyjama bottoms and a baggy jumper.

'A woman from RTÉ News has been calling here all morning looking for me,' she said. 'One of your lot must have said something, because I didn't.'

Swan immediately thought of Beasley. 'It wasn't us. Maybe someone in the hospital recognised you from the *Late Late*.'

'Oh, my fault, is it?'

'I didn't mean that. Look, could we have a chat?'

Ali turned and walked back into her room. They took it as an invitation.

'Dr Beasley took things further than required,' he said, as they followed her. Strictly speaking, he shouldn't be admitting any fault to her, but the guilt was itching him. He'd been taken aback at the full gynaecological detailing of Beasley's report, which had arrived promptly that morning.

He hadn't really thought it through, had left it to Considine and the doctor and had allowed himself to assume there were less invasive ways to determine these things.

238

'You insisted that she was examined,' Considine had countered. 'What did you think a gynaecologist would do?'

She managed to get the home number of the consultant at Holles Street who the pathologist knew. Swan read Beasley's findings over the phone to him before he showed the report to anyone else. The consultant laughed off the idea that the girl described had delivered a full-term child a fortnight before.

It was as Swan suspected. After Elizabeth's last miscarriage she had been in bed for a week and the bleeding had gone on and on. That was after only four months, and the baby would have been no bigger than ... than something that could be in your palm, perhaps. He hadn't seen it himself, the little thing, just stood outside the locked bathroom door as Elizabeth wailed with a ferocity that made her a stranger to him. That was when the chill had come down between them, that second time.

The consultant from Holles Street said a scan wasn't even necessary to clear Alison Hogan, but Swan was wondering if it might still be useful to kill Beasley's report. Close the door on it.

'Why did it have to be him?' Ali was asking now. 'And that nurse was so horrible—'

'I think maybe we should get another doctor – perhaps a woman doctor – to look at you. Give you a scan.'

'I could stay in with you this time,' offered Considine, but Ali ignored her.

'How could I have a baby and not know it?'

They were all standing in the middle of her bedroom.

'Can we sit down?' asked Swan.

There was more floor showing than before, an attempt at tidying, but no surface was completely clear. Ali walked over to a mound of clothes and produced a little basket-weave stool from underneath, which she brought back to the middle of the room for him. She flounced down on her bed and started to comb her fingers through her hair, inspecting the ends. Meanwhile Considine had drifted off to lean against the shower cubicle in the corner, out of the girl's line of sight, disappearing her presence.

'Do you know what a poltergeist is?' Swan asked.

'I saw the film.'

'It was a little girl in that film, if I remember right, but your paranormal experts would claim that poltergeists are more attracted to teenage girls – that the power of adolescence stirs up all kinds of commotion.'

'Is this about the state of my room?'

Swan laughed, relieved that she would joke. 'No, no … what I was trying to say – badly – is that you remind me of one of those girls: so many bits of this case keep leading back to you. See, I don't believe in poltergeists, Ali, but there's a hell of a lot of disturbance happens around you.'

She shifted her eyes slightly to meet his, a veneer of defiance.

'I want to show you something.' Swan opened his brief-case and took out an evidence bag. 'You said the baby was wrapped in a white cloth.'

'Is that it?'

'You tell me.'

He placed the bag on his knees and slowly drew out the white blouse her mother had given him.

'I suppose,' she said.

'Actually, this is one of your own school blouses.'

'Oh. All I saw was some white cloth.'

'There's something I need you to explain.' He beckoned her over, tilted the material towards the light of the window. 'What are these?'

At first she seemed to be just staring at his fingertip moving over the material.

'These little holes,' he persisted, and she bent closer. She lifted one hand to the right side of her chest.

'Badges.'

'What badges?'

Ali went over to a gaping chest of drawers and took out an old leather collar box. She sat cross-legged on the floor in front of him and opened it, dipping her fingers into a tangle of plastic beads, outsize rings and knotted chains, selecting four round badges from the bottom, which she held out on her palm like coins. Swan put the blouse back in the envelope and took them from her.

One was very small, the size of a five-pence piece. It depicted a feminist symbol of a clenched red fist inside a circle, with a cross at the bottom. Two middle-sized ones said *Free Nelson Mandela* and *Art is Revolution*. The last was the largest – a scrawl of punkish writing against a black background; 'SPUC OFF', it said.

'A little bird told me that the school doesn't allow badges.'

'They can't see them under my tunic.'

'What's the point of that?'

She shrugged. 'I know they're there.'

*A timid rebel*, thought Swan.

'Do other girls do the same thing?' He willed her to say yes.

'I don't know.'

He held up the SPUC OFF badge. The initials stood for Society for Protection of the Unborn Child.

'Does this mean that you're pro-abortion, Ali?'

'I think women should have a choice.'

'Is it what you would do?'

'Depends. Maybe.'

'How would you know where to go? There's a ban on information now.'

'The small ads in any British women's magazine have phone numbers. I've seen them.'

'Have you now? And what if your pregnancy had gone too far?'

'What did Dr Beasley say to you?'

'He said he couldn't rule you out.'

'I didn't have a baby. Jesus! Look at me.' She stretched her arms out from her body. Swan wondered what he was supposed to be looking at; what he saw was a well-built girl in a jumper so baggy she could be concealing a toddler.

'A blouse exactly like yours – holes and all – was found in the shed. How could it have got there?'

'Dunno.'

'Did you ever change your clothes there?'

'Yeah, we could wear rough clothes for gardening. But I don't think I ever left anything there.'

'And what exactly were you doing in St Brigid's that Sunday night?'

Ali went back to sit on the bed, started fiddling with her hair again. The colour rose in her face.

'I was with my friends. We were drinking in the trees by the hockey pitch.'

'And you saw nothing?'

She turned to look at Considine behind her, hoping for intervention perhaps, but Gina's face was a perfect blank. Ali turned back to him with a bullish expression.

'I didn't give birth between beers!'

'Detective Considine here said you mentioned something about some trouble down in Buleen – the place you were staying.'

'The Gardaí said someone drowned after a dance. Was that the person you knew?' asked Considine, coming round to stand beside Swan.

The girl's chin wobbled a little, her state so volatile now that any questioning seemed overbearing. Yet necessary.

'It was Joan,' she said eventually. 'Joan Dempsey. She used to cook for my aunt. Then she was in a mental home, a hospital, until last week.' She made a little broken noise like a hiccup. 'They say that she jumped into the river. I don't know.'

'Why was she in a home?'

Ali was raking the fingernails of one hand down the pale inside of her opposite forearm, red lines rising to the surface of her skin.

'The baby I found ... back before, you know – it was Joan's. She told me so last week.'

Swan and Considine looked at each other for a minute. There was the distant sound of footsteps climbing the stairs.

'So you see, Mr Swan, you're not so far off with your poltergeists – I do have special powers—' Whoever was coming up the stairs was humming now, signalling their approach. 'People die around me.'

The door swung open to reveal Deirdre Hogan with three mugs and a packet of biscuits on a tray.

'I know you said not to, but there were these Jaffa cakes staring at me from the shelf, and I thought: well, if they don't eat them, I might, so I better bring them up to the guardians of the peace and my slim daughter *toot-sweet*. And a cup of coffee to wash them down. Only instant, mind.'

During this patter she wandered deep into the room, trying to clear a surface, tutting and laughing. But her eyes kept checking on her daughter. Ali seemed to have fallen back into herself, staring down at the mug that her mother had passed her.

'You're not going to take her anywhere, are you? I'm not happy about what she was put through yesterday … And now the phone keeps ringing.'

'I took it off the hook,' Ali said. Her mother nodded. They were allies now, Swan noted.

'We were just here for a chat, Mrs Hogan.' He got to his feet. 'Get some rest, Ali.'

'Bit of a dead-end, don't you think?' said Considine when they reached the pavement. 'She didn't have a baby. And there's an innocent reason her blouse could have been lying in the shed.'

'I just don't know. What are you up to?'

'I think I'll go and revisit the doctors' surgeries round here. There's a chance some woman might have come in by now. I don't know, either, but I feel like we must have missed something.'

Swan sat in his car for a while before turning the engine on. To believe Ali Hogan or not?

He counted up the infanticide cases he'd had experience of – the baby by the canal, the one under the garage in Clondalkin two years back. Oh, and there was that case in Drimnagh – two tiny skeletons in a boarding-house cupboard, fishbone ribs covered in paper-thin skin. The woman from Achill who had put them there twenty years before said she hadn't known anyone in Dublin at the time. That was her only explanation.

He remembered the words of a farmer he'd met once in a bar in Athlone. He'd said that it used to be a common thing for the bog-strippers to turn up the remains of infants. The little bones scattered over the flayed land.

He thought the man was being morbid in drink, but maybe it was he who was naïve. Perhaps the whole country was dotted with tiny corpses waiting to be found – babies tucked behind gateposts, eased under floorboards or thrown into sacks, with the company of stones to take them down into brown water. An Irish solution to an Irish problem. Grown secretly in the dark, and to the dark so quickly returned, some never surfacing at all to feel air inflate their lungs, the trickle of warm milk filling new stomachs.

And what of his own babies: would they ever make it into the world or would there only be more pain? Two conceived, both faltered in the womb. Two months. Four months. He was forty-three. Elizabeth thirty-eight already. Perhaps they were too old, or a bad match. All he knew was that he couldn't bear it to happen again. She wanted to try – argued that they didn't have the luxury of waiting – but he couldn't go near her, for fear of it. They hadn't been intimate for so long now, he wasn't sure it could be mended.

He wiped a hand over his eyes and turned the ignition, driving without focus until he was away from Ranelagh, waking again to the world beyond the windscreen only as he turned down by the canal.

He noticed a woman sitting on a bench in a short skirt and boots, her hair dyed a chemical auburn, her mouth clasped passionately around a cigarette. It reminded him of Sister Bernadette and her good work with the working girls of this area. The ice-queen moving among them. Community projects, the old nun had said. Not so very far away from the convent, really. He wondered if anyone from the team had had time to check it out.

Percy Place was where she said St Jude's, the drop-in centre, was – just nearby. He took a left fork out of the main traffic flow and cruised slowly to where the handsome Georgian terrace faced onto the canal. Halfway down he spotted a round plaque on the wall – a famous writer remembered.

Swan parked. It was a lovely street, especially in the quiet of a late Sunday morning, like a film set, the way the whispering trees watched over the little stone bridge. The start of a Kavanagh poem learned at school came to him:

*Leafy-with-love banks and the green waters of the*
   *canal*
*Pouring redemption for me …*

Ah, redemption. A pint of that would be welcome.

The house was tall and wide, and a little brass sign at the top of the steps said *Order of the Annunciation*, in letters you would have to be closer than two feet away to read. Very discreet. He knocked. Nothing happened. He knocked again.

A door opened somewhere below and Swan looked down over the railing into the paved basement area. A young woman with very short hair walked out and put something in a bin. Even from above, he could see how her stomach domed out.

'Excuse me? Do you know if there's anyone in up here?'

She looked up, shading her eyes with a hand. She was much younger than he had first thought.

'It's all the one. Who are you looking for?'

'Sister Bernadette?'

'She's had to go away.'

'Do you work here?'

'Naw. I'm a *resident*.' She didn't look like a prostitute, not at all. She looked more like a schoolgirl.

An awful thought struck him.

# 25

After the police detectives left, Ali collected up their mugs and put the tray outside the door. She turned back to the mess of her room, a mess she'd become newly aware of through strangers' eyes. Clothes spewed from the rucksack she had brought with her from Buleen. That was a good place to start.

When she shook out her jeans, the little medal that Joan's mother had given her fell out of the pocket, followed by the flutter of Mary O'Shea's business card. Ali picked up the white rectangle and stared at it.

She sat back down on the bed, all energy fled. She rubbed the edge of the card back and forth against her lips. Mary would be very interested in what Beasley had subjected her to. But what would Mary do with that? How could she control where that story went? How could she be sure she wouldn't come out of it looking suspicious, stupid – both? She shouldn't trust Mary, and she couldn't trust the police. The police thought she might have had a baby. Beasley had looked inside her and thought so too. Swan was talking about poltergeists and dark forces. All of it was awful – everything that had happened since she stepped into the garden, or was it the night before that when things started to fall apart?

She should have told the police about being at St Brigid's that night; it just never occurred to her. The awful sight of that baby had put everything else out of her head. Fitz and she had met up with Bobby and Ronan outside the Berry-bush pub while Davy had been inside buying a naggin of vodka for them. The boys had beer, and it was their idea to go to the school grounds, not hers. Ronan had been paying her a lot of attention, slagging her, pretending to be interested in her bangles, that kind of thing. Usually boys paid more attention to Fitz.

He stole one of her bracelets and she had chased after him, running over the grass in her bare feet, leaving Bobby and Fitz behind at the hockey pitch, drinking beer. When she caught up with Ronan, he grabbed her, pressed her into the bark of one of the big cedars. They were only messing about, nothing serious. He was kissing her neck, and she was starting to feel kind of floaty with it, watching the branches above her moving against the darkening sky – that deep, deep blue that comes before black. One of Ronan's hands was at her chest, twisting the buttons of her shirt. She wasn't wearing a bra. Ronan laughed and stepped back from her. She looked down and saw with a shock that one breast was exposed, lolling out, almost luminous in the dusk.

It was then that they heard the footsteps on the path, a soft gritty rhythm coming towards them. Ali turned quickly and crouched into the tree, signalled to Ronan to hide too. She didn't dare move until the sound had faded well beyond them. Ronan claimed it was a nun who passed – perhaps the ghost of a nun – but that wasn't what she had seen. The half-glimpsed figure looked more like a man to her.

She couldn't tell Swan she had gone off with Ronan – he thought she was a right tramp already. She'd caught him staring at that damn love-bite on her neck. Anyway, she couldn't really be sure she had seen anything.

She tore Mary's business card into little pieces. It was better not to have that temptation after what happened last time.

She didn't know what to do with herself. She didn't want to tidy. The muffled sound of the radio floated up from her mother's room downstairs. She would be sitting there among her broken things and saucers of glue. A spider in her web, fiddling, mending.

The gate to the passageway squeaked. Ali went to her window and looked down. A familiar bright head bobbed up the passageway.

As Ali ran down the first flight of stairs, the doorbell rang.

'I'll get it!' her mother shouted.

'It's okay,' Ali called back, 'it's only Fitz.'

When she pulled the big door open, Fitz was picking at the labels on the rack of old bells.

'When you going to get rid of all these?' she asked.

Ali gave her friend a quick hug and pulled her inside. She could hear her mother moving around on the landing, so she pushed Fitz into the front room. She didn't want her mother hearing any more than was necessary, especially now that she was being so nice, treating Ali as lovingly and carefully as a piece of her broken porcelain.

'Have I been in this room?' asked Fitz, looking around at the stripped single bed, the tilting empty shelves.

'Davy was staying in it last,' said Ali.

'The foxy uncle,' said Fitz, and ran a palm sensually over the bare mattress before sitting down on it.

Ali laughed obligingly. This is how they always were together, joking, mock-sophisticated, but it felt newly awkward, like she couldn't find the rhythm of their usual dance.

On the wall over the bed, Davy had stuck pictures from newspapers, a collage of faces that he had added to day by day, like a bulging cloud. He stuck them on with toothpaste. She noticed Mary O'Shea's picture in the centre, little fangs and horns drawn on in black felt-tip.

Fitz followed her gaze.

'Did he do all that? He's mad. Where's he gone?'

'He had to go back down to Buleen. Work.'

'Pity. I think he fancied me.'

Fitz was probably right, but Ali wasn't going to add to her vanity. When she'd brought Fitz home with her that night she'd noticed how flustered Davy was, tripping over himself to take them out for a drink. If only they'd managed to get served in the Berrybush, they wouldn't have ended up going to St Brigid's with the consolation prize of the vodka he'd bought them and those stupid boys. Davy refused to come with them. Why would he drink like a kid when he could sit in a pub, he said. Maybe he wasn't that keen on Fitz after all.

'Anyway,' Fitz was saying, 'I came here to say I was sorry I said anything to the Guards about the boys, but they were pretty fierce. I was worried they'd do me for under-age drinking.'

'I'm not angry with you,' said Ali, 'but it is creepy, don't you think? I mean … someone else was there that night. And the baby turned up in the shed. I just don't know. Maybe it *was* me that did it and I've blacked it all out. Have you noticed anything strange about me in the last few months?'

'No, but I'm noticing it now.'

'I'm serious.'

'Unless you're completely schizophrenic, or something. Ali, you'd *know*. And I'd certainly know.'

'You'll testify in court then?'

Fitz laughed and rolled her eyes. 'You've got to get a grip, sweetie.'

She wanted to tell Fitz about Joan, but where would she even start to explain it all?

'Aren't you're worried about your results?' said Fitz.

Ali's first thought was that Fitz somehow knew about Beasley and all the tests they did on her, but as Fitz went on to say how she hadn't done enough revision, Ali realised she was only talking about the Leaving: the exam results, the thing she'd been so obsessed about before all this. Her future.

'They'll be here next week. I can't believe it. Do you want to meet up? We could go into town …'

Ali imagined sitting with Fitz on a red settee in Bewley's, eating almond buns, laughing about nothing and watching university boys go by.

'I can't go out, Fitz, I can't see anyone. You could come here. I'm sure Ma would let us have some wine.'

'I guess I could, but Allanah and Rachel were talking about Captain Americas, which would be fun. Come *on*.'

'Don't worry. You go out. I'll phone you.'

'Do that.'

Ali walked her to the door.

When Fitz reached the bottom of the steps she turned and cocked her hand like a gun. '*Ciao*, baby. Don't take any shit.'

Ali stood for a while with her forehead against the closed door. She missed the way they'd been.

She went back into Davy's room. She missed him too. Maybe when all this was past, he would come back and get a proper job in Dublin. Anyone could see there was nothing for him in Buleen, only an ugly half-finished bungalow. And the place did something bad to him, made his humour bitter and careless. She stood and looked at the pictures he'd put on the wall until her mother called her to the kitchen for lunch.

Ali ate the soup put in front of her. Tomato, sweet and bland.

'I talked to Una on the phone just now. She says Joan's funeral is tomorrow. So quick. But I don't think she was suggesting we should go.'

Joan's funeral. Coming back to Dublin had been forced on her. She should be in Buleen, should be there to acknowledge all that she hadn't done for Joan.

'I think I should be there, Ma. I spent time with Joan in Buleen. I even spoke to her the night she died.'

'I'm concerned about you, pet. You've been involved in too much – too much *grimness*.'

'We could go together. You haven't been back in a long time.'

'Ha!' said her mother. 'I don't care if I never see that hole again.' She quickly put her hand up to her mouth. Ali stared back at her. It had never occurred to her that her mother didn't love the place she came from.

'Why not?'

'Oh, I don't know – lots of things. The baby, of course. Other bad associations. Do you remember your granddad at all?'

'Sort of.' What Ali remembered was an old red-faced man propped in an easy chair in Una's front room. His stillness and silence were frightening.

'He was fairly diminished when you knew him. When I was a girl, he was a bit of a brute, to be frank. No affection. Thought a father's role was to toughen you up.'

Her mother pushed her half-eaten plate of soup away to one side.

'I remember once – I'll never forget it – he had this notion that being able to deliver a good death to a beast was an essential skill. He thought the whole family should know how to do it, even his children.'

Ali put her spoon down. She wanted to tell her mother to stop talking, but no words came.

'One of the cats brought a bird into the kitchen, maimed. It was a little wren, hopping around under the table with it wing sticking out. I was only five or six. My father fetches a bucket from the scullery, fills it with water. Then he bends down and catches the bird, calls me to him. I thought he was going to mend it somehow, so I wasn't scared until he presses the little thing into my hand, tells me to hold it under the water. I wouldn't do it, no matter how he argued that it's the right thing.

'So he puts his hand around mine and forces them both into the bucket, and I can feel the little thing fluttering, panicking, inside my fingers, but I can't open my hand. Finally it stops moving, and I look at my father. He takes our hands out of the bucket, pulls my fingers apart and the bird is stretching out in my hand, its little claws uncurling. You know, I don't think I ever felt the same about him after.'

'Did he make the others do that?'

'Oh yes. He made Una kill a lamb that was ailing, but she would have done anything for her daddy. Davy went trapping rabbits with him from the time he could walk, learned how to dispatch them. But it was different for him.'

'How different?

'Ach, he's a boy, it doesn't seem to go so hard with them. Anyway, it was enough to give me a stomach full. I never miss the place at all. But if you want to go back, I won't stop you.'

Ali went upstairs to pack. As she changed her clothes, she spotted the little Lourdes medal on the floor. She picked it up it and put it in her shirt pocket, happy to take any protection that was going. From somewhere in the chest of drawers she found a black skirt to wear for the funeral.

'There's a train in an hour.'

Her mother was standing at the phone. She put the receiver down and turned to take Ali into her arms for the first time in years. Ali hugged back.

'Be careful,' said Ma. The phone started to ring again. Neither moved to answer it.

'If my Leaving results come,' said Ali, 'don't open them. Wait till I get back and we can open them together.'

# 26

Swan took his badge from his inside pocket and held it out towards the pregnant girl. She squinted and shook her head. It was too far away. Swan went down to her, could hardly ask her to climb the steps up to him.

'Someone was supposed to meet me here,' he lied. 'I need to take a quick look round. Are any staff about?'

'One of the nuns'll be coming to make the dinner, but there's nobody here now. Never is on a Sunday.' Her accent wasn't Dublin, more southerly – Corkish. She inspected his ID diligently and smiled a cheeky smile.

'I'm not in trouble, am I?' Flirty, despite her condition. Swan didn't respond.

He stepped towards the open basement door, peered in – he could see a washing machine and a chest freezer.

'Can I just have a look?'

'I suppose it's all right – but don't go into any of the girls' rooms, they're private.'

'How many?'

'Many what?'

'Girls are staying at the moment?'

'There's three of us.'

Swan followed her into the basement of the house, through a large, functional-looking kitchen. Beyond that there was a big sitting room, with a hatch through to the kitchen. The curtains had been drawn to block the light from the TV screen, but even in the blue-washed gloom, the pregnant state of the two young women slumped on the sofa was the first thing he noticed. They were planted deep in the cushions, as if their distended bellies had fallen on them and rooted them there. The girls stirred at his entrance, and one drew a hand up over her stomach in a protective gesture.

'He's just having a look round,' said the crop-haired girl and shot Swan a grin as though his motives were slightly suspect. She went over to an armchair and descended into it slowly, taking the strain on her arms. It seemed he was free to wander. Through the next doorway a staircase led up to the rest of the house.

On the floor above, next to the main entrance, he found two nicely proportioned rooms, furnished for the most part with bland desks and filing cabinets and those low easy chairs with no arms – perhaps this was the drop-in centre that Sister Bernadette had mentioned, but the two floors above that looked like an upmarket B&B: nice carpet, another living room or parlour and a series of gleaming doors with numbers on them and tiny brass frames below. A few of the frames held yellow cards with names inked on them in cramped Gothic calligraphy – Jenny Mooney, Esther McDaid, Sharon O'Higgins – just like the writing on the Reverend Mother's door back at the convent.

He tried a door with no name on it and peeked into a simple bedroom. The single bed was stripped back to its floral mattress. The white wardrobe and matching bedside and dressing table all had the same gold squiggly handles. If not exactly luxurious, it was comfortable and fresh, a lot better than most charity gaffs.

A home for pregnant girls. What were those bloody nuns at – not telling them about this place? Or was it the unit's fault for not locating it? He was sure it hadn't turned up in their checks of mother-and-baby homes.

'Are you finished yet?' The girl had come to keep an eye on him.

'Seems a nice place.'

She made a non-committal noise and leaned a shoulder against the wall.

'Are you from round here?' asked Swan.

'Naw. I'm from Clonakilty.'

'How are you liking Dublin?'

'We don't go out much. They think someone might spot us. From home.'

'Which one are you?' Swan pointed to the doors with names on them.

'Esther McDaid. No longer a maid.' She gave a little laugh. 'You got any money?'

'What do you need money for?'

'They don't let us have any. They say it might be stolen, if we had it.'

'Maybe I have. Tell me, who was the last girl here to have a baby?'

Her bold smile dimmed and she examined him closely. He stared her out, trying to simultaneously look kindly and hide the eagerness he felt. He wondered whether he should be so blatant as to take out his wallet.

She turned round and headed for the stairs, looked back at him over one shoulder. He followed her down. On the landing of the last flight of stairs she stopped and opened a door he had presumed was a bathroom. It led to a corridor, an extension on the back of the original house, and the end of the corridor was a little chapel, with miniature pews for about eight people. A hanging candle in a small red glass signalled Christ's presence. Esther bobbed a quick genuflection, leaning back to balance her bump.

She led him to the left, to a blunt little offshoot passage with a door at the end.

'She stayed here, not for long. A couple of weeks ago. We weren't even supposed to know about it, but she came out some nights and talked to us, once the nuns were gone or asleep. One day I heard a baby cry in there. She didn't give it up. I heard her arguing with Sister Bernadette about it.'

'Are you going to keep yours?'

'They won't let me. They tell me it'll ruin my life. I told Bernadette that wasn't fair, and she told me that I would spoil the baby's life too, if it grew up as a bastard. She used that word.'

There was a name-holder on this door too, but the little card was blank. Swan tried the handle. It opened into a bedroom larger than the ones upstairs, with a sofa and a double bed. The carpet that ran seamlessly between the skirting boards was a rich cornflower blue. He let out a whistle, then walked to the centre of the room and slowly looked about. His veins hummed with excitement. There were no personal belongings, nothing that drew his eye.

He opened the wardrobe door. It was empty, except for a padded plastic rectangle with teddy bears on it. Inexperienced as he was, Swan recognised it as a changing mat.

He closed the wardrobe and looked round. Esther had disappeared. Instead, Sister Dreyfus stood there in a grey anorak, her habitually tense expression turned to frank alarm. He suppressed a terrible urge to laugh.

'Can I help you, Detective?'

He backed her out of the room, closed the door behind him. Esther McDaid was sitting on one of the chapel pews, pretending to pray. He would have to remember to slip her some money. At least enough for a train fare.

'I need a telephone, and then I need to see Sister Bernadette. Here. Now.' He tried not to shout it.

Mother Mary Paul was having extraordinary difficulty backing the convent's station wagon into a quite generous space across the road from St Jude's. Swan watched her efforts through the window of the front office that he had commandeered as his own.

More than an hour had passed since he hit the phone. Sunday was a bad day for excitement – the world wasn't geared up to meet it. Considine was at home, and offered to locate Barrett and come to Percy Place as soon as they could manage. Rathmines Garda station would send two uniforms over to secure the scene. There was nobody in the technical lab, so he left a message at the duty desk. He was tempted to phone Goretti Flynn at home, but she would probably just tell him to lock the bedroom door and wait for morning.

The nuns had been elusive too. Nobody answered the main phone in the convent, and it was only by bullying Sister Dreyfus that he managed to reach Mother Mary Paul on a private line. Mary Paul said Sister Bernadette was on retreat across the border in Newry, but she would come herself right away, didn't bother to fake surprise or ask why. Sister Dreyfus was supposed to be downstairs making lunch for the residents, but kept appearing at his elbow with cups of tea. Hovering.

Mother Mary Paul finally gave up her struggle with the car, leaving it at an angle to the kerb. She slammed the driver's door with surprising force and shifted her shoulders back, military-style, before heading towards the house. Swan opened the front door and directed her into the front office.

'Monsignor Kelly is on his way,' were the first words out of her mouth.

He was about to shut the front door when he heard a little skid of tyres, and Considine jinked her Mini into a small space at the kerb. Barrett was with her. Swan asked Mary Paul to wait in the office and went to meet them.

They clustered on the pavement. He turned to Considine first, couldn't resist a bit of finger-pointing.

'You were supposed to check out every lying-in home and refuge in the land. Remember this one? Run by the nuns from – where is it? – oh yes, St Brigid's, where the baby was found!'

'There's no central register, boss. No proper system. This place wasn't on the adoption-board list and didn't come up in any enquiries.'

'If the Rosary Baby was born here, we've wasted a lot of time. I want you to go in there and talk to the residents. They're down in the kitchen. Get me some background on the girl who stayed here two weeks ago and left with her baby.'

Considine flared her nostrils slightly and walked stiffly up the steps while getting her notebook out of her shoulder bag. Barrett smirked.

'And I've no time for *that*,' Swan said, finger in his face. 'You come with me while I talk to the Reverend Mother.'

He took a chair opposite the nun.

'So when were you going to let us in on this little secret?'

'It wasn't – isn't – a secret. We've nothing to hide.'

'Did you not think that the fact you were running a home for pregnant girls might interest us?'

'It's nothing like that. Just a few referrals from the country – nothing formal. The few residents here are in a fragile state; there was no point in putting them through police questioning. There's no connection between St Jude's and the child in the garden, I'm perfectly satisfied with that, and you will be too.'

Mother Mary Paul's hand disappeared into the folds of her habit and emerged with a ring of keys. She rose and went to a quaint cupboard in an alcove beside the fireplace and unlocked one of the doors. It was empty except for a couple of files, a book and what looked like a petty-cash box. Mary Paul pulled out this book – a black ledger, the paper dyed a rosy-pink along the edges. She flicked through it, arriving at the place she wanted, handed it to Swan.

'I checked this myself. Afterwards.'

265

The list of names ended halfway down the left page. In the columns next to the names was written the name of a town, a priest, then two columns of dates. At the top of the first column of dates it said 'Arrival'. Above the second column were the letters 'DLV'. The last three entries were the same names as those he had read on the doors upstairs. They only had an arrival date next to them, nothing in the column marked DLV.

'This second date …?'

'That's the date they gave birth.'

The latest delivery date recorded was 3rd June 1984, more than six weeks before the Rosary baby was born. That might explain why this place hadn't turned up in Considine's investigations of recent births. Swan flicked back through the earlier pages. The register went back seven years. The busiest year was 1978, when twelve girls stayed. Not exactly an avalanche.

'The information here seems a bit minimal, Mother. What about the girl's addresses, the details of adoption?'

'We just provide a place for the girls to stay. They are referred by their parish, and all adoption details are dealt with privately.'

'Privately between whom?' he asked.

'I think you need to talk to Monsignor Kelly, if you wish to pursue this.'

The doorbell rang, and Swan answered it to two flush-faced young Guards from Rathmines. He sent one down to the back door and told the other to stay on the steps and prevent arrivals and departures.

He sat down again to face the nun.

'The thing is, Mother, a girl stayed here recently who isn't on this register. She had her baby in her room with her, and now she's gone. Disappeared about the time that the baby was found in your convent grounds.'

'She must be on the register. Sister Bernadette wouldn't allow it otherwise.'

'Well, she's not. Though the other girls remember her. It's a pity Sister Bernadette's not here to explain yet. We've sent a car up to Newry to collect her from the retreat house. Seems they don't believe in answering phones there, either.'

'It's a silent retreat,' said Mary Paul. To one side of her, Barrett rolled his eyes.

'I'll leave you here with Detective Barrett,' said Swan, 'in case anything pertinent comes to you.'

In the basement kitchen, Considine sat at the table with the three pregnant girls, while Sister Dreyfus busied herself by the stove, a big blue apron practically brushing her sensible shoes. The cloying smell of packet minestrone permeated the room. A plate of white sliced bread and some industrial-looking cheese were laid out on the table.

'What have we got?' said Swan, taking a place at the table.

'The girls say she arrived about a month ago, and mostly kept to her room.'

'Do we have a name?'

'She wouldn't tell us,' said a girl with very fine blonde hair.

'Who brought her here?'

'Don't know,' said Esther McDaid. 'She just came down to the kitchen one day …'

'And she had a baby with her?'

'Not when she arrived,' said Considine. 'As far as I can establish, cries were heard from the room two weeks after, not long before she left.'

'We never saw the kid,' said Esther. 'I think she was keeping it away from us, you see, out of kindness.'

'What did she look like?' Swan asked.

'She was older, twenty-five or so, I'd say. Lovely thick hair – like a conker.' This from the blonde girl. Considine wrote quickly in her notebook.

'Was the baby delivered here or in hospital?' Swan was wondering if this girl could be someone they had already accounted for, someone who had come up in the hospital searches. He needed to keep a lid on this exultant, head-long feeling. The girls looked at each other and shrugged.

'Sister Bernadette would know. They got on well,' said Esther.

'Who got on?'

'Sister Bernadette and the Peggy girl. I heard them talking in her room a few times – when I was praying in the chapel.' The two other girls looked at Esther sceptically.

Swan looked at his watch. T. P. Murphy had volunteered to fetch Sister Bernadette from Newry. He would be there within the half-hour. With Sunday traffic, he could get her back to Dublin by four or five.

'So when did this Peggy leave here? Tell me about that ...'

The girls looked at each other.

'Dunno,' said Esther. 'It was about two or three week-ends ago, we just sort of realised she wasn't here any more. Gone home.'

268

'Home to where?'

Esther checked silently with the other two. 'Dunno. Nowhere near me. Galway, maybe?' The quieter girls just shook their heads.

Swan became aware that Sister Dreyfus, standing by the kitchen sink, had given up any semblance of lunch preparation and was listening intently, completely still.

'Sister?'

She turned to face them, clutching a dish brush in her yellow gloved hands.

'Did you know this girl?'

She nodded.

Considine asked the girls to wait in the TV lounge, assuring them that they would get their lunch soon. Sister Dreyfus removed her rubber gloves and sat at the table, looking simultaneously nervous and determined.

'It was a Sunday, because there was only me here. I was on my way upstairs, after the girls had their tea, and she came out of her room. She had a big coat on and she had a bag. She was holding something inside the coat – I thought it might be the baby. She didn't notice me; I was on the lower stairs. When she closed the door, I went to the window. There was a car waiting across the road. She got into it and drove off.'

'When you say she drove off, did she drive the car herself?'

Sister Dreyfus thought for a moment, her face a scowl of concentration. 'She can't have. She was holding the baby still. There must have been someone driving. Yes.'

'And Sister Bernadette wasn't here at the time?'

'No.'

'Did you see the baby move, or hear it cry?'

Sister Dreyfus's eyes grew large behind her glasses as she realised the implications of what he meant. She shook her head.

'She would never harm her child.'

Above them he could hear male voices, raised. The Guard at the door fending off Monsignor Kelly, it sounded like.

'Did you discuss this with Sister Bernadette?'

A quick shake of the head, a cowed look.

'Did you not think, when the baby was found in the convent, that there might be a connection?' said Swan.

'No, I thought she had decided to keep her child. That was why she sneaked off. By rights, she should have left it with us.'

An idea was beginning to form in Swan's mind, something that would make sense of the convent's secrecy.

'Who adopts the babies, Sister?'

'I don't know anything about that. Mother Mary Paul, you should talk to her.'

'We'll do that.'

Swan waited for Considine to finish her notes, thanked the nun for her time.

Sister Dreyfus held a pale finger in the air. 'Wait!'

'What is it?'

'Her name!' The nun went to a drawer in one of the kitchen cabinets and took out a notebook. Several nibbed pens were bound to it by a thick rubber band. She brought it to the table and opened it. It was a kind of copy book, where names and letters were drawn in the mannered thick-and-thin stroke calligraphy that Swan recognised from the name signs upstairs. Sister Dreyfus flicked through the pages and stopped, put her finger to a name repeated three times in three varied styles – Peggy Nolan. Peggy Nolan. Peggy Nolan.

'That's her. I make the name signs. I made one for her door, but she took it off.'

It was a common name. There must be hundreds of Peggy Nolans throughout the land. Maybe it had already come up in the investigation.

'Familiar?' Swan asked Considine.

She frowned. 'I'll have to check.'

'Please go ahead with your lunch, Sister, and thank you. Your help has been invaluable.'

Sister Dreyfus smiled, a mercurial spasm.

As they climbed up to the first floor, Swan turned to Considine and shook his head in wonder.

She gave him an answering grin. 'Unbelievable.'

Up in the front office they found that Barrett and Mother Mary Paul had run out of conversation. The nun gazed anxiously out the front window.

'Monsignor Kelly is being kept outside, waiting,' she complained.

'How much do they pay you for the babies?' asked Swan.

She glared at him, full beam. 'How dare you! That's not the way it is – even slightly! If the new parents choose to show gratitude, that is completely—' She jerked in her seat. 'I think you should talk to Monsignor Kelly about this.'

'We can't let anyone else into the house now, Mother, we need to search it. In fact it might be an idea for you to take the other girls back to the convent with you.'

'I can't take them back to St Brigid's – it's not suitable.'

'I'm sure you'll sort it out. By the way, does Sister Bernadette drive?'

'Yes, she drives. And I hope she gets back soon to help me sort out this … *misunderstanding*.'

'We'll be first in line to talk to Sister Bernadette. Tell me, is the name Peggy Nolan familiar to you?'

'It is not.'

Swan showed Barrett and Considine the back bedroom, where this Peggy Nolan had stayed. They didn't enter the room, but stood close together on the threshold.

'Can you find out about locking this, Declan? And supervise the exit of the girls and nuns. I'm thinking the baby could well have been killed right here, in the bedroom. There's no immediate signs – it's all been cleaned. It might account for her hiding it under her coat, wouldn't it?'

'Could be,' said Barrett.

'Gina?'

Considine was frowning at the carpet, miles away. At the sound of her name she quickly met his eye.

'It's odd, but I'm pretty sure there was a girl down in that town in Clare called Peggy Nolan. The guy I met to talk about the Buleen baby was Dr Nolan, right? And his daughter, the receptionist, she was a Peggy. I remember thinking it was an old-fashioned name for a girl.'

They looked at each other for a few seconds. Weighing the idea.

'Sister Bernadette,' said Swan, 'where would you say her accent was from?'

'I'd say Tipperary,' said Barrett.

'Could it be east Clare? It's soft, though.'

'It could be Clare,' said Barrett.

'If the nun was from the Buleen area, maybe she knew your Peggy Nolan already. Did your girl have hair like a "conker"?' Swan asked Considine.

'Yeah, dark-reddish. She was the right age, too.'

A phone was ringing downstairs. Swan raced down the steps. When he got to the office, Mother Mary Paul was holding out the receiver to him. T. P. Murphy was on the other end.

'You've got the nun?' asked Swan.

'You little bollix,' replied Murphy. 'A complete wild-gooser. And now I've got the RUC on my back. They insisted on accompanying me to Newry, and now they want me to fill in a stack of forms, threatening me with cross-border infringement. It's going to take me hours to get home.'

'Where is she?'

'She wasn't there at all. The priest who finally deigned to break his silence said she phoned last week to cancel. You owe me, big time.'

*Damn.* Where had she got to? Mother Mary Paul had no answers for Swan. Considine and Barrett were waiting in the hallway.

'Barrett, stay here until it's secure and empty. Make sure forensics are coming, even if it's tonight. Gina, I want you to put out a call for Sister Bernadette, but we also need to get the team to trace all the Peggy Nolans you can find, just in case your one's too good to be true. Then come join me as soon as you can.'

'Where?'

'Buleen, of course! Wherever the hell it is. Oh, and give that girl with the short hair a tenner – no make it twenty. I'll see you right.'

On the doorstep Monsignor Kelly was pacing and smoking – an expensive-looking brand with a gold band around the filter. He threw down a long butt as Swan emerged and came forward to shake his hand. Cufflinks in the shape of crosses.

'Bit of a mix-up with your officer here,' said the monsignor, as if they were old friends temporarily kept apart by a harsh world.

'Sorry about that – thing is, I've got a lot on, so perhaps we could catch up later.'

'Is everything all right?'

'Smashing, Father. Lovely place they have here, beautifully kept.'

Monsignor Kelly looked relieved, grateful.

'My officers are taking a few statements from the nuns and residents, so Garda O'Malley here can keep you company till that's finished.'

'But it was you I needed to speak to.'

'No can do, Monsignor.'

Swan set off down the front steps. At the bottom he turned back.

'Must take a good lot of donations to keep a place like this in the style, eh? Regular donations. From couples.'

Monsignor Kelly's determined smile dribbled off his face.

'But as I said to the Reverend Mother, we'll talk later, eh? After I've seen the adoption board.'

Swan went to the office to keep on top of the paperwork, then headed home. He couldn't see the end of it yet, but he was starting to see the beginning. Peggy Nolan could have known Sister Bernadette of old and persuaded the nun to help her, to let her stay at Percy Place without telling anyone else. She delivers the child there, with the nun's help, because the nun knows nursing, but three days later someone – one of them – beats the baby to death. The nun sneaks her away. Bernadette knows the Rosary Garden well. It's her idea to bury the child there, but for some reason it gets left in the shed.

But *why* – why kill it?

At home Swan poured himself a finger of whiskey, searched out a couple of clean shirts, underwear, razor. He had hoped, without too much hope, that Elizabeth might be there. The only sign of her presence was a small sheet of paper torn from a notebook, the left edge frilled where she had ripped it from the spiral. Auntie Josie had taken another dip, it said; she was needed there, it said. With luck, she'd be back tomorrow.

He made some calls and packed his things in a briefcase, sat on the bed for a time. He might as well sleep now and leave early, than navigate in the dark. And he didn't want to go away, with things so strained between Elizabeth and himself, without doing some little thing to thaw the ice, though he wasn't sure what.

He woke before dawn, relishing the idea of driving the empty roads west as the sun rose behind him. He made a cup of coffee and fed the cat, stood looking at Elizabeth's note on the table as he supped. He washed his cup and put it on the draining board, then turned the note to the blank side and wrote quickly:

*It's not just there you're needed. I need you.*
*I'm sorry for my coldness. We'll do as you want.*
*I love you,*

V

He stared for a moment at his hokey words. She'd think he'd gone mad. Fuck it.

He left the note on the table and ran out the front door before he could change his mind.

# 27

Father Philbin's homily didn't mention Joan's time in Damascus House. He also avoided anything particular to the circumstances of her death, but opted instead for generalised gravitas and veiled allusions to 'a young life snuffed out in its prime' and 'which of us knows the time and the place of our calling'. Under this roof, in these circumstances, there could be no question of Joan having had a conscious role in whatever slip or fall took her into the river's flow. If her death was suicide, they would not be having this mass; therefore it was not suicide.

The church was already packed when Ali arrived. Many more than at that Sunday mass Una had dragged her to when she first arrived. A little over a week ago, but felt like so much longer.

As she took her seat, an uneasy silence reigned among the congregation, torn here and there by muffled coughs. Finally the moan of the organ washed down on their heads and she turned to see the small coffin being carried in on the shoulders of six men, one of whom was Ivor. His hair was combed back and flattened with some lotion or oil that darkened it. His expression was full of effort. She looked down at her hands as he came level, couldn't bear the chance that their eyes might meet. It seemed unbelievable that Joan lay inside that box. All through the mass she berated herself for her role in freeing Joan from Damascus House, and again for making her angry outside the dance. It would be easier to think it an accident – join in the church's version – but she just could not.

A choir of reed-voiced pensioners struggled into the sweet first lines of 'Bring Flowers of the Fairest'. The coffin was hoisted once more and the men stepped it back down the aisle. Ivor was on the opposite side of it now, screened from view. After the coffin came Joan's mother, the thin woman who had pressed the medal on her, not knowing she'd need all of Mary's compassion for herself. A ruddy-faced man in a tight black suit walked in line with her, presumably Joan's father. They didn't touch or lean on each other, staying as far apart as the aisle would allow.

Ali joined the rest of the congregation in following the coffin as it was carried down the street, an empty hearse driving behind the crowd. The graveyard was the new one – a field at the edge of town with two and a half rows of shining stone tablets adorned with wreaths, small statues and domed displays of plastic flowers. Most of it was plain mown grass awaiting the dead to come: many of those in this crowd, no doubt. Her mind was turning morbid. Ahead she could see the two mounds of earth that marked the hole where the procession would end.

The women of Buleen gathered close around the grave, murmuring Hail Marys together, a decade of the rosary. The men were scattered to the periphery by some invisible force, many solemn with clasped hands, observing the backs of the women, others starting to chat in low voices, just like they were attending any village occasion – the perpetual banter. A soft, sieved rain billowed down the valley, but few took shelter under umbrellas. Coat shoulders darkened. Ali hadn't even a jacket to protect her, was soon soaked through in her black cardigan and skirt. She moved into the crush of bodies for shelter.

She caught sight of Roisín and Una on the other side of the crowd, but otherwise didn't know many people there. Joan's family came from Ennisbridge, two miles up the road and a world away. On the opposite edge of the graveside she recognised Peggy Nolan's pale-blue mac. The woman beside her shared her umbrella, holding the big black wing of it low over both their faces. Dr Nolan stood several paces behind them, straight as a soldier.

Ali wondered how well the Nolans had known Joan. She thought of Dr Nolan on that Christmas Day, the present in his hand, the daughters in their good coats. Had he been brought into the secret of what had been found? She vaguely remembered the two Nolan girls sitting side-by-side in the living room, obediently bored. Their father out of the room, possibly with Joan.

The first note of a laugh broke through the air and was immediately stifled. Ali wheeled round to see Davy looking down at the ground, kicking a stone away. The fellow beside him had a guilty hand near his mouth, and his eyes checked the crowd. They couldn't keep quiet for ten minutes; always the jokes, always the bit of crack, even here. She turned back to the gathering at the graveside and noticed that a few of the women were also looking over to Davy and his crony, among them Peggy Nolan, whose placid face was unusually alive, eyes burning as she looked at the boys. Ali thought of Peggy standing at the edge of the dance floor in the marquee, that same still attention. At that moment the woman beside Peggy lifted the umbrella that hid her face.

It was just for an instant.

The woman's eyes met Ali's and the umbrella dipped down again. She was wearing her veil as usual, looked no different than when she stalked the corridors of St Brigid's, but Ali's first shocked thought was: *Antoinette Nolan.*

It was as if two different photographs – one of Peggy's prim, dimly remembered teenage sister and one of Sister Bernadette – had been superimposed and found to be identical. Sister Bernadette was who Antoinette Nolan had grown up to be: the colouring, the posture, the pale hand that still rested on Peggy's shoulder, all so vividly obvious now. Peggy had said her sister was in Dublin; that was all. She didn't say she was a nun.

The prayers ended and the crowd loosened, moving back from the grave as two men with shovels approached the hole. Ali pressed forward through the shifting bodies towards the spot where Sister Bernadette and Peggy had been standing, but when she got there, they were gone.

Most mourners had regrouped around the Dempsey family, queuing to shake hands and express their sympathies. Ivor was standing beside his father, his tallness marking him out. Ali was tempted to leave, but the right thing was to pay her respects, to let him know she had shown up. She pulled her damp cardigan around her and pressed into the mass of bodies once more.

She was an arm's length away from Ivor before he noticed her, his eyes locking onto hers as he reached for her hand, pulling her close.

'You. You're here.'

'I'm so sorry—'

An old man pushed in beside her and started to talk into Ivor's face. He was saying how Joan was in a better place now, and Ivor was answering, but his fingers held Ali's firmly, keeping her close to him. On the other side of Ivor stood his mother, her eyes bloodshot, her expression congested with grief. A woman was talking to her, head nodding sadly, yet Joan's mother suddenly turned, as if Ali had called her name, and looked straight into her eyes, then down to where Ivor's fingers were entwined with hers. Mrs Dempsey's mouth opened and it seemed some accusation was about to come, but no noise came from her throat.

Ali tried to pull her hand from Ivor's, but he wouldn't let go. The old man finally moved on and Ivor bent his head to her ear.

'I couldn't find her,' he said, his voice cracking.

He released her hand and she sank back into the crowd. She had no right to be upsetting these people. No right to push herself into their lives. If she hadn't agreed to take Joan on that stupid picnic … hadn't brought up the lost baby … Tears blurred her view as she hurried down the wet path to the cemetery gate.

She walked away from the town, over the bridge and out towards Caherbawn. The rain blew off. She didn't want to go back to the farm, she wanted to go somewhere she could be alone, where she could try to forgive herself. A beam of sun caught the tops of the trees beyond the farm and she remembered the ruined cottage, the place where Joan had been full of hope and Ivor had smiled his gold-flecked smile.

# 28

There wasn't a living creature to be seen on the streets of Buleen. Swan finally spotted the blue Garda sign over one of the doors on the main street. The station was locked. A handwritten note said that Garda Fitzmaurice would be back after the funeral.

He walked along the wide pavement, peering at the few sad shops until he came to the doctor's surgery. Dr Nolan was not in residence – another door locked against him. It must be a popular funeral. Then Swan remembered the Hogan girl becoming distressed about the woman who had drowned herself. That must be it. A tragedy would always fetch a crowd.

*Patience*, he told himself. Garda Fitzmaurice had confirmed by phone that Peggy Nolan was in Buleen with her family. *Where else would she be?* – there was no reason to think she'd fly the nest. And, no, there was no sign of a baby.

Swan walked all the way down one side of the street and up the other. He noted the press of cars around the ugly pink church.

That was all the patience he could tolerate. He needed a phone. In the comfortable-looking hotel, he asked for the use of a room. The German proprietor showed no particular surprise, just walked him upstairs to a high, simple bedroom whose two windows overlooked the main street. With this view, he'd be able to see Garda Fitzmaurice return. Swan picked up the telephone and leaned against the window casing.

Barrett was in the office. He said Sister Bernadette had not been located yet. He also said that Considine was on her way, that she would arrive at two o'clock at Birdhill.

'Birdhill?'

'There wasn't a car to spare. Kavanagh's on an efficiency drive – he told her to get a train and you could pick her up from the station …'

'How the hell would that be efficient?' Swan said.

'It wasn't me who told her!'

'Just tell me how to get to this Birdhill place. Never heard of it.'

Swan hung on the line while Barrett consulted a map. Down in the street, men in sombre clothes gathered outside a pub. The funeral aftermath. He leaned closer to the glass, looked sideways. The cars were leaving from outside the church. Below him, a dark-clad figure appeared around the corner, arms wrapped around herself, hair bedraggled.

Swan cursed, hung up and ran downstairs. He arrived on the pavement in time to touch her shoulder as she passed.

Ali Hogan jumped at the contact, and the face she turned to him was full of fear.

'Aren't you supposed to be in Dublin?' he said.

'Have you come to get me?'

'Get you for what?'

'I don't know …'

Clots of cobweb adhered to the sleeves of her cardigan, and the front of her skirt was streaked with mud and grass stains.

'Are you all right?'

She looked down at herself, started to wipe ineffectually at the stains on her skirt.

'I – I was in the woods. There's an old cottage – I think I found something. Will you come with me?'

'I'm waiting to meet up with someone.'

'Oh.' She didn't seem curious about what had brought him there, caught up in her own drama.

'What was it you found?'

She shortened the distance between them, looked full into his face and said, 'I think it's a grave.'

The Garda station was still closed, Considine wasn't due for an hour and a half.

'Is it far, this place?'

'Not very.'

'I've a car near here.'

'It's just a walk.'

Swan followed the girl over an old bridge and out of the town, towards scattered houses and patches of woodland. He should have insisted on the car.

'Does your mother know you're here?'

An impatient nod. He took in her black clothing. A car came towards them and they stepped onto the grass verge.

'Were you at the funeral?'

'Yeah.' She stepped back onto the tarmac and walked off at a lick. Swan hurried after, regretful now about this country detour, unsure how to manage the girl.

She led him up a rough track that cut through pine woods, then along a path to where the remains of a cottage stood in a mossy clearing. It looked like it had been abandoned long ago. A few jagged stubs of beam were all that was left of the roof, and the walls were starting to fall in.

Swan followed Ali across the derelict threshold. The girl stood in the middle of the space and started to talk.

'This was where Joan brought me the day she got out – so I came back to remember her, because we were happy that day, and I was looking at that hut that she said Ivor built and I noticed there was a bit on the end that was planked up, and I don't know why, but I thought I'd have a look and the planks came away ...'

As she spoke, Swan walked over to the bit that she had described as a 'hut'. It was just a lean-to of corrugated iron and wood cladding resting against an end wall. The kind of thing you would build to shelter a few sheep or some fodder.

One end was open, and a filthy mattress lay inside, as repulsive as a carcass.

'They used to stay here, the two of them, Joan said, when there was trouble at home. It was their place, so she must have made the grave too, don't you think?'

Swan stooped and made blinkers with his hands, to see better into the dark. Beyond the head of the mattress was a wall made of short lengths of horizontal planks. He stood and cast his eye over the outside of the shelter. Sure enough, it was longer than the space he had just looked into. Ali waited for him at the other end.

The boards that clad the outside of that end were

vertical, and two of them were now lying on a flattened area of nettles and grass, leaving a gap into the dark space.

'They were loose,' Ali was saying. 'I just put a hand to them …'

Kneeling on the bruised ground, Swan twisted his shoulders and pushed his head through the gap. The air was colder inside, heavy with the smell of damp clay. The space was as small as a cupboard, no more than three feet deep and empty.

Light crept in over his shoulder and his eyes adjusted. He hadn't noticed the slate propped against the cottage wall. It was an ordinary slate, might have been part of the cottage's roof once, but the bottom of it was embedded in the earth. As he tipped his head, a little light struck it and he could see marks scratched into it – the spidery double outline of a cross, and beneath it a heart. The ground in front was slightly mounded.

He pulled back out of the small gap and started to wrench away the other planks. They came easily, the old wood crumbling under force.

'And what exactly do you think is in here?'

'I think it's Joan's baby – it must be,' said Ali.

Swan thought they were more likely to find someone's dog or kitten beneath the slate than a child.

He was so close to solving the mystery of one dead baby, but had somehow let himself get diverted into this other tale. The wise thing would be to leave this little slate as it was, get on with the matter at hand. Garda Fitzmaurice could come and check it out another day.

'I'll run back and get more help,' said Ali.

'Wait.' A fuss was the last thing he wanted. He was only a couple of hours away from moving in on the Nolan girl.

A flat stone lay in the weeds beside him, the size of his palm. He picked it up and started to scratch experimentally at the earth in front of the little slate.

'I can't watch.' Ali walked away.

Hopefully there would be nothing at all here, thought Swan, scraping methodically now. He was only an inch down when his makeshift spade encountered a small, pliable obstruction, a pale nub that had an odd pinkish tinge to it. He put aside the stone and took his penknife out of his coat pocket. By prodding about, he loosened the earth about this small protrusion and brushed it away in one movement. There, in the scooped-out hollow, a perfect little hand emerged.

Swan's heart missed a beat. Each finger was less than an inch long. Tiny pricks of clay filled a row of four dimples on the back of the palm. Warm relief trickled through him as he made sense of it. He pushed the tip of the penknife against the flesh-toned – it was obvious now – plastic.

As he started to dig out the rest of the doll, he called out to Ali, 'It's only a doll.'

She came to kneel beside him as he uncovered the whole arm, and next to it a forehead started to emerge. Here and there the plastic was marked with bright-yellow streaks, some kind of ageing. Once the head was free, he prised the rest of it from the soil, shook it free of insects and dirt and handed it to her. The body felt heavier than it should, as if soil had gradually sifted inside during the time it lay in the ground. The doll had a flannel nappy still wrapped around its bottom, a filthy scrap.

Swan poked around below where the doll had lain, to check there was nothing else there. Behind him, Ali muttered something.

'What's that?'

'Baby Joy,' she repeated, 'this is Baby Joy.'

'Was it yours?'

'No, but it was supposed to be.' Ali brought the grubby body up to her chest, embraced it.

He should get her back to her family. The girl wasn't right, it was plain.

'I need to get on,' he said. 'I'll walk you back to town, to where you're staying.'

'My aunt's house is just near here.'

'I'll walk you to that, then.'

He was glad to get away from the desolate cottage. As they walked, he rubbed his hands together to get rid of the soil that stuck to them. His trousers were mucky too. He offered to take the doll – to get rid of it for her – but Ali wouldn't give it up.

Halfway down the forestry track she stopped still. 'Have you come here because of Joan?'

'Joan? No.'

'You have, haven't you?'

'I don't know your Joan, Ali. I'm still after the mother of the Rosary Garden baby.'

'So what are you doing here?'

Swan hooked his hand into the crook of Ali's arm, forced her to carry on walking.

'There's someone here we need to talk to.'

'Oh,' said Ali, looking down at the movement of her feet. Then she said in a small voice, 'Is it Sister Bernadette?'

'What about Sister Bernadette?'

'I saw her this morning.'

It was Swan's turn to stop walking.

'She's here?'

'Yea, it's stupid, but I never realised before that she's from here – I even met her when I was small, only then she was called Antoinette Nolan.'

'Antoinette Nolan. With a sister called Peggy?'

'You know Peggy?'

'Not yet,' said Swan.

Now it made sense. Nuns had families – you forget that. Mother Mary Paul even talked to him about nuns taking new names. But families had loyalties that outlasted those new vows; a girl in trouble would naturally seek out her sister.

Garda Fitzmaurice must be back at the station by now. They needed to make a plan for handling the whole Nolan family, Sister Bernadette included; get in some extra Guards from Kinmore. And there was Considine to collect.

'Where's your aunt's house?' They had reached the roadside, and the town was in sight.

Ali raised a hand slightly from her side to indicate something not far away. The other arm still cradled the filthy doll. She looked a forlorn sight.

'A bath is very good for the spirits,' he said, hurrying away. 'Ask your aunt to run you a bath.'

290

# 29

Cathal was blethering on about some woman he'd met in Limerick, about the unusual sexual offers she'd whispered in his ear at some drinking dive. Davy clutched his pint and watched the Dempsey family gathered on the other side of the pub, the centre of attention. It wasn't the usual post-funeral lark of ham sandwiches and slices of cake in someone's tidy front room. There was nothing to eat, and the Red Rock Saloon was the roughest of venues. Perfect for the Dempseys. He hadn't really meant to come along, had sort of drifted in with the crowd.

Joan's brothers kept throwing him filthy looks. He had the feeling that a fight was brewing, and he welcomed it.

Some aul' fella appeared at his side. 'Your sister says can you come outside.'

Davy squinted at him. 'Right you are.'

The old man moved off.

'I'm thinking maybe now she was only a prostitute,' Cathal was saying. Davy studied the crush of people around the Dempsey family, offering drinks and words of wisdom about death. Their tiny, ignorant opinions. He looked at their mouths, their squirming wet lips. He understood so much now about the rottenness of it all.

Davy tipped his glass to his lips, swallowed deep. Cathal

had disappeared without him noticing. He was standing alone and people were staring at him openly now. The old man reappeared.

'Go on now, son. Your sister needs you.'

Una was waiting outside in her car, clutching the steering wheel but going nowhere.

Davy walked over, put his palms on the car roof and hung down from them to peer in at her. 'What's up with you?'

'You're drunk. Get in,' she said.

'I've got a pint on the go.'

'Please, Davy.'

'Oh, please, is it?'

The man who had ushered him out of the pub was standing in the entrance now, barring it. Davy started to laugh as he made his way round to the passenger side of the car. When he got in, Una rolled her window down, as if he stank, and maybe he did. She looked all keyed up, like she could snap if you twanged her.

'This feels familiar.'

'Don't bait me,' said Una. 'It's not right for you to be in there.'

'Free drink and weeping – it suits me fine.'

'Who's in there? Did anyone say anything?'

'Ach ... everyone's scrambling for their bit of the blame. The ma's not there, but the men are. I'll bet you a quid there's a fight before closing.'

'Do they say she jumped?'

'Sure, isn't that what happened?'

'Don't mess me about.'

'Wouldn't dare mess about with *you*. Someone told me Ned Greevy's saying he spotted her alone on the bridge that night. What do you make of that?'

'My nerves are in bits. I didn't push her, you know that.'

Davy combed his hand through his fringe, cleared it from his eyes. 'I was looking the other way.'

Her mouth opened in protest, but she seemed to change her mind and swallowed it back. She turned the key and the engine shuddered into life.

'Hey, let me out,' he said.

Una pulled out of the car park, her hand clumsy with the gears. 'I can't trust you not to say something stupid when you're like this.'

'What you going to do – *kill* me?'

The old Ford barrelled up the road towards Buleen, Una's grip on the wheel as tight as her jaw.

'Sorry. That was crude of me,' he said. 'It was just a convenient accident, let's put it that way. First the child, then the mother.'

'I've told you before. The baby was dead when I got to the kitchen. It was Joan's hands on it.'

'Drop me at Melody's,' he said as they passed the church, but Una ignored him, turning down towards the bridge at speed.

'For fuck's sake!'

'You don't need any more drink.'

The car bucked over the top of the bridge. Una braked hard and pulled into the grass verge beside the old chapel. With the car stopped, she turned to face him.

'Do you want me up before the Guards – would that make you happy?'

Davy met her eyes, found himself examining the black holes in the centre of them, the bit of someone that was supposed to show their true self. Nothing. She was staring back, right into his black holes. It was stupid to think you could know a person. The sound of the river flowing behind them grew in his ears, an unbearable noise.

'A baby's not really a person, is it, Una?'

She shifted her eyes to look out the windscreen. 'Of course it's a person, it has a soul.'

'Did you confess what you did to the priest?'

'I protected Joan. Protected you. God will be my judge.'

'You got away with it.'

'You've no idea what it is to live with something like that. I got away with nothing.'

They drove on towards the farm.

'I'll drop you at your house,' said Una, 'you can change, then you'll come down to the farm for your tea.'

A man was walking towards them on the roadside. He had a beige raincoat on, open and blowing back from a pale grey suit. Not the kind of clothes anyone wore around here. The knees of his trousers had mud on them. As they drew closer, Davy recognised the detective from the Dublin police station. He quickly raised a hand to his face. Una looked in the rear-view mirror. The man stood gazing after them, his coat billowing against the cow parsley that gushed from the hedge.

'Who's that?'

'*I* don't know. Just drop me at the track.'

As he got out of the car, Davy looked back down the road towards town. The man was no longer in sight.

'Come down in about an hour,' said Una.

'I'm not hungry,' said Davy. He banged the car door shut and started up the track towards his bungalow.

# 30

Ali ignored Detective Swan's advice. A bath would fix nothing, and she didn't want to face her aunt. Instead of going to the farm, she walked to Davy's house. He wasn't there. She sat down on the cement stump that stood like a sentry by the unfinished threshold. The afternoon was mild, but she couldn't stop her hands from trembling. Down on the road, a car door slammed and soon afterwards Davy appeared through the trees, walking fast. He was still wearing his dark funeral suit, but it looked baggier than when she'd seen him at the graveyard, and his tie was gone.

He started to raise a hand in greeting, but then blinked and stood still, looking at her with an expression somewhere between disgust and confusion.

'What have you got there?' he called.

Ali looked down. The doll was lying across her knee.

'It's my doll.'

He closed the distance between them. In the light of the clearing he looked ill, his skin doughy. He stood over her, staring down at the filthy remains of Baby Joy. He brought his hand up and swung it in slow motion towards her face. His fingers delivered a light flick against her cheek.

'You little joker,' he said, but he wasn't smiling.

Ali stood up. 'You've been in the pub, haven't you?'

'Where did you find that aul' yoke?'

'This yoke is the doll I was supposed to get that Christmas. I found it buried in the cottage on the forestry road.'

Davy started to laugh, low and empty. 'So that's what she did with it. What a retard. So you're all on your own here?'

'Yeah.'

'Only I saw a man on the road, heading for the village – he had city clothes.'

'That's Detective Swan – he's from Dublin.'

Davy took a small bunch of keys from his pocket and bounced them rhythmically in his hand. 'I hope he's not going to take you away from us again?' He hopped past her up onto the doorstep and busied himself with the lock.

'Nah, he's here to talk to Sister Bernadette from my school. She's Dr Nolan's daughter. Well, you probably know that.'

Davy was taking a while to unlock the door. 'Why don't you come in for a coffee,' he said, his back still turned, 'tell me all about it.'

'Davy?'

He looked round.

'Who's a retard? When I said I'd found the doll, you said something like *she's a retard*.'

He lifted his shoulders, then relaxed them in a long, exaggerated sigh.

'Joan. God rest her soul. I gave her that doll to help her get over losing the baby that night. Something to hold while she was wailing. We needed the box. I didn't think she'd go and bury it.'

Ali shivered. *We needed the box*. So matter-of-fact. She did a sum in her head. Davy must have been sixteen when Joan had her baby.

'Do you know about … where her baby ended up? When we found this doll, I was thinking, *Where's the real one?*'

'Who's we?'

'Detective Swan and me – he helped dig it up.'

Davy stepped down beside her.

'You're some kid, do you know that? Okay, so …'

Sliding an arm round her shoulder, Davy started to walk her along the rough path towards the farm. The doll hung from her hand, brushing through the grass. Everything was both ordinary and extraordinary, and she felt that she was being carried along on some kind of irresistible current, that even though she could speak and move, she couldn't affect the flow of things. Even Davy seemed strange, full of flippant cheer.

'Joan used to stay in that broken cottage with her little brother, like a pair of tinkers. I don't know what you see in him, by the way; he's closer to livestock than human. He thinks it was me that shafted her. Got her up the pole. An altar boy like me.'

'I don't think I feel right, Davy. Do you?'

He squeezed her closer to him, but kept walking. 'He'd rather think that than the truth. Better than knowing it was your old man or your uncle, or even one of your brothers, doing her. That's why Joan used to stay over in the kitchen – she didn't want to go home. She knew an awful lot for her age, sex stuff. She was very keen to teach it, too.'

The path widened and the trees gave way to farm

buildings. Davy released his hold on her, looked about at the barn and outbuildings as if they were new to him, rubbed at his chin.

Ali walked ahead onto the concrete screed of the farm-yard, and the view opened up around her – the soft rise of hills, the lines of hedges and, closer in, on her left, the pig sheds. Davy came up to stand beside her.

'Technically speaking, I might have been the father, but I know in my heart it wasn't mine. It was a sickly thing, and its end was sad. I won't have that one associated with me. I won't.'

Gold sunlight slanted across the fields, but here in the shade of the barn it felt cold. Ali tucked the doll inside her cardigan and drew the cloth tight around her. A tractor came into view, crossing the high meadow. Cut grass spewed out behind the reaper blades to form quilted lines.

'Looks like everyone's back from the funeral,' she said, her own voice high in her ears. 'Let's go down to the house.'

She took a step forward, but Davy's hand fell on her shoulder, as she half-expected it would, holding her in place.

'You asked me a question,' he said, 'at least let me answer.'

Ali turned to look at him. Davy jumped to one side and landed on a drain cover. It rang from the blow, like a gong.

'Do you know what this is?'

As he said it, her nose opened to the familiar smell. Under the square drain cover was the tank that took all the pig waste. Cement channels ran down from the sheds and under the concrete rectangle they were standing on.

'It's the slurry tank,' said Ali.

'Good girl. Three fathoms deep of shit and piss. The magical thing is you never need to empty it, because the shit eats itself.'

Ali remembered a fear she had when she was little, when she was helping to brush the slurry down the channels, that she would slip through one of the narrow slits at the end into a dark pool of stink. But that had been a groundless fear, the stuff of nightmares, easily dissolved in the light of day. Nothing like what she felt now, lurking, wide-awake.

'That so?' she managed. Her hand moved to embrace the curve of the doll's back beneath the thin wool of her cardigan, some animal sense in her feeling a small presence there. The tractor thrummed out of sight.

Davy drew her close and lowered his voice. 'Una's not a very sentimental person, you know that. It was the middle of Christmas Day when you found it. Guests arriving and all. She did what she had to do.' He tapped on the metal with the toe of his scuffed black brogues.

Ali stepped back from the metal hatch, couldn't block out an image of the baby's body sinking slowly into the brown muck, lit by a square of daylight. Una standing above it, the grimy box in her hands.

'That's horrible.'

'Women do horrible things, though your Mary O'Shea libbers don't think so. *Oh, the poor mistreated women … Oh, the terrible men that oppress them …* If you hadn't stuck your little nose in, it could have waited. I might have buried it properly on Stephen's Day, when things were quiet.'

'You knew it was under the bed?'

'Course I did. I said I'd deal with it. And I would have...'
He turned from her. 'Ach, you were only a child, it wasn't
your fault.'

Ali stared at him. Davy was quieter now – the antic
spirit had gone out of him as suddenly as a wind dying.
He'd been too young to be involved in something like that,
younger than she was now, and she didn't believe that
callous tone he was trying to muster. He was still her Davy.

'Let's go down to the house,' she said.

'I don't want to see my sister right now.'

The tractor noise was moving closer, though the machine
itself was hidden behind the sheds. The light of the day was
fading, shadows gathering in field hollows and the lee of
buildings.

'You look tired,' Ali said.

'I'd like to sleep for a thousand years, but I can't even
manage an hour. Come back to the bungalow and have a
drink with me.'

He held out a hand to her, and after a moment she took
it. She had asked, and he had told her. That should be
worth something. Truth should be worth something.

They walked back through the trees, Davy humming a
meandering slow tune. His grip on her hand was reassur-
ing, tight.

# 31

The Nolan home was on a rise of land to the north of Buleen, half hidden by a lush hedge. It was double-fronted, with wide bay windows, a large brick-arched porch and a thick creeper straddling one corner. They left two police cars blocking the driveway, and the Kinmore Guards quickly fanned out in the grounds. Swan, Considine and Fitzmaurice walked round to the front door. An old blue-and-white vase took centre stage in one of the windows, holding sprays of gladioli. In the deep of the room, a pale face turned to their passing.

After a short wait, it was Sister Bernadette who appeared in the porch, her expression guarded but calm.

'Good afternoon, Detective.'

'Well, it's been quite a hunt to track you down. We'll need to talk to you further, and your sister Peggy.'

She stood for a moment as if running through reasons to refuse them. Her eyes moved to take in the police cars.

'Come in.' She stepped back to allow them into the house. The broad hall beyond the porch was wood-panelled, with a grandfather clock and a carved oak bench. Discreet good things, handed down. A brass plaque on one door read *Surgery*. Sister Bernadette was attempting to show them into the room opposite, but Swan hesitated.

303

'Who else is in the house with you?'

'My father's in his study, working,' she said, indicating the door with the brass sign. 'My mother's shopping in Limerick with a neighbour.'

'And your sister?'

'Having a nap,' said Sister Bernadette. A board creaked above their heads. Swan raised his eyes to the sound.

'Peggy?' Bernadette called.

Bare feet appeared at the top of the stairs, slowly followed by the rest of a young woman. She wore a nightdress and a shawl around her shoulders. Her hair was indeed the colour of a conker and curled thickly around her shoulders. She registered no surprise to see them there. Her face was still as wax.

'Peggy, we're going to have a chat with your sister,' said Swan. 'Perhaps my colleague Gina here can keep you company in the meantime?'

Considine was on her way up the stairs when a man with white hair stuck his head out of the surgery door. Garda Fitzmaurice greeted Dr Nolan in an easy-going way and reassured him that no emergencies were in progress. Swan introduced himself and said he'd be obliged if the doctor could remain in the house for the moment.

Nolan exchanged a furtive glance with his eldest daughter before retreating behind his door.

Sister Bernadette led Swan and Garda Fitzmaurice into the living room and took a seat on the very edge of a chintz-covered armchair, hands demurely clasped over one knee. Swan experienced a surge of impatience in the face of her composure, an urge to shout or throw some delicate ornaments about. Instead he wandered past her to take in the view from the window, settling his breathing. When he spoke, he addressed the windowpane.

'Your nuns think you're in Newry.'

'I needed to come home.'

'To check on your sister?' He turned.

She gave him a steady look. 'Yes.'

'I've been to St Jude's. Your sister had her baby there, didn't she?'

A quick nod. 'My sister's not well.'

'How do you mean?'

'I think having a child disturbed her – disturbed the balance of her mind.'

'Can I ask: where is that child?'

Sister Bernadette looked over at the dried flowers arranged in the empty fire grate. 'You have it.'

'The baby in the shed?'

The nun turned to look at him, her eyes full of rising tears. 'I recognised her the moment I saw her lying in that basket. I delivered her myself. Held her in my arms each day she lived.' She pulled her black sleeve down over the knuckle of her thumb and wiped her cheeks quickly.

'You misled us. You lied.'

'I was worried about Peggy. I discovered she disappeared the same day the child was found. I came down here as soon as I could get away, to find out what had happened.'

'Do you know for certain that your sister killed her baby?'

'We argued about the child. I thought Peggy should bring her back home, despite what people might say, but she wanted her to *disappear*, that's what she said.'

'Your sister's not married – wouldn't it be tough for her to keep a child and raise it alone?'

'We would have managed. I told her I'd help.'

'But you're up in Dublin.'

'I could have come home.'

More tears appeared and Sister Bernadette swiped at them irritably.

'That seems mighty liberal of you. We spoke with someone who saw your sister leave St Jude's with the baby. She saw her being driven off in a car. You drive, don't you, Sister?'

Sister Bernadette looked at him, plainly surprised or acting it well. 'That wasn't me.'

'Who else did she know in Dublin?' he asked.

'No one.'

'Did she tell you who the father was?'

'I asked her, but all she would say was that they couldn't be together – yet.' Sister Bernadette took a breath. 'I think he must have been a married man, but she still had hopes for him. The hope was more precious than the child. Maybe I pressured her too much.'

'Did she admit to killing it?'

Sister Bernadette shook her head quickly. 'But having a baby can bring on depression, even psychosis. Peggy was – not herself. Like she didn't have her feet on the ground. I didn't *think* she could something like that, but what do I know?' There was bitterness in her voice.

'And what does Peggy say?' asked Fitzmaurice.

'She says the baby in the shed wasn't hers, that her baby was adopted and taken abroad. It's a fantasy. I held Grace in my arms, so how can she be in another place and happy? She wasn't just Peggy's, she was *something* to me too …'

'Grace?'

'Peggy wouldn't name her, but I call her Grace.'

They sat in silence for a minute while Sister Bernadette struggled to control her breathing.

'Why did you unwrap the coverings from the baby?'

'I needed to see what was done to her.' She brought a curled fist to her mouth, pressed it hard against her lips. 'I wish I hadn't. I don't know why I hid the blouse; I think I was in a panic in case it was Peggy's. I sent the Hogan girl away for water so I could have some time. Just an excuse – she'd been baptised already in the little chapel at St Jude's, only the three of us there.' She smiled briefly at the memory.

There was a knock at the door and Considine stuck her head in, asked to see Swan for a moment. They went into the small front porch and kept their voices low.

'I was making small talk, boss, wasn't trying to do my own interview, but she just started talking about the kid.'

'Okay. What's she saying?'

'She says the one found in Dublin wasn't hers. Says that hers was taken to England. She won't say who took it.'

'Do you believe her?'

'It's pretty unlikely.'

'Did she talk about being picked up in the car?'

'No – I wanted to hold off till you were there. How's the nun?'

'Chatty. Now she says she recognised the baby in the shed as her sister's. She thinks her sister snapped and killed it.'

'Wow. Just like that.'

'I'm not so sure,' said Swan. 'She's assuming no one else was involved, but who was driving the car that picked Peggy up from St Jude's – if it wasn't her sister? Time to bring her downstairs.'

Peggy Nolan sat in the corner of a small sofa in a bright room off the kitchen, her bare feet tucked under her. The room was painted yellow with little mirrors and pictures livening the walls, the kind of old-fashioned things Elizabeth would like. Swan remembered the sentimental note he had left for his wife and quickly bundled her from his mind.

Apart from her russet colouring, Peggy was quite different from her sister, made from some heavier element, her face full and sensuous but lacking animation. Moving quietly, Swan took a chair opposite. Considine sat on the sofa beside Peggy, while Fitzmaurice lurked somewhere behind him.

'This is Detective Swan, my boss,' said Considine. 'Can you tell him what you told me?'

Peggy moved her gaze slowly from Considine to Swan. 'My baby is in England, in a house by the sea.'

Swan wondered whether the girl was doped. Her dark eyes were hard to read.

'That sounds pleasant. Who took her there?'

She opened her mouth slightly and closed it again, her gaze dropping to the floor.

'Can't say.'

'Was it someone you met in Dublin?'

A slight shake of her head.

'Your sister doesn't think the baby was adopted. She says she recognised her as the one found in the Rosary Garden.'

'That baby was NOT mine.' Although Peggy didn't raise her eyes, an edge of defiance had come into her voice, an anger stirring.

'Look at me, Peggy. We have a way of proving the baby in the garden wasn't yours. You want that, don't you?'

'Yes.'

'All we have to do is take blood from you and from your child's father.'

'No.'

'I thought you wanted to prove the dead baby's not yours?'

'Is that the only way?' The girl was agitated, slurring her words slightly.

'We'll take care of the arrangements, if you just tell us his name. You don't have to see him.'

'Come on now, Pegeen,' said Garda Fitzmaurice from the doorway. His voice was low and managed to convey an infinite reasonableness. Peggy looked at him in hope.

'He said we'd have a fresh start. It was him found the good home for it.'

'Of course he did.'

'But now he won't talk to me at all.'

'I could have a word with him,' said Fitzmaurice, 'straighten things out for you.'

'Could you really?'

'No bother.'

Tears tipped suddenly from Peggy's eyes as she got to

her feet and shuffled over to put her arms around Garda Fitzmaurice. Swan held his breath and prayed that no one would enter the room to see this.

'Where is he today?' Fitzmaurice asked, smooth as a breeze.

Peggy shook her head, rubbing her forehead against his uniform jacket.

'Remember that lovely mild evening, Peggy, back in the autumn. When I saw you up in the quarry wood? You were parked in your father's car with someone, weren't you? Davy Brennan, I think it was.'

Peggy had gone very still. Her hands dropped from the Garda's shoulders and came to cover her face.

'He'll be angry with me. Don't tell him I said.'

'Was it Davy Brennan who took the baby away to be adopted?' asked Swan.

She nodded. 'In England. He gave me a photo of the couple. They have a lot of money, he said, and they're Catholic.'

Swan gave silent thanks for Garda Fitzmaurice and old-fashioned vigilance. The detectives retreated to the hall.

Garda Fitzmaurice said he'd seen this Brennan lad in Buleen that morning, but that he'd been up in Dublin for a while.

Dublin. Swan's heart quickened.

'What's he like?'

'Bit of a boyo, but from a respectable family. As you know.'

'What do I know?'

'Sure, he's one of the Devanes at Caherbawn. Mrs

Devane's maiden name is Brennan. Like your one on *The Late Late Show*, only she goes by the name of Hogan. He's her uncle.'

Swan's brain raced to absorb this information, throwing up a picture, a memory, from Rathmines Garda station on the very first day of the case. When he walked into the reception area after interviewing Alison Hogan, there had been two people sitting in the chairs. The emotional Deirdre Hogan had shaded her companion into obscurity. But he had been sitting right beside her. Swan tried to conjure him back into memory, but could only see the way his fringe fell forward to hide his features, the dark slouch that he had read as boredom.

He asked Fitzmaurice to phone the farm, to check if Davy Brennan was there.

'Pretend it's nothing important.'

The Garda came back after a short exchange.

'His sister says she hasn't seen him, says he might be away to Kinmore. She was very keen to know why I wanted him, though. I'll put a call out, if ye want.'

'Yes, but no hanging about – let's just go to the farm. Leave two of the lads here and round up the others. I'll join you in a minute.'

# 32

Davy pushed Ali through the hall of the bungalow and into the kitchen. 'I need a drink. We both need a drink.'

He worked his way along the line of cupboards, opening and shutting doors on empty shelves.

'Is there beer?' said Ali, laying the doll on the dirty counter. The place seemed even more of a wreck than when she first saw it. A bucket beside the sink overflowed with rubbish and the cement floor was splashed with brown stains. A queue of bottles stood against the skirting board.

'No beer – I've whiskey somewhere.' He twirled round to face her. 'I've never told anyone about the slurry pit. It's stupid for you not to know. You're not a child any more.' Davy walked over to the small fridge, opened the door and stared into it, even though he had searched it a moment before. 'That's not to say I'm not a little bit annoyed with you.' He addressed the fridge, not her.

'What have I done?'

'You've been bringing policemen sniffing in your wake.'

'What's that to do with us?'

'What indeed!' Davy slammed the fridge and walked out of the kitchen. Ali followed. From the hallway she watched him do a circuit of the small bathroom, searching.

'I don't want you to be annoyed with me,' she said.

She hoped he would calm down, hoped he wouldn't find any whiskey and that not finding it wouldn't make him angry. She followed him into a bedroom. Davy got down on his hands and knees and started going through his suitcase and the pile of clothes beside it. She needed to ask him something. She wasn't sure she wanted the answer, but the question kept nagging around her head.

'You said that Joan's baby was sickly. But she told me it was stillborn.'

Davy sat back, cross-legged on the floor. 'They made that up afterwards, Una and herself. I know what I saw … I saw its little arm waving – I saw it. They treated me like an idiot. Never took a breath, Una says, but I saw it. I was looking through the window at them. When Una laid it on the table it wasn't moving any more. I don't know what they did to it, or which one of them did it. Una said I didn't see what I thought I saw.'

Ali moved to the mattress on the floor, crawled over it so that she could sit with her back against the wall. She needed to sit very still. Davy was looking at his hands. She remembered him as he was at sixteen, a tall hero. She tried to figure out the likely truth of what he said – was he mistaken, or spinning a tale? She thought of her mother's story of her grandfather forcing them to kill animals as a mercy.

Minutes passed.

'When I went back into the kitchen, Una was tending to Joan. She told me to put it away – so I did – I hid it for her. Christmas Day, after the hoo-ha, I saw her coming back down from the pit with the box and she says to me, *It's in a better place*, with that pious bloody face on her. My sister. My sister is ... remarkable.'

Davy turned to look at Ali, his eyes refocusing.

'Aaah!' he cried and lunged in her direction, stretching flat out on the mattress beside her. His hand came from behind a pillow, gripping an almost-full bottle of Paddy by the neck. He rolled away and spun the metal top from it with one rub of his palm. He threw back a slug and held out the bottle to her. 'You look like you need it.'

'I don't like it straight.'

'Don't be a fairy.'

She took the bottle and swallowed. It burned inside her mouth and made her lips sting, but as it went down, she felt a warming in her chest, like coming back to life. She took another sip and Davy smiled. She wanted to change the subject.

'Hey,' she said, 'aren't these my mother's sheets?'

'Must've taken them by mistake.'

'Mistake?'

'I don't know why you're bothering to go to university; with that nose on you, you should go straight into the cop shop – or the Gestapo – go snooping with the piggy pigs, oink-oink.' He grabbed the bottle from her, swallowed deep and wiped his mouth with the back of his hand.

Ali tried again to think of something light to talk about, something to make Davy come back to himself. And then she thought of him laughing in the graveyard, the sound of it carrying over Joan's open grave. And how Peggy had stared at him, her eyes burning; and Sister Bernadette

315

beside her, looking too, angry with Davy for something more than just the laugh.

She stood up, wobbled on the mattress.

'Where're you going?'

'I'm going to get some water – water for the whiskey.'

Ali let the tap run. The night of the marquee dance, she had seen Peggy on the edge of the floor, looking out at the dancers with the most miserable expression. And when Ali had taken her place, Davy was two feet away dancing with Valerie, the woman who had broken it off with him for his wandering eye. What was the connection between Davy and Peggy?

She heard him move about the house, then a loud crack of splintering wood. She didn't know what he was up to, but stayed at the sink, moving the glass under the water's flow, filling it and emptying it again and again. What was it that Joan had said to her? *You know nothing. Nothing at all.*

'You got a lighter?' He was in the doorway.

She wiped her hands on her skirt and took her lighter and cigarette box out of her pocket and offered them up.

'Bring us a glass too – I'm lighting a fire in the front room.'

Ali sat on the sofa, smoking, supping her whiskey and water steadily while Davy assembled a pile of thin wood and newspaper in the rough hole where a fire surround might one day go. He hummed as he touched the flame to the edges of the paper. The wood crisped and spat.

'That's cosy now,' he said, balancing two peat briquettes

over the flames. He came to join her on the sofa, filling the tumbler she'd brought for him with whiskey before settling back against the cushions.

'You're very quiet, but it's better you know. Young girls can be very naïve. This is what the world is.'

Her tongue in her mouth was clumsy. 'Did something happen between you and Peggy?'

'Aw, Jaysus – that too? Let me make one thing clear: I never fancied her. It was a moment of weakness. You know I'm given to moments of weakness.'

Davy put his hand on Ali's knee and gave her a rueful smile. She didn't smile back, but glimpsed a foggy image of Davy's face very close to hers in the darkness. He sighed and removed his hand, picking up the tale.

'It was just once or twice. In the back of her daddy's Jag; what can I say – the surroundings appealed to me. Should have fucked the car instead. She said she was on the pill, said her daddy got her a supply, and I believed her. Next thing she's up the pole, and telling Valerie about it. And I got no say in any of it. That's not fair, is it?'

'I don't know.'

'I said she should get rid of it, and do you know what she said to me? She said she would *if* I'd be her boyfriend. She was trying to hijack my life. *My whole life.*'

Davy thumped the arm of the sofa so hard the drink in Ali's glass trembled. She raised it to her lips and tipped all the liquid into her mouth.

'I convinced her to get it adopted – had a place set up for her in some residential place out in Connemara. Might have led her on a little bit about my feelings to get the job done, okay, but then Antoinette takes Peggy off to Dublin with her, says she doesn't want her to make any rash decisions …'

Ali thought of the Rosary Garden, of Sister Bernadette standing bereft outside the shed with a dead baby in her arms.

'… like I've no rights, like I'm some fuckin' plank of wood. You women think it's all down to you – *dominion over life and death*, eh? I was just trying to get my say. It was half mine.'

Ali tried to get to her feet, but Davy grabbed her hand and pulled, holding her down next to him and pointing a finger in her face.

'You listen: I'll tell you how it was supposed to go, and then how *you* messed it up.'

'I feel sick.'

'I don't care.'

Davy looked round for the whiskey bottle, but he couldn't reach it and keep hold of her at the same time.

'Bugger. Anyway, Peggy goes to Dublin to have the baby, and I follow after. Her sister's trying to persuade her to keep it, to come back to Buleen and live openly with her little bastard in my own town. I'd never be rid of her.'

'What did you do?'

'I sorted something out. It was perfect. I told her I had a family in England, rich people desperate for a baby, who would give it the life of a princess. We do a deal. I persuade Peggy to give me the baby one night in Dublin and tell her I'm going to take it over on the ferry.'

'Did you?'

'Of course I didn't. I would have been stopped at the first post. It was just a tale. No, I had a better plan. I figured I could drive as far as Portlaoise and back without your mother missing her car. Drop the baby near the hospital in the dark. I even had a wee bed set up in the back of the car, a towel to wrap it in. I'm not a monster. They'd be searching the midlands for the mother. Nothing to connect it to her or me.'

'It's still alive?'

'It would be, if you hadn't arrived at the door with your little blondie friend.'

'*What?*'

'Your house. That night. The thing was screaming – a noise that would strip the skin off you. I popped back to yours, figured I could get some milk and whiskey down it. Just dope it, like. I knew no one was in. But still it won't stop crying. I was in the laundry room with it when I hear the key in the door and you two giggling in the hall. You made me panic.'

His voice was accusing, but he wouldn't meet her eye. Ali remembered coming in with Fitz that night, because Fitz wanted to meet Davy – wanted to meet any man she could – and him coming out of the scullery all flustered, and her thinking it was shyness.

'What have you done, Davy?'

'I've done no worse than thousands of women, than my own sister did. What difference is there between a foetus and a just-born baby that knows nothing or no one – days, that's all it is.'

'There *is* a difference,' said Ali.

319

His hand grabbed the back of her neck and tightened.

'Don't give me crap. You don't know enough to keep your knickers on, either. I had to leave it somewhere, so I thought I'd put it in that little garden you talk about so much. A nice present for Sister Bernadette and her meddling. And there you were, under a tree, getting your titties out for some boy.'

It felt like being punched. He had been there, the figure walking on the path down to the Rosary Garden. He had seen her with Ronan. This wasn't made up.

Davy let go of her, turned away. When he spoke, his voice was barely there. 'I just needed it to shut up.'

'Davy, it wasn't an "it".'

He wrapped his arms around his head as if warding her off. 'It wasn't my fault—'

Ali leapt for the hall, grabbing at the jamb to pivot herself towards the front door. She fumbled with the snib while he called her name from the living room, a forlorn wail that almost made her waver, but the door was opening now and she could see the dusky sky and the path through the trees beckoning her out of there.

She stepped out into air, forgetting that the ground would be so far. Her body pitched forward, flying down towards the cement boulder that suddenly filled her vision.

# 33

Swan knocked on Dr Nolan's study door. Outside, in the dwindling light, his small team readied themselves for the short trip to Caherbawn.

'Come in!'

It was more of a library than a consulting room, though an examination bench covered in nasty beige vinyl lurked against one wall. The sight of it reminded him of Ali, and what she had been subjected to on his orders. But the girl and the mother hadn't been quite honest with him – they had never mentioned an uncle being with them in Dublin.

Dr Nolan was sitting at an old-fashioned writing desk, a fat reference tome open before him, a brass lamp casting a civilised light. He slid off some wire-rimmed reading glasses as Swan approached. There was a ring of falseness to the pose, as if he had been waiting to be interrupted.

'I'll assume you know why we're here, Doctor.'

A nod and a shrug. *I do, but I don't.*

'Your daughters have given contradictory statements to me about the fate of the baby your daughter Peggy was carrying. What do you know of it?'

'I would think that Bernadette would be your more reliable witness. My younger daughter's state of mind isn't strong.'

'She didn't seem very focused. What have you given her?'

'She's on a prescription tranquilliser. All above board.'

'When did you notice she was pregnant?'

Dr Nolan hesitated a moment. 'She concealed it from us. I didn't know till quite late along.'

'I thought the signs would be more obvious to a medic,' said Swan.

The doctor tightened his jaw. 'The girls tend to rely on their mother for those kind of confidences.'

There was no regret for his lost grandchild, nor did he seem inclined to protect Peggy against her sister's implied accusation.

'We'll need to take a statement from you and your wife tomorrow at the station.'

'Can't it be done here?'

'I'll see – it might be possible, if you can help me with another matter.'

Nolan nodded.

'Twelve years ago at Christmas time another baby was found, at Caherbawn. I believe you were there.'

'Your officer asked me about that previously. Una Devane called me to Caherbawn and I examined the mother.'

'Did the child's body have any marks on it – any signs of violence?'

A hesitation. The doctor shook his head.

'You didn't inform the Guards.'

'The child never lived, didn't attain independent existence, as such. Some people's lives are hard enough. I don't see that there's any benefit in making a song and dance.'

'What happened to the body?'

'I can't recall. It was left with the family. You should see Una Devane about it.'

'Are you sure you actually examined the child?'

Dr Nolan picked up his glasses as if eager to get on with his reading. 'I don't see the point in all this.'

'Did you see the baby?'

'Una Devane is a reliable woman … it was Christmas. A house full of children.'

'You didn't.'

'I was shown it briefly,' he finally conceded.

'The mother of the child that you didn't record was buried this morning, drowned. Did you sign off her death certificate?'

'There was nothing to suggest Joan Dempsey's death was anything other than an accident.'

'Don't you need an autopsy to determine that?'

'I examined the body and spoke to Father Philbin and the police. We did not deem it necessary.'

A big man in a small town, thought Swan. Practised here all his life, knew all the secrets. Decided what was best. Deemed it.

'Well, I'm just going to have to order one myself.'

As he rose to go, Swan noticed the little wire glasses trembling in the doctor's grip.

# 34

Branches moving against a deep-blue sky. Twilight and shifting air, everything mobile. She thought she was back in the convent grounds with Ronan, that he was about to kiss her and that this time it would be lovely. A face hovered over her, Ronan's face approaching, blocking out her view of the sky. The face wavered, became Davy's, so close to hers that all the light disappeared and she was floating in blackness again.

When Ali woke, she was aware of stones under her, and although the air was mild, her head was cold and clammy.

She raised her fingers to her scalp, felt her hair clumped together, sticky. Now she was properly awake and could recognise the outside of Davy's bungalow. She put a hand to the concrete stump beside her, used it to lever herself to sitting. Her hand left dark prints on the grey. She wanted to be sick.

The house was in blackness; the door stood open. Ali got shakily to her feet and tried to think. If he was still there in the living room he could see her through the dark window, might be looking straight at her. She knew now that he would hurt her, if he felt he had to.

Ali turned and hobbled away, picking up speed as she reached the trees, ears straining for steps behind her. Halfway along the path she held onto a sapling and stopped to look behind. She couldn't see him, but branches and their shadows swayed in the breeze. He could be very close by.

If she could reach the farmhouse, surely her family would protect her. But Davy was family too, closer to the rest of them than she was. A line of fresh blood dripped down her cheek, and she held a hand to it. She had no choice – she might even be dying. Ali staggered in the direction of the farm. She would not die alone out here.

The barn loomed up behind the trees. Not far to go, she told herself. Her feet hit the concrete of the yard and she could see the light from the kitchen window fall across the patch of grass at the back of the house. On the ground to her left, she registered two squares of darkness where the awful slurry tank was. There should only be one square, the drain cover, but now there seemed to be two, one darker than the other, and something else – some object – beside them.

Keep going, she told herself, but her eyes clung to the squares, halting her feet, wanting to make sense of it.

The slurry tank had been opened. One square was the metal cover, pulled aside; the other was the black void it should be covering. She took a few steps towards them. Except for her own ragged breathing, all remained quiet, nothing moved. From six feet away, she peered at the open hole and what was left beside it. It was hard to make it out in the dim light, and Ali moved closer. At first she thought it was a stone, then she saw it was a shoe, a black brogue. She knew she'd seen one like it recently, but her head was so fogged it took another long moment until she could make sense of it and remember where.

A tremor ran through her body and her throat opened to unleash a wail. In answer to her scream, a raw light burst from a lamp on the side of the barn, raking across the ground. A voice called her name and she turned to see Una running from the house towards her – her face distorted in panic.

But even as she turned towards her aunt, Ali couldn't rid her eyes of what she had glimpsed as the light burst across the yard. A dark shape like a sack, or perhaps a rounded back, lolled in the glossy brown swill of the slurry.

# 35

The scene that greeted Swan at Caherbawn was like some twisted medieval altarpiece – suffering and gesture stamped in light against the grainy dark.

Four figures were lit up by harsh white floodlights. Two men, smeared with muck, laboured with wooden poles twice their height. They seemed to be prodding the ground, but the poles kept changing lengths and Swan realised they were probing some kind of hole. At their feet crouched two female figures, one middle-aged, kneeling with her arms cast out to either side of her in a kind of supplication, her hair wild and her eyes to heaven, the other on her hands and knees, staring into the hole, a shining trail of blood caking one side of her milky face. Ali. His heart contracted at the sight.

Before Swan could fully absorb what he was looking at, Considine leapt out of the passenger seat, the two Guards from Kinmore following her. Ali shouted something as they approached, pointing into the hole in the ground. The two men with the long poles froze where they were. The woman got to her feet and stepped behind the men.

The smell was awful, thick in his nose and throat, intimate and revolting. By the time he reached the group he could feel it soak his clothes and skin. One of the Gardaí stepped away to retch, affording Swan a view of the dark pit that all attention was centred on. Two feet below the opening he could see the stewing surface of some vast reservoir of faeces. The men had been stirring this with their poles, trying to fish something from it, and in the ordure was a form more solid than the rest. At first glance he took it to be a cat or dog that had somehow fallen in, a suggestion of matted fur or hair.

He lifted his eyes. Considine had her arms around Ali, was trying to inspect her head injury even while she spoke to calm the shivering girl. The younger man was wearing a blue boiler suit. His red hair and arms were streaked with slurry as if he had been half-dipped into the tank.

'What's in there?' Swan asked him.

'She's says – she says it's Davy,' he replied, gesturing at Ali, but never taking his eyes from the hatch.

'It can't be Davy,' the older woman said.

'Well, it's someone,' said one of the Guards and the older man turned away at his words, trailing the hooked pole after him, heading off into the darkness, his shoulders heaving.

They eventually persuaded the family to go into the house, even the older man, Joe Devane, who they found shaking in a corner of the barn, still gripping his smeared pole.

Fitzmaurice put a call in for an ambulance and the fire brigade. He asked Swan if it was worth getting the Garda divers too.

'Let's see what the fire boys can do first.'

It took two hours to get him out – two hours of argument

and speculation, of ropes and pulleys and improvised scaffold. The young fireman who volunteered to go down neck-deep and attach a line to the body deserved a medal. At last they managed to haul it out by a rope looped under its armpits, and it hung for a while under the scaffold in the lights, slowly rotating as the muck dripped from it, sliding off in gobbets. Swan checked again that the curtains were closed in the farmhouse.

Four men lowered the corpse onto the ground next to the opening.

'That's Davy Brennan all right,' said Fitzmaurice.

'Should we hose him down, clean him up a bit, for the family, like?' asked one of the firemen.

'No. We need him as he is,' said Swan. 'The Guards will take care of it from here.'

Two paramedics leaned against their ambulance, waiting. The yard and driveway were jammed with an assortment of vehicles now, a static pile-up.

'Don't touch the drain cover,' he said to one of the firemen who had bent to grasp it. 'Leave everything now, and thanks for your help, lads.'

The body was photographed before being lifted into the ambulance. Swan watched it move away, lights blazing, then he turned and entered the farmhouse. Considine was waiting for him.

'I have them in separate rooms, now. The Guards are ready to take initial statements. No one saw him go in, apparently. Ali was the last to see him alive, they were drinking together in the next house along. Davy Brennan's own house.'

'It would be her. Christ. Did he give her the crack on the head?'

'She says she fell running away from him; says he told her he killed Peggy Nolan's baby in the Ranelagh house.'

'Do you believe her?'

Considine screwed her mouth up. 'Well, it fits with what the Nolan girl said. He was the last person to have the baby, as far as we know. '

'Where is she now?'

She nodded her head towards a closed door.

In the old-fashioned living room beyond, they found Ali Hogan sitting on a sofa while Dr Nolan stood over her, bandaging her head. Swan had the odd sensation that he was watching a play with a very small cast, the same faces appearing again and again.

'They called me,' Nolan said immediately, defensively.

'That looks very neat now,' said Considine, and opened the door to the hall to hurry him out.

Dr Nolan quickly tucked the end of the bandage in, picked up his bag and left.

The girl was horribly pale, and her eyes were blurred-looking, pupils wide and black. She still wore her dark funeral garb, even more stained than it had been when he saw her last, spatters of blood and muck now added to the smears of grass.

'We need to go through everything with you, Ali.'

'Where will you take me?'

'We can do it here if you like,' said Considine.

Ali shook her head, clamped her jaw.

They decided to take her to the hotel, to leave the rest of

the family to Fitzmaurice and his recruits for this evening. The body of Davy Brennan was on the road to Limerick, to a morgue and a post-mortem exam. Swan had ordered another for the body of Joan Dempsey – that would involve disinterring her from her new grave.

Swan guided Ali out of the room while Considine collected some clothes for her. Hanging onto his elbow, Ali staggered, so he adjusted the arrangement, put an arm about her waist to support her better, his fingers resting on her ribcage. She was skinnier than he had imagined, and he found himself pondering who it was he was holding so intimately – an innocent caught in the crossfire of other people's desperate acts or someone more deeply involved.

They waited on the front doorstep for Considine. Fitzmaurice was conducting traffic at the side of the house, looking ten years younger than he had that morning. Another police car had arrived, and Ali's aunt was manoeuvring a car out of the way to make more space. Swan thought that, in the circumstances, one of the Guards should have offered to move it for her.

'Little more,' said Fitzmaurice, gesturing the car back, '… little more. That's it!' He rapped the boot sharply with his hand and the woman hit the brakes – one brake light shone white where the red plastic had come away.

'Need to get that fixed, Una,' said Fitzmaurice automatically. At that moment Considine appeared with a purple rucksack and headed for the car. Swan started to follow, but Ali seemed stuck to the spot, her eyes riveted to the back of her aunt's car as the lights died and the engine stopped. She seemed terrified.

He looked round and could see nothing that would account for it. She was probably just overwhelmed. Ali suddenly walked out of his embrace, hurrying after Considine without a backwards look.

# 36

Swan sat in a winged armchair in the lobby of the Buleen Hotel, waiting for Considine and the girl to finish breakfast. He was all set to drive back to Dublin, bringing Ali Hogan back with him. When he looked over the top of his newspaper he could see them through the dining-room doorway, among the sunlit tablecloths and the sheen of china. Ali didn't appear to be eating, but Gina was making up for her, addressing the big cooked breakfast with the relish of a woman who rarely got one.

Considine deserved someone who would be good to her, he thought; at thirty, she shouldn't be sharing with a female flatmate. You needed the solid ground of a good relationship in this job. He caught his own sanctimony in time, and hid his smile behind his paper. He was hardly the boy to pontificate on personal relations. And yet.

He had phoned Elizabeth first thing, wary of her reaction to the little note he'd left. But she practically cooed down the line at him, asking when he was coming home, flirting almost. He was stunned at how simply their marital winter could be thawed, just by telling her that he loved her. But even as she hinted that she'd be staying in Dublin more, he found himself wondering how such a thing could be sustained. Would he have to say it all the time – and if he did, wouldn't it wear out?

He turned to the television listings. With any luck he'd be home on the sofa tonight. The killer of the Rosary Baby was dead, it seemed. Between the statements they had gathered and what a forensic examination of the Hogans' unkempt laundry room would tell them, he was satisfied they'd find it had died at Davy Brennan's hands, like the girl said.

What had happened to Davy Brennan was another question, one he was happy for Considine to supervise for now. A bit of a step up for her.

All evening they had questioned Ali Hogan in the little TV lounge of the hotel, Considine writing down a torrent of words on borrowed paper, not just about what Brennan had said he had done with Peggy Nolan's baby, but also her account of Joan Dempsey and of how her baby had been disposed of in the same slurry tank that Brennan had ended up in.

Ali had been scrupulous in her details, like that first time in Rathmines, but last night she kept stopping, scanning the tastefully grained wallpaper as if something was eluding her. Occasionally she asked them questions too, testing her own account.

'Do you think he could have been the father of Joan's baby?' she said at one point.

'It's possible,' Swan answered. 'Our forensics people say that the bones of the child may well be at the bottom of the tank, even after all these years. They'll start draining it tomorrow.'

Ali's eyes grew wide in the lamplight. 'I think maybe he thought he'd killed me too. Or that he'd be blamed for it. He saw me lying outside his house.'

He would have been in desperate state, Swan thought. The baby, then the niece, knowing the police were in town. There are easier ways to take your own life, though.

'You say it was your uncle put the first baby in the tank?'

Ali had hesitated, squinted away, nodded briefly.

It made some kind of dark sense, thought Swan, the first baby brought back into consciousness by the killing of the second. And maybe he killed the first one also, this Davy Brennan, and followed them both to oblivion.

The dead had a strong pull on the living, even the smallest of them. Joan Dempsey too – following her dead child to the grave of her own will, or possibly made to follow. Davy Brennan had been at the same dance the night she died, but no one had seen them together. There was only one sighting of Joan alone on the road, heading towards Buleen. The body might tell them something more of her death.

But none of it might ever get to court with Davy Brennan dead. Four lives lost, four furrows ploughed through those who remained.


'Put on your seatbelt, now.'

He had to say it twice. The girl didn't seem to be hearing properly. She still had a little tremor to her movements, and the bandage around her head made her look even more of a tragic waif. Swan hoped that the doctor who came to the hotel the previous evening was right, that she wasn't concussed. He wasn't going to take Dr Nolan's word for anything, so he got a young guy in from Kinmore, who held up various fingers for her to count, and looked deep into her eyes at close range, briefly bringing an embarrassed flush to Ali's cheeks.

Considine stood on the pavement beside the car, arms folded and brow furrowed. She tapped on Swan's window and he rolled it down. Dipping her head, she spoke across him to the girl.

'If you feel sick or anything, just say, and he'll stop.'

'Of course I'll stop,' said Swan. What was he, an ogre?

'I'll ring you later this afternoon for an update, boss.'

'Thanks, Gina.'

Swan turned the key in the ignition and pulled out, unsure for a moment which direction to take. Ali pointed at the road over the bridge.

'Is that the best way?'

'I need to pick up something from Davy's house.'

He parked where she told him to, on the side of the road just past the farmhouse and out of sight of it. She wouldn't come up to the house herself, but gave him very exact directions of where to find what she wanted.

The Guards had stretched perimeter tape around the bungalow, but there was no one about to see that the barrier was observed. Swan gazed at the unfinished house, the lump of concrete smeared with dried blood in front of it.

The doll was where she said it would be, lying on a kitchen surface. This house was almost as depressing as the ruined cottage where they dug it up. A defeated kind of place. And the dirty old doll in the middle of it. He had a notion to just throw it away, to tell the girl it was gone.

He lifted it into the crook of his arm and went over to

the stainless-steel sink that tilted from one wall. He took his handkerchief out of his trouser pocket and wet it, then wiped the doll clean of dirt as best he could. It was an ugly little thing, the pouchy eyes shut fast.

'What's to become of us?' Swan said, wiping its plastic brow. 'What's to become of us at all?' He had rarely held a baby, didn't know how he felt about holding one. *It's different when it's your own*, they always said. He couldn't imagine the pleasure ever being more than the worry.

There was a plastic carrier bag lying on the floor. Swan left his muddy handkerchief by the sink and quickly dunked the doll in the bag, head-first. You could think about things too much.

Ali slouched down in the passenger seat and waited. There was a chance that Una had seen them pass, might come down to the road to talk to her. Ali sank her head lower, fingered the edge of her bandage, wondered what was keeping Swan.

If her aunt came down, so what? Una didn't know what Davy had told her, about the child on the kitchen table and Una disposing of it. She didn't know that Ali had seen her car with its broken brake light outside the marquee, had heard a familiar voice call for Joan.

No one would know.

Last night, as they tried to get Davy's body out, in the stink and panic, her aunt had taken Ali in her arms, folded her into her body so that they were crying into the crook of each other's necks, rocking there on their knees in the dark, like being at sea, like being washed in the storm and the salty sea. All of it flowing from her, jagged pain turned to water. And a thought had come clearly into Ali's head. *I won't give her up.*

A sharp tap came on the glass by her temple and she jerked away, raising her hands to protect her head.

Swan walked round the front of the car and got in.

'Sorry, that was stupid. You didn't see me coming.'

He leaned over and placed a plastic bag in the footwell beside her legs. Two little feet stuck out of it. She picked up the bag, wrapped it more tightly around the doll and twisted round to put it on the back seat. She couldn't bear to look at it.

Swan drove back to the village and turned left, passing Melody's pub and the pink church. *Goodbye*, Ali thought as she counted off the landmarks. *Goodbye. Goodbye.*

The regimented field of the new graveyard was next. There was a large yellow digger in the middle of it, next to where Joan was buried. Swan slowed the car down to look.

'You'll be glad to know,' he said, 'we're going to give Joan Dempsey a proper post-mortem. There'll be an investigation, too, see if they can't find out a bit more.'

Ali didn't dare meet his eye, just kept looking at the digger.

'I thought you'd be glad.'

'I am glad,' she mumbled.

But he made no move to drive off. 'I wonder how they're getting on. Looks like they've made quick progress.'

Ali prayed he wouldn't get out and keep her waiting when they were so close to escape. She turned her head away, and there, on the other side of the street, stood Ivor, his wild hair flowing in the wind. He was looking at the digger too, showed no signs of noticing her.

She remembered his fingers on her lips, the tang of tobacco in his hair. Their time in the van together that night seemed tawdry now, worse than tawdry. He should have been minding Joan. She shouldn't have gone with him.

'Can we go?'

Swan looked at her, but didn't say anything, just pressed his foot on the accelerator and they eased away. Ivor saw her then, turned and took one step after the car. She watched him grow small in the side mirror.

She didn't know if the body of Joan would somehow lead them back to Una. She couldn't be certain that Una had anything to do with it, anyway. She hadn't lied to anyone. If she had sinned, her sin was one of omission. And by that omission she had chosen to save her aunt. She needed to save someone.

'There's a kind of wheel on the side of your chair there,' Swan was saying. 'If you turn it, the seat will tilt back and you can get a bit of a rest maybe – rest your head anyway. Three hours and we'll be home. Your mother will be glad to see you.'

Ali tipped back her seat, removing herself from Swan's eyeline. She watched the reflection of overhead branches slide down the windscreen. She would be glad to see her mother but was dreading the house, knowing what Davy had done there. She would go up to her room as soon as she could, lock the door and climb under the covers.

And in the middle of the night, when everything was still, she would get up and go downstairs to the garden and dig a hole between the roots of their apple tree. The place where she and Davy drank and laughed, and perhaps kissed in the warm July nights.

She would bury the doll there, bury it all.

# ACKNOWLEDGEMENTS

I want to especially thank the Scottish Book Trust and their New Writer Award scheme, for providing the cash, encouragement and mentoring that helped develop the first draft of *The Rosary Garden* some years ago. Thanks also to the Dundee International Book Prize and the staff of the sadly defunct Cargo Books, who first published and supported it. To my editor Miranda Jewess and all the Viper team, endless thanks for your commitment, fine minds and good cheer. Lastly, gratitude and respect to the best of agents, Jenny Brown.

# ABOUT THE AUTHOR

Nicola White is a writer, former curator and documentary maker. She won the Scottish Book Trust New Writer Award in 2008, and in 2012 was Leverhulme Writer in Residence at Edinburgh University. *The Rosary Garden* won the Dundee International Book Prize, was shortlisted for the McIlvanney Prize and was selected as one of the four best crime debuts of the year at Harrogate Festival. She grew up in Dublin and New York, and now lives in the Scottish Highlands. Find her on Twitter *@whiteheadednic*.